~ Mt. Hope ~

Stephen St. Clair

Also by Stephen St. Clair

Contemporary Action Romance
The Sight of Love

Kindred Souls Trilogy
*Voyage of the Scotsmen * Trials of the Scotsmen
* Redemption of the Scotsmen*

The Wondrous Attic Series
*Tales From the Wondrous Attic
* Reflections of Reality*

Collaborations
*Have Fate Will Travel: Chances Are
with Sadie K. Frazier*

Flash Fiction Anthology
*Ethereality: An Anthological Treasury of Flash
Fiction Fables*

Published in the United States by Inked Faerie Press under Traveling Realms Media.

ISBN: 9798859966820

stephenstclairauthor.com

Prologue

The world, as it seemed, was always in chaos. Always in turmoil. A select few were called to deal with such madness, but only one knew how to extinguish both in one shot. Literally.

It was hot. Hotter than usual in the Syrian mountain range and surrounding areas. Gabriel Sterling had been called upon one last time to take out a potential target - one of the deadliest terrorist groups in the world. Due to the lack of intel, mission parameters could never be set for the main objective - take out the Vulture.

No one had ever heard of the Vulture's real name, which made it harder to do any real intel. Due to the lack of definitive info on the suspected terrorist leader, it was thought his/her name remained unknown, so it would be harder to find them.

It wasn't until late one night that C.I.A. monitoring team members overheard a conversation from remote listening stations that would give them the exact info they needed.

The name of the terrorist leader had been disclosed over the air but quickly followed by an execution. Someone in the Vulture's group messed up and messed up big.

Plans were put into place- send a sniper to take out the Vulture.

But not just any sniper, *the best* sniper; that's when Staff Sergeant Gabriel Sterling was called upon for one last mission.

He was set to retire, but the thought of claiming the victory kill of the Vulture would put him in the military record books, if there was such a thing.

Gabriel was onsite just twenty-four hours after he was given orders to report. He had received intel that the Vulture was moving his base of operations to a nearby town in Syria.

Forty-eight hours later, Gabriel found himself in his element, hiding in the mountains and waiting for the kill shot.

Gabriel almost always had his earpiece in, in case Ops had new satellite relay images come through, notifying him that the Vulture was on the move and headed in his direction.

It was dark when the call finally came through. Gabriel moved into position so he could verify what Ops was relaying.

"Alpha One, this is Ops. Target is approaching. Look for a convoy with multiple vehicles. The Vulture is reported to be in the middle vehicle. High altitude recon will paint the target for you," came a voice in his earpiece.

"Thanks, Ops. I'll let you know when I have confirmation of the target," Gabriel replied quietly.

Gabriel, in the prone position between two massive boulders and protected from overhead and side view, had his scope trained on the convoy. He watched for the target to come into sight.

"Come on, hurry up," Gabriel whispered to himself.

Finally, a vehicle became visible. It was an old military troop truck, a Russian Ural-4230. Overhead recon had painted a nice big laser target right on it for him.

"Ops, this is Alpha. I see the vehicle, waiting for a visual of the target," Gabriel said.

"Roger that. Orders are still standing - you are to eliminate only the Vulture. No one else," Ops said.

"Understood," replied Gabriel.

Gabriel followed the vehicle with his scope until he could see the rear occupants. Unfortunately, he had no photographs or digital renderings of the Vulture. Any proof of the suspect came from satellite imagery and intel behind that imagery.

Finally, the convoy stopped, and the occupants started getting out of their vehicles. One single person didn't seem to stand out as the group's leader. Gabriel had almost always been able to pick out who the leader was. They seemed to have an air about them or mannerisms that gave away their position in the group.

Suddenly, a break in the crowd formed, and a lone individual could be seen.

Gabriel's earpiece crackled with voices.

"Alpha, your target is visual. You have the shot," said Ops.

What Staff Sergeant Sterling was seeing was a boy, not more than sixteen or seventeen.

"He's just a kid," Gabriel said.

"Staff Sergeant, you have the shot, take it!" came a different voice in his earpiece.

"Who's on the line?' Gabriel asked.

"This is General Holder. Sergeant, take the shot. It's an order. We will never get a chance again if you mess this up, so I suggest you *don't* mess up," warned the General.

Gabriel looked through his scope again at the suspect. He was still standing by himself. He knew that if he messed this up, bad things could happen, and with his retirement on the line, he could very well have refused or worse.

"It's a damn kid," Gabriel whispered.

"Sergeant, take the shot before he moves!" the General commanded.

Gabriel drew a breath, lined up his scope again with the target, and took the shot.

He watched as the body fell.

There was too much noise around the group to notice at first. Finally, someone in front of the body turned and saw the boy lying in a pool of blood. That's when all hell broke loose.

"Ops, mission complete. Please verify," Gabriel said. "And make it quick. I'm going to have company in a minute or two."

"Confirmed. Congratulations, staff Sergeant Sterling, you just took out the world's most dangerous terrorist," the General said.

"Great, now come get me," Gabriel said.

"Rendezvous is five clicks north of you. You better hustle if you're going to make it," said the other voice from Ops.

"I'll make it. I always do," Gabriel replied.

He had his rifle stowed away, and all traces of him being there were wiped out in a matter of seconds. The trick now was to get down without being seen. Shouldn't be too hard for him. You don't get to be the top sniper in the United States Marines by getting caught. Lucky for him, he was dropped at the location with his getaway vehicle - an old motorcycle. He made sure and stashed it not too far from where he had been holed up.

He had his rifle and his gear bag strapped to his back. He climbed onto the motorcycle, turned the key, and it sputtered to life. He took off like a bat out of hell.

Gabriel nearly raced the motorcycle across the desert when he heard vehicles coming up behind him. They were out of range, but the RPG rounds they fired off weren't. He could feel the heat from the explosion as one raced past.

"Sergeant, this is Lieutenant Marshall. I hear you need a ride?"

"Yes, Sir. I do. I have bogies on my six, and they're making things rather difficult for me," Gabriel shouted into his microphone.

"We see them. Try to steer clear. We got a little surprise for them," replied Lieutenant Marshall.

Suddenly, fire from the sky rained down in the form of an M3M mounted machine gun. There would be no survivors from that.

"You're in the clear. Sergeant. See you soon," said the Lieutenant.

"Roger that. Hope someone brought me a victory drink. I'm going to need it," Gabriel said.

"We got steaks on the grill waiting for you back at the base," informed Lieutenant Marshall.

"Sounds good. I'll take two," Gabriel said.

Gabriel was almost there. He could see the chopper just ahead. It was a CH-53E Super Stallion.

He pulled up and slammed on the brakes, launching himself off the motorcycle. A few quick strides and he was home free.

They didn't quite make it without a few rounds pinging off the side of the chopper, though. The enemy was again met with a few more bursts of the M3M, and their story was over.

In the same instant, Staff Sergeant Gabriel Sterling's would begin.

Despite his soon-to-be-famous kill, some harsh words would no doubt be said, but he no longer cared.

He would nod and accept whatever blame he had coming.

He had completed his final mission and made it out alive.

He would soon be officially retired.

Chapter One

Gabriel waited at the railroad cross bars in his old V10 Dodge Pickup truck. He named it Fury because, once upon a time, his mom and dad used to be furious when he would peel out in the street. Twenty years later, it still had some power, but it likely wouldn't be peeling out and racing down the highway anytime soon.

He had been there for over twenty minutes when he heard someone honking behind him. The train had finally passed by, which meant his nap was over. He waved at the person behind him, quickly sat up, and threw his truck into drive.

Retirement from the United States Marines was not as easy as he thought it would be. He wasn't sure if it was because he was the sniper that took out the Vulture or because he had just served his country for twenty years, and there was twenty years' worth of paperwork to catch up on.

Either way, he was home free, and there shouldn't be the need to have his head on a constant swivel or his trigger finger trying to recall from muscle memory when to pull the trigger.

He was headed back home to where his family lived in upstate Montana. They owned a ranch - or used to, anyway.

When his parents died, the ranch hands all left except for one - Rex Dansbury. He had been a lifelong friend and third generation to work on the family ranch.

Unfortunately, Gabriel was the only known Sterling left in his mom and dad's bloodline, so there was no one else to take things over, and with him being in the military, that didn't help. He did have an opportunity or two to retire early, but he hadn't exactly stayed in his parents' good graces. Not after he said he would stay in for just one more tour. That was two tours ago.

He stopped at the top of the long gravel driveway, sitting next to the mailbox that had so much mail it was lying on the ground. Gabriel got out and gathered up all he could find. There were more bills than anything.

One piece of mail quickly got his attention. It was from an attorney. He opened the envelope and started reading. It looked like there had been a lean put up against the property, and unless forty thousand could be put down, the ranch would go to the bank and then later auctioned.

The date on the notice was just two days ago. There was still time.

He pulled up in front of his house. It was a one-story ranch with a large wrap-around front porch. A man was sitting in the rocking chair. It was Rex.

"Rex, you old dog, don't you have some fences to mend or something?" Gabriel called out, teasing the old ranch hand.

"Not no more! Seems that I'm out of a job, and you're out of a ranch," replied Rex.

Gabriel met the old ranch hand at the stairs and clasped hands with him.

"It's good to see you, old friend. How have you been?" Gabriel asked.

"Well, aside from not having a job anymore, not too bad. Heard you retired from the military. You get one last kill did ya?" Rex asked.

"Something like that. I got the mail, by the way. It looks like the ranch has a lean on it," Gabriel said.

"Yep. Attorney from the city stopped by. He said to have you call him, and he'd work out a deal with ya since you served in the military and all," Rex said.

"Yeah, I'm sure he will. I'll call him later. Let's go inside and get out of this heat," Gabriel said.

"Sounds good. I left a beer or two in the fridge. Oh, and yer pa left you something on the table," Rex said.

His words caught Gabriel off guard. He and his dad were on the outs after his last reenlistment, but in the end, his dad understood. He had been a Vietnam veteran.

There was a box on the table. Gabriel opened it and saw that it was his dad's service medals. Medal of Honor, two purple hearts, the Congressional Medal of Honor. He knew these meant a lot to his dad, so for his dad to give them to him, he knew it was his dad's way of saying he was proud of him.

On the other hand, his mom had been mad at him from the moment he broke the news he was enlisting. She stayed very distant as if he were never coming home, which was always a possibility.

Gabriel put the lid back on the box and set it back on the table. He went over to the fridge and opened it. Sure enough, there were two beers. He removed the caps and handed one to Rex.

"Thanks for serving, son. I'm proud of ya," Rex said as he tapped his bottle against Gabriel's. Rex had also been in the military, so he understood what it had cost Gabriel.

"Thanks. I'm glad to be out, though. Now maybe I can start living," Gabriel replied.

"Maybe you can get yerself a girl too. I know what it's like to be stuck in the military and not want to commit to anyone," Rex said.

Rex was only in for four years, but in those four years, combat seemed to be the only thing he saw.

"We'll see. I need to get the homestead back in working order first," Gabriel said.

"You get things squared away and a few horses running around, and I'll come back and keep an eye on things like I used to for yer folks," Rex said.

"You got yourself a deal. Are you staying in the bunkhouse still, or did you finally get a place of your own somewhere?" Gabriel asked.

"Shoot, no. I ain't stayed in the bunkhouse for years. I bought an acre off your pa a couple of years ago and built myself a small cabin. Even got me a small lake to fish out of," Rex replied, smiling.

"Sounds like I need to come over to your place and do some fishing then," Gabriel replied. He knew that was all Rex ever wanted to do - own his own place and go fishing whenever he wanted.

"Come on over. It's by that lake I caught you skinny dippin' in when you was a kid. Who was that girl you were with that night? She sure was pretty," Rex asked with an ornery look in his eyes.

"See, now, why'd you have to bring that up?" Gabriel said as he recalled from memory the night in question.

"Well, I just thought, you know, in case you had forgotten what a woman looked like," Rex said, smiling as he took another pull from his beer.

"I'm well aware of what a woman looks like," Gabriel replied.

"You sure you ain't one of them funny fellas?" Rex said, trying to goad Gabriel even more. He always had a way of saying things that made you want to either want to walk away shaking your head or punch him in the jaw. Either way, Gabriel knew Rex was just messing with him.

"Nah, that's the other branch of the military," he replied, smiling straight at Rex.

"Watch it there. You ain't too big I can't turn over my knee," Rex said.

"I bet you told all the boys on deck that," Gabriel fired back.

Rex didn't answer. He just sat in his chair and shook his head.

A few more minutes of silence passed, then Rex got up, said his goodbyes, and headed out. Gabriel stood on the front porch and watched his friend walk back to his place. It was a weird turn of events to be standing there with Rex and no one else. The old man had been as much a father figure to him as his dad had been. Maybe even more so.

Gabriel took in the sights for a bit longer. It was too quiet, though. There was always a distraction being in the military, some dangerous mission to carry out. He needed a distraction again. First thing, though - deal with that attorney.

He returned inside, grabbed the paperwork from the table, and found the number to call.

"Yes, this is Gabriel Sterling. I'm calling about the lean on my parent's ranch.

"Hi, Mr. Sterling. It's good to talk to you finally. I'm assuming you understand why the lean was put on the property?" the attorney, Clive Butterbaugh, asked.

"Well, I'm guessing my parents didn't pay their taxes?" Gabriel asked.

13

"You could say that. It looks like they owe quite a bit, too," Clive said.

"How much are we talking?" asked Gabriel.

"About forty thousand dollars," the attorney stated.

Gabriel swallowed hard.

"I know it's a lot of money. I think with your years of service, you might be able to qualify for a loan from the bank," Clive said.

"I also have my retirement pension. I have quite a bit to draw from too. Let me look things over, and I will call you back first thing tomorrow," Gabriel said.

"Sounds good. Oh, and I do believe the lean on the property can be suspended with a certain percentage down. Keep that in mind as you look over your finances," the attorney said.

"That will help. I will give you a call tomorrow. Thanks for speaking with me."

Gabriel said goodbye, then hung up. Problem one was taken care of. It was on to the next - get some dinner. Gabriel jumped in his truck and headed back into town.

There was only one grocery store and a couple of fast-food places at that end of town. The other end was more the touristy end.

He was never much of a grocery shopper, but he knew how to get the basics. Steak was his favorite, though, so he loaded his cart with red meat. Potatoes and onions were another staple, and then, of course, some beer.

Satisfied that his cart was full, he headed towards the checkout stands. He paid for the groceries and saw a bulletin board on the way out. There were the usual ads for this or that, but two caught his attention. One was for anyone looking to adopt Blue Heeler puppies, and the other was for a handyman needed at the Mt. Hope church. Gabriel was pretty good at building and fixing things. He tore off a piece of paper for both advertisements and headed to his truck.

The church was on the way home, so he called the number and inquired about the job. Pastor Nick Parker said he was the only one that had called on the job, so it was his if he wanted it. Gabriel said he was close by and would be happy to stop by.

Gabriel pulled up to the church, got out of his truck, and headed to the front doors. Pastor Nick was waiting for him and officially introduced himself.

"Very nice to meet you, Gabriel. You're not new in town, are you?" Nick asked.

"No, sir. My parents own a ranch just north of town. I actually just retired from the Marines and decided to come back home," Gabriel said.

"Well, I'm thankful for your service, and if you ever find yourself in need of a second home, this one is always available," Nick replied.

15

"Thank you. I'm afraid God might have a few things to say about what I've been doing with my life," Gabriel replied.

"Oh, what makes you say that?" Nick asked.

"Because I was a sniper in the Marines, and well, they're known for only a couple of things," Gabriel answered.

"You do know there were wars in the Bible, right?" Nick asked sarcastically.

"I know. It just seemed different each time I carried out the order," Gabriel said.

"Well, I would say thanks for serving, but those words don't seem to be enough," Pastor Nick said.

"It's okay. To be honest, I'm glad I'm done. I have a chance to start fresh, and I'm going to enjoy life a little instead of always looking through a rifle scope," Gabriel said.

"I understand. Well, look, let me show you what needs to be done, and then we can go from there," Nick said as he led the way to the front of the sanctuary.

As the two men headed up front, Gabriel saw a woman coming out of a side room from the stage area where the pulpit was. He immediately slipped into his old sniper routine - size up the individual in front of you. The problem this time was that she noticed him sizing her up and flashed him a smile. Most people Gabriel sized up didn't smile back.

"Ah, there's my secretary. Rose, got a sec to meet our handyman?" Nick asked the woman.

She looked up again and smiled. There was a hint of redness on her cheeks. Clearly, she did not like being put on the spot.

"Garbiel, this is Rose Callahan. She's my secretary when I need a hand with things around the church. I believe you also work at the library in the evenings. Isn't that correct?" Pastor Nick said.

Gabriel reached out to shake her hand, mentally taking notes on how soft and warm her skin was. He looked her in the eyes and noticed her pupils were dilated. A sure sign of nervous excitement. His sniper skills were still working overtime as he picked up a hint of perfume. A soft subtle hint of rose. Gabriel smiled when he recognized the smell.

Fitting perfume for a woman also named Rose.

"Nice to meet you, Mrs. Callahan," Gabriel said.

"Please, just call me Rose, and I'm not married either. It's just me and my dog."

"Sounds good to me. I was actually thinking about getting a dog. I just retired from the military and not used to things being so quiet," Gabriel said.

"Well, I'll keep my eyes out for anyone needing to get rid of a dog. Hope to see you around." Rose said and walked away.

Gabriel watched as she headed towards the back of the sanctuary, giving a glance over her shoulder and a smile one last time. He felt a strange feeling in the pit of his stomach, which was not uncommon for him considering what he had done for the past twenty years, but this feeling felt more like something he would have felt when he was a lot younger.

He took mental notes as Pastor Nick continued the tour and showed Gabriel the jobs that needed to be done. They were easy enough, a little time-consuming, but easy. Most jobs required nothing more than a minor repair or a hole in the wall patched and then some paint. Gabriel scheduled a time to come back and start working on the needed areas. He would have to round up tools. He recalled his dad having a well-stocked tool chest back home in the garage, so hopefully, the tools he needed would be there.

He said goodbye to Nick, then silently wished he would have an opportunity to see Rose again. Their meeting was brief, but something about her made his head spin, but only in a good way, which was quite the opposite of how he normally felt.

Chapter Two

The next morning came with a loud knock on the front door. Gabriel slowly climbed out of bed, threw on some clothes, and headed to the front door. Rex was standing there waiting with a thermos and a bristly smile that suggested he was up to no good.

"Good mornin' sunshine! How's about me and you drive around the property and check things out. If yer gonna get things back and running, you're gonna want a refresh on things," Rex said.

"Yeah, I guess, and good morning to you too. What the hell is in your coffee, by the way?" Gabriel asked.

"Whiskey. I'm not sure about the ratio, but it gets the job done. Want me to make you some?" Rex asked.

"No thanks. I'll stick to just coffee. You eaten breakfast yet?" Gabriel asked.

"Yep! Beans and bacon," Rex replied.

"You don't say," Gabriel replied with a wrinkled expression. Rex was notorious for being gassy, especially after eating beans.

"Sorry about that. I grabbed a can of spicy beans instead of the regular kind. I don't think they agree with me," Rex replied.

"Better hope they start agreeing. You don't want to be five hundred acres out and nowhere to go," Gabriel replied.

19

"Nah, I always keep a shovel and a roll of teepee in the truck," Rex replied without missing a beat.

"Good to know. I called the attorney, and he thinks I can get a bank loan. If I put enough down on the debt that my parents owe, I can have things back up and running in no time," Gabriel said.

"Great, let's go! Oh, I forgot to tell you, there was this business fella that passed through the other day. He said something about wanting to buy some land for something called wind farming. You ever heard of such a thing?" Rex asked. Rex was a smart guy, but not in the technology field.

"Yeah, I know what those are. It's a pretty good investment if you can get in on something like that," Gabriel replied.

"Here's his card if you want to call him back. Have you thought about what you want to do with your folk's land? They have quite a bit. I wouldn't blame you if you wanted to sell some of it off," Rex said.

"Honestly, I haven't thought much about it. Is horse ranching even a thing anymore?" Gabriel asked.

"Honestly, I always felt there towards the end that your dad should have bought cattle versus horses, but you know how he was," Rex replied.

"Yeah, I do. Well, let's go drive around. I need to head back into town this afternoon. I'm going to repair some stuff at the church," Gabriel said.

"You turnin' into a handyman?" Rex asked, surprised.

"Nah, I just saw a flier at the grocery store. Said something about the pastor looking for someone to come in and make some repairs, and figured I could use some cash now rather than wait for my military pension to get to my bank," Gabriel replied.

"Are you trying to say that our government is slow?" Rex asked, smiling.

"Something like that," Gabriel replied. "Let me go get some work clothes on, grab some coffee, and we can head out."

"Take your time. It's not like I got things to do anymore," Rex said as he took a long sip of his coffee.

Gabriel headed back to his bedroom. Despite the lack of food or coffee, his brain was already running a few scenarios that would help his ranch turn a profit.

A few minutes later, he and Rex were heading out. Gabriel was keeping two things in the forefront of his mind: what section of land he would want to sell and whether he wanted to run cattle on the rest of the acreage. Both were worthy ventures, but he wanted to do it right.

The drive was pretty uneventful. They talked about irrelevant things, mainly what each of them had been doing the past few years, but Rex had a funny feeling something was on Gabriel's mind.

"You gonna tell me what yer really thinking about, or should I just assume it's about a girl?" Rex asked.

This snapped Garbiel back to the present.

"No, uh, no girl," Gabriel said, which was a lie. There was Rose at the church, but she was not what he was thinking about. It was more about what he really wanted to do.

"Okay, so what then?" Rex asked.

"Okay, so hear me out. You've worked the ranch for a long time. How much land, bare minimum, would we need to run, say, three hundred head of cattle on?" Gabriel asked.

"Well, shoot, ask me something hard, why don't ya," Rex said. He stopped the truck and tried doing some math in his head.

"Your parents have about 2500 acres. That's a lot of land. I would say about eight hundred to one thousand acres, just to keep things healthy," Rex replied.

Gabriel thought for a minute about those numbers. He pulled out his cell phone and did some number crunching of his own.

"Okay, so what if we sell some of the land to the wind turbine company, if they are offering a fair price, obviously, and then take that money they give us and put it into some cattle. We could start out with a hundred or so, then see how things are going?" Gabriel asked.

Rex looked at Gabriel like he was speaking a foreign language.

"I'm not sure if your dad would outright disown you or punch you in the jaw, but then again, he ain't here, and it ain't his land no more. It's yours, and you need to do what's right for you. *And* me, of course," Rex said.

"Oh, you're not going anywhere! And you're right. It is my land, and as far as I'm concerned, it's yours too. You've worked it for nearly fifty years, so you have a say in this as well," Gabriel said.

"Why don't we head back and give that sales guy a call, and then we can figure this out. If yer gonna do this, you need to do it right. I also want to make your parents proud. I know if they were alive, they wouldn't get it, but money is money, and that wasn't always your dad's strong suit. Shoot, you shoulda heard your mom go after your dad when he wanted to buy a new truck," Rex said.

"Yeah, Mom was the hot head of the family, that's for sure, but my dad... he was a silent storm waiting to happen," Gabriel replied.

One particular memory came to mind - one time when his dad and mom had gone into town to buy some meds for a downed horse, someone tried picking up on his mom. It only took half a second, and his dad laid the other guy out on the ground. There were no actual words exchanged, but the man came to with Gabriel's dad standing over him.

The two men nodded, and they went on their way. Lesson learned. Of course, the real conversation came when they were driving back home, and Gabriel's mom informed his dad that she could have handled things herself. His dad nodded but then informed his wife that her honor was at stake and his job was to protect it. Lesson learned.

Rex pulled the truck into what had become his usual spot, and both men jumped out and went inside. Gabriel dialed the number on the business card, and an automated voice answered. Gabriel left a message, then hung up. Five minutes later, his cell phone went off. It was the number he had dialed.

"Hello, this is Gabriel Sterling. I'm trying to reach Marcus Rogers."

"What's this about?" said a voice on the other end.

"Well, he stopped by a couple of days ago and left a business card. I'm just calling him back."

"Okay, Mister Sterling, I'll have him call you. Is this about a wind farm by chance?" asked the voice on the other end.

"Yes. I was wondering if there was an interest in about six hundred and twenty acres plus or minus a few," Gabriel said.

"Sweet Jesus, yes! I mean, um, yes, I'm sure our company would be interested. As soon as Marcus gets back in the office, I will have him call you," said the voice on the other end.

"Sounds good, thank you," Gabriel said, then ended the call.

"Did I hear the person on the other end say, 'Sweet Jesus'?" Rex asked.

"Yeah, they sounded a little excited but then tried to cover it up," Gabriel said.

"Of course they did. Well, look, if we're just gonna be sittin' around waiting for a phone call, I think I might go check out some lots that I know are selling some cattle. I'll let you know if I find anything," Rex said.

"Sounds good. I'll see ya later," Gabriel replied.

Rex headed out, leaving the front door open. Gabriel could see his front yard and beyond - the Rocky Mountains. They were his favorite place to go as a kid. The problem was, half the time, it was Rex that took him there. His dad was always busy on the ranch, and his mom was always at home cooking meals for all the ranch hands.

Gabriel noticed the clock on the wall and saw it was nearly 3 p.m. He jumped up and headed to his dad's garage, where all his tools were. He rummaged through a few things and assembled a decent toolbox full of odds and ends. He was better at being a sniper, but if there was one thing he learned, it was to think on the fly and go. If he was trapped in a corner with no weapon, what could he use within reach? It was basic improvisation.

He jumped in his truck and headed to town with tools in hand, plus a saw or two. He stopped first to get a bite to eat. Coffee was no substitute for actual food. Sitting in the restaurant parking lot cramming in a cheeseburger, he noticed the church across the street and someone going in - Rose.

He felt his stomach start to knot.

"Seriously?" he said out loud. He shook his head and drove across the street to the church.

He found a spot to park that was close to the door. His toolbox was not small, but it wasn't so big he would throw his shoulder out of socket trying to carry it in.

As he headed inside, he nearly crashed into Rose. She was in a hurry and had an armload of books that scattered to the ground as they ran headlong into each other.

"Oh, I'm so sorry. I knew I had too many books in my arms," Rose said as she turned multiple shades of red.

"Nope, it's on me. I should have looked before entering," Gabriel said.

"Are you okay? I hope not too many books landed on your feet," Rose asked.

"Nah, I've had worse land on me. I was in the military for twenty years. I can handle a few books," Gabriel replied. He was only telling her half the truth. A couple of big books landed hard and hit his toes.

"Are you taking these to your car?" he asked.

"Yep. Pastor Nick said that he wanted to donate them so we could make room for new ones," Rose answered.

"That sounds like a good idea. I like to read in my downtime. When I was traveling about, I used to pick up a book or two from the different countries I had been to," Gabriel said.

"What branch were you in?" Rose asked, curious.

"I was in the Marines. Sniper division," he replied.

"Wow, I bet you saw some interesting things," she said.

Gabriel didn't reply. His mind went straight to his last mission - the Vulture.

Rose noticed Gabriel went somewhere in his mind and put her hand on his.

"Hey, you okay?" she asked, concerned.

Gabriel shook his head to clear out the memory.

"Yep, all good. Sorry, some things still come to the surface. You can't bury those as easily sometimes," he said.

"I understand. My ex was in the military, and he couldn't always handle things very well, but, um..." Rose didn't finish talking. It was Gabriel's turn to realize she, too, had stories she wished she could keep buried.

They successfully made it to her car without a mishap, quickly placing the books in the trunk.

"Well, it was nice to see you again. Are you coming to church tomorrow? I hear Pastor Nick has a whopper of a sermon," Rose said.

"I'm not much for going to church; that is, I don't think the good Lord would want me amongst His fellow saints, not after what all I've done," Gabriel said.

"That's not how you're supposed to look at going to church. The Bible teaches us that no sin is too great for the Lord to forgive. Look, if you were in the military and on active duty, I have no doubt you saw and did things that most regular folks can't imagine, but in there, we are all free from transgressions and are allowed to bask in God's love," Rose said.

"You sure you aren't giving the sermon tomorrow?" Gabriel said, smiling.

"No, but I do help with the prayer service sometimes on Wednesday nights. Maybe that would be more to your liking?" Rose asked.

"You know, I might. I got some things to talk to God about anyway, so I might just stop in," Gabriel said.

"I'd love to see you there," Rose said. She stuck out her hand to shake his. Gabriel shook hers in return.

As he extended his hand, his tattoo came into view on his right bicep. It was an image of his sergeant stripes that he had on his uniform. It wasn't uncommon for military personnel to have tattoos, but it was unusual for them to have their rank tattooed on their arms. He had it done right after receiving the final word that his retirement was approved.

They released their handshake, and Gabriel stepped back as she walked around to the driver's side of the car.

He watched her drive away and got lost in thought, mainly the thought of her. She had a beautiful innocence about her, but Gabriel was picking up on something she was trying to keep buried. It was what he called his sniper's sense that he tended to use to read people. He had many targets that had come under his sight and would always watch them for a quick second or two. He learned quite a bit about mannerisms that way.

Gabriel headed inside and pulled from memory what he needed to repair. He pulled a small notebook from his pocket he remembered to grab on his way out the door. The notes he ended up taking weren't too long. After looking at everything, he figured it would be a solid two days of work. He was sure the pastor was going to be happy with this.

"Gabriel, is that you?" came a voice from behind. It was the pastor.

"Oh, hey. I thought I would stop by and get a shopping list together of everything that I needed. I think it's only gonna take about two full days to get all this down," Gabriel said as he glanced at his list.

"Oh, that would be great. The church is having a picnic next Saturday. It would be good to have all of that done by then," Pastor Nick said.

"Count on it then. I'll make sure everything is nice and neat for you and the congregation," Gabriel replied.

"That would be great! Hey, you coming tomorrow? I have one heck of a sermon planned. I think you might like it," Nick said.

"I'm starting to feel like I should. I ran into Rose on my way in, and she invited me too," Gabriel said.

"Well, then, I guess you better come then. Main service starts at eleven, but if you get here early enough before, there is coffee and donuts downstairs in the kitchen," Nick said, adding a little incentive.

"You had me at coffee and donuts," Gabriel replied, smiling.

"Good! I'll see you tomorrow," Nick replied, patting Gabriel on the arm, then heading back out of the sanctuary.

"What did you just get yourself into?" he said quietly to himself.

Gabriel tucked the notebook back in his pocket and headed out. He needed to get back to the ranch in case the person from the wind farm company called him back. He also needed to find some clothes worthy of going to church. It was going to be an interesting day tomorrow, for sure.

Chapter Three

Gabriel set his alarm to get up nice and early. He wanted to make sure he was clean-shaven. He treated it more like he was going to a military ceremony, which was as formal as it gets.

At nine-thirty, he was dressed and ready to go. He had found a nice pair of slacks from his dad's dresser and a button-up shirt and tie. To finish it off, he also found one of his dad's cowboy hats that he only wore on special occasions. All in all, he considered himself ready to go to church.

Gabriel made it in time to find one last spot to park. He had missed coffee and doughnuts, but that was okay. He wanted to get into the sanctuary and find a place to blend in.

Someone else had different plans for him. He stood at the back until he spotted a seat clear up front. Exactly where he didn't want to be. He really wasn't in the mood to be seen.

He was committed, though, and he was there, just as he said he would be. Gabriel sucked in his pride and headed up front to the first pew. Smiling faces turned to see him as he sat down.

As he sat there wondering when the sermon would start, he noticed everyone around him was wearing less than formal attire. Some even had on jeans.

He took a deep breath and hung his head. To most, it looked like he was in prayer, but he was really cursing at himself for not asking what acceptable attire for church was. Things had definitely changed since he had been gone.

The piano started playing, and everyone stood up to sing the opening hymn. It was a familiar hymn he probably sang half a dozen times growing up, but unfortunately, the words weren't exactly coming to him. After the hymn, the congregation bowed their heads as Pastor Nick stepped up to the pulpit and gave the opening prayer.

Gabriel forgot to grab a church bulletin. He had no idea about the order of service. The piano started playing again, and then as he looked up, Rose was standing up on the stage.

She was wearing a white dress with blue polka dots and a pair of high-heeled shoes. Gabriel was quite sure she was the prettiest woman he had ever seen, and he had been to quite a few places and seen plenty of women. She was definitely it.

Gabriel got lucky. She hadn't seen him. He had the sudden urge to get up and leave, but then she finally spotted him. All he could do was smile and nod. He noticed that her cheeks turned multiple shades of red again, but she quickly composed herself.

That makes two of us! Gabriel thought to himself.

She started singing *How Great Thou Art,* but it sounded different than he remembered. It was like she had rewritten the music to it.

Gabriel immediately became entranced by her voice. The light coming in through the stained-glass windows at the

32

front of the church shone around her like she was surrounded by a multi-colored aura.

Rose ended the song with a soft finishing note. She looked one last time at Gabriel and smiled. He knew the smile was meant for him. He smiled back and slowly nodded. She left the stage and headed somewhere out of sight.

Pastor Nick stepped up to the pulpit, thanked Rose for the song, and went straight into his sermon. Gabriel listened and found Nick's topic interesting. He even discerned that his sermon would revolve around meeting God halfway, something that Gabriel very much needed to do if he was going to make any recompense for the things he had done over the past twenty years.

Like so many other people, Gabriel became lost in his own thoughts. He still tried to listen to the message, but his senses became even more distracted by a light, sweet scent of perfume. The scent had not been there just a few minutes ago.

He suddenly felt a slight tap on his left elbow. He looked over and down and saw a note tucked under his arm. He grabbed it before it fell to the floor and discreetly opened it.

Hi! I'm so glad you decided to make it. I wasn't sure if you would. You look really nice, by the way. The next time, though, you could dress down. You aren't at a military parade. Things get crazy after the service ends, so don't leave without saying hi to me!

-Rose

Gabriel smiled. It was almost like being a teenager again and passing notes in church. He got out an ink pen from his suit jacket and wrote back:

I may have to start coming more often if you're going to be up there singing! You were amazing up there. I'll have to remember next time to wear something different. I'm blazing hot in this suit coat. I'll stick around, just don't leave. I might need you to revive me.

-Gabriel

He passed the note back secretly and then decided he couldn't take being hot anymore. He slid the jacket off his broad shoulders and hung it over the back of the pew. He gave another sigh of relief. The cool air from the open windows immediately washed over him.

By placing his jacket behind him, Rose took advantage of putting another note in his suit coat breast pocket. She hoped he would find it after he left.

The sermon went on, and knowing Rose was behind him, comforted him a little, yet he found himself again distracted by her perfume. His sniper senses kicked in and he could almost hear her breathing. He could hear her move in the pew and even cross her legs a couple of times.

34

Pastor Nick's sermon was winding down, and he thanked everyone for being in attendance. He even glanced over in Gabriel's direction and smiled. He was now noticed by the two people who wanted him there the most.

The closing hymn started playing, signaling that church was officially over. Gabriel, relieved that he had accomplished his goals for the day, smiled as he listened to Rose singing behind him. She truly had a voice from on high.

He was glad that he had survived the service. More was to come, though. He still had to talk to Rose, but that would probably be the best part of going to church.

The final prayer was given, and then with a great sigh of relief, everyone headed for the rear door. Everyone except for Rose.

He turned to grab his jacket and found Rose already standing in the aisle.

"Hi! I'm glad you decided to make it. I hope it wasn't so bad having to sit there," Rose said.

"No, I enjoyed the service - and the people around me," he said, emphasizing the last part.

Rose understood what he meant and smiled.

"How did I do as far as singing? I get so nervous up there in front of people. I think Pastor Nick said there were like three hundred people in attendance today.

"Well, as they say - you stole the show. No offense to Pastor Nick or God, but you were my favorite part," Gabriel replied.

Rose started turning red again. He was guessing she got embarrassed easily, but there was something else that Gabriel was beginning to pick up on. There seemed to be a fire hidden behind her eyes.

"Thank you for saying that. I've only stood up in front of everyone a couple of times," Rose said with modesty. "So, do you have any plans this afternoon? A few of us usually pick up some food and go to the park for a picnic," Rose said.

"That sounds nice. I wish I would have brought some extra clothes, though," he replied.

"Nah, don't worry about it. It's nice enough. You should be okay," Rose said.

"I'll take your word for it. It looks like just about everyone has left, shall we?" Gabriel said.

"Oh, yeah, we better. Nick locks up the church on Sundays. He lives in the house behind the church, so most days he leaves it open, but since he usually goes to the picnic, he locks everything up," Rose replied.

"Good idea. Even small towns have been known to have their issues," he said.

They both made their way out of the church and to the parking lot.

"You want to ride with me? I think I know what park you were talking about. I used to go there when I was a kid," Gabriel said.

"You didn't say you lived here growing up," said Rose, surprised.

"Oh yeah, my parents own a ranch about thirty minutes or so out of town," he answered.

"Well then, yes, I'll ride with you!" Rose said.

They headed to Gabriel's truck, which happened to be on the far side of the parking lot. He didn't mind the walk, though.

As he walked alongside Rose, he looked over at her a couple of times in his peripheral vision. He caught her smiling once as she looked up at him.

"What are you smiling at?" he asked.

"Were you watching me as we walked?" she asked.

"I was a sniper, remember? I was trained to see everything around me," Gabriel replied.

"So, do you have me in your sights then?" she asked, teasing him.

"Well, that depends," he replied.

"On?" Rose asked.

"Whether or not someone has a ransom out for you?' he replied.

"Meaning if someone finds me valuable?" she asked.

"Believe me, you're valuable, but maybe someone should have done a better job showing you that," Gabriel answered, quickly wishing he could take it back.

"I'll keep that in mind. And thank you for that; that was a good answer. Have you ever used that line before?" Rose asked, now giving it back to him.

"Line, what line?" he asked, knowing she was messing with him.

"You know what line I mean! Besides, I'm just giving you a hard time. It's been a long while since anyone has halfway said anything nice to me," Rose replied.

"I find that very hard to believe," Gabriel replied, sincerely surprised.

"Remember when we first met the other day when I said it was just me and my dog? Well, it really is just me and my dog," she answered softly.

Gabriel noticed he had hit a sore spot, so he tried to crawl out of the hole he had dug.

"I'm sorry, I didn't mean to pry," Gabriel said, quickly trying to regain some ground he may have lost.

"No, it's okay. I don't like to talk about my past, so it's on me for baiting you," she replied. She leaned into Gabriel, giving him a partial shoulder nudge.

"Me either. Although, you wouldn't have guessed that with all the psych docs I had to have a sit down with before I was allowed to retire," Gabriel said.

"What do you mean?" Rose asked.

"I killed people for a living. Someone somewhere assumed that I would have baggage," he replied.

"Do you?" Rose asked.

Gabriel stopped and turned to face Rose. His jaw was set hard, clenched from the anguish he suddenly felt in his chest.

"Rose, I've done things that would make most people's stomach turn. I'm not the kind you take home to meet your mom. I joined the military to get away from here, but when I retired, all I could think about was coming back home. Why? I don't know. I just did. I guess a part of me was looking to heal from the past and try to make some good out of not being here for my parents when they needed me the most," Gabriel explained.

Rose stood looking at the man in front of her. She noticed his jawline and how tight the muscles were. She saw more, though, like the sadness in his eyes. The pain that he must be carrying.

She took a huge risk but stepped forward, wrapped her arms around him, and held on tight. Gabriel was caught off guard, but not in a bad way. He knew what she was trying to do, and as he felt her body press against his, he felt his own starting to relax. He felt his arms tighten slightly around her but then released at the last second. She had been the first woman he had been that physically close to in years.

"I'm sorry if that made you uncomfortable. I felt the strange urge to try and make you feel better," Rose explained.

"It's okay. I didn't mean to dump that on you. I've had twenty years of training that basically forced me to keep things packed tight. So, I did," Gabriel said.

"But you're here now. You can unpack things a little at a time. I promise it's safe," she said, trying to reassure him that things were okay.

From where he was standing, things did look a little safer.

"Thanks. You actually may have saved me a psych visit. I was supposed to call in over the next couple of days to report in on how I'm adjusting," Gabriel said.

"See, it's already started," Rose replied, smiling.

Gabriel laughed. He had a feeling that she was what he needed more than anything.

They made it to his truck and climbed in. Rose had him stop by a fast-food restaurant and wait outside as she ran in. A few minutes later, she came out with what looked like a grocery cart worth of food.

She hopped back into the truck and smiled.

"Got everything we need, let's go!" she said.

Rose had picked up enough fried chicken to feed a small village and all the trimmings. Gabriel would be eating pretty well before too long, or so he hoped.

Chapter Four

When they pulled up to the park, Gabriel was quickly reminded of why this was *the* place to go after church. There was lush green grass and tall, tall trees. Most of the people from the church had congregated at or around the gazebo that sat alongside a small stream. The backdrop of the mountains was a nice addition.

"I'll let you lead the way," Gabriel said.

"Well, I usually just sit next to anyone that looks hungry, and we share what the other has brought," Rose said.

Gabriel looked down at the food he was carrying and smiled.

"I think there are going to be a lot of people sitting by us," he said.

"That's what I was hoping for," she replied, smiling.

Gabriel was instructed to set stuff down on a table in the shade of the gazebo. He stepped back and watched as Rose got out all the food. She quickly found herself swarmed by hungry people.

"I think you're a hit," Gabriel said, amazed by how many people converged on the table.

"We better join in, or there won't be anything left," Rose said.

Gabriel agreed as he stepped up alongside Rose and grabbed a plate and plasticware. He didn't want to seem greedy by loading up his plate, so he only took a couple of things. He was going to have to eat more when he got home.

Rose stayed in front of him the whole time but managed to look back and noticed his plate wasn't that full.

"Now, I know you eat more than that. My ex was military, too, remember? If there was food, he was there and not shy about how much he took," Rose said.

"What branch?' he asked.

"Army," she answered.

"Infantry?" Gabriel asked.

"I think so. Why?" she asked.

"Any Army guys I ever knew ate like they were on death row and eating their last meal. Snipers, on the other hand, or at least me, ate like I was going into the desert- food conservation," Gabriel explained.

"Makes sense. Well, you're not going into the desert, so eat up, or I'll feed you myself!" Rose said.

"Ha! Is that a promise or a threat?" Gabriel asked.

"Both," Rose said as she shrugged her shoulders. "Dark or light? Breast or thigh?"

"Huh?" Gabriel asked, confused by the sudden shift.

Rose looked back with a bucket of chicken in her hand.

"There are only two kinds of men in this world - breast men or thigh men," she said.

It was his turn to be embarrassed. His mind quickly went elsewhere, and Rose could tell by the partial smile forming in the corners of Gabriel's lips.

"How about a breast, then? You seem like the kinda guy that likes breasts," Rose said.

"Oh, sweet Jesus, help me," Gabriel mumbled under his breath, except Rose heard him and quickly became aware of what she had just said.

She set the chicken down after putting both pieces on his plate and then grabbed one of his arms and escorted him to a picnic table farthest away from everyone else.

By the time they got to the table, Gabriel was about to bust from laughter, and Rose was red head to toe.

"Why didn't you say something?" she asked.

"And what, miss the pretty shade of red that you now seem to be covered in? Heck no. For the record, I like legs. Don't get me wrong, I like breasts, chicken breasts, that is, but I like long, slender legs," Gabriel said. He was egging her on now. He could see on her face that she was about to pop from embarrassment, so he stopped.

"Okay, I'll stop. I'm sorry. You did set yourself up, though," he said, handing Rose a napkin.

She had started crying, which made Gabriel feel bad. He didn't think what he had said actually hurt her.

He held out his hand and put it on her arm.

43

"Hey, don't do that. Come on now. I was just teasing you. I'm sorry," Gabriel said.

Rose sniffed one last time and then socked Gabriel in the arm.

"Hey! What was that for?" he asked.

"For making me think I had embarrassed you! There were so many people staring at us, I had to get us out of there," Rose said.

"First of all, it was kind of funny, and yes, you kind of embarrassed me, but it was all in good fun. Besides, it was fun to watch you squirm," Gabriel said.

"Oh, you are so going to get it," Rose said, hinting at retaliation.

She leaned in and bumped her shoulder against his.

They spent the next hour or two eating and talking, but not in that order. It had been years since Gabriel had been allowed to let things go like he was doing and in a personal manner. She made it easy for him to open up, but he wasn't about to let out all his dirty laundry.

Death was hard to just open up and talk about, especially when you were the one causing the death.

Peppered throughout their conversation, Rose dropped several hints of trauma in her life. The more he let her carry the conversation, the more he felt off about Rose. Something that made his sniper senses go on high alert.

She mentioned a couple of times her ex's name and a couple of other things that cued him into her possibly not feeling safe. He even caught her slipping up when she mentioned moving to their town and starting life over. When a woman says things like that, there is a good chance they were starting life over for a reason, not just because they picked a spot out on a map.

The sun started setting, and they realized almost everyone had left. Everything in the gazebo had been cleaned up, so they headed back to Gabriel's truck, got in, and headed back toward the church.

"Do you mind if we make a quick stop? There's a place I want to see real quick," he said.

"Sure. I'm in no hurry," Rose replied.

A road on the outskirts of town led up to a mountaintop that overlooked the whole town and beyond. He decided to try to end the night on a good note, but he knew he was taking a chance with Rose. He did only just meet here a day or two ago.

The sun was setting by the time they got to the top of the mountain. He walked around, opened Rose's door, and helped her get out. He quickly grabbed his suit coat from the back seat. It was getting chilly, and he thought it might come in handy as most things go with potential intimate moments.

He noticed she had slipped her high heels off at some point and was now barefoot. He saw the perfect spot and led her to an area near a tall pine tree.

Gabriel heard Rose gasp, knowing she was watching the sun set over the mountain range.

"I, uh, wanted to say thank you for today, and please don't think I'm trying to be too forward, but this was the only thing I could think of that would explain how I felt being around you today," Gabriel said, his rich bass voice slipping into a near whisper.

Rose was visibly shivering, so he wrapped his suit coat around her shoulders. She pulled it tight around herself and snuggled deep within the recesses of the coat. She turned and looked up at Gabriel.

"I don't know why you are home besides retiring, but something tells me there is a specific reason you needed to come back. Like you said earlier, even though we only met a day or two ago, I hope I get to be a part of the reason you came home," Rose said. She, too, was taking a huge risk, but both were feeling like the stars were aligning, so they did what most people do when the stars are moving about - they made a wish.

The horizon was turning from a yellow-orange hue to pinks and purples as the sun sank slowly out of view. Just as it was almost gone, a shooting star looked to kiss the top of the sun.

"Quick, make a wish," Rose said.

Gabriel looked down at Rose and smiled.

"I already did," he replied softly.

Rose leaned in, wrapped one of her arms around Gabriel's waist, and pulled him into her. She leaned up and softly kissed his cheek.

"What's that for?" he asked.

"My wish came true," she replied.

It was Gabriel's turn to reciprocate. He positioned himself and wrapped his arms around her, then pulled her for a tight embrace.

In the heat of their embrace, Gabriel's stomach let out an awful sound.

"Was that you or me?" Rose asked.

"I think it was me," Gabriel answered.

"I told you that you should have grabbed more food!" Rose reminded him.

"I know, but I wanted to make a good first impression," Gabriel said.

"I think you have surpassed that," Rose said, smiling. "Come on, I know an all-night diner we can go to. Plus, I have a friend that works there, so we might get a discount," Rose said.

"Sounds good. I have yet to have bad diner food," Gabriel said as they headed toward his truck.

"Is there such a thing?" Rose asked.

Gabriel stopped suddenly and looked at Rose, then shook his head.

"There was a diner I went to, or the equivalent of that in the Middle East. I had just gone out on patrol, and we passed through this small town that was supposed to be troop friendly. The owner came out and spoke pretty good English. He told us that if we wanted something to eat, to come inside, and he would feed us," Gabriel paused as if trying to focus on the memory.

"The place smelled pretty good, but we knew better than to let our guards down, and it paid off. Armed men came from the back with guns pointed at us. The good part is, we had the advantage."

"Why is that?" Rose asked.

"Always have a sniper on your team because they don't always keep long-barreled rifles on them; they usually have at least one side piece too. I managed to get shots off, killing five of their guys before they could even fire once. By then, my guys had drawn their weapons and pointed them at the remaining terrorists. One of my guys quickly told the shop owner that we would like to take our order to go, hinting with the end of his gun that there would be more consequences.

"So let me guess, the service sucked?" Rose said, trying to stifle a laugh.

"Yep, but surprisingly the food wasn't too bad," Gabriel replied.

"Well, I can promise you that the diner my friend works at won't have terrorists working in the back," Rose said.

"Good, because I left my sidearm at home," Gabriel said.

"You don't carry a gun on you, do you?" Rose asked, concerned.

"No. If I have to start carrying a gun in my hometown, then we have bigger problems," Gabriel said with a serious tone.

"Agreed," Rose acknowledged.

They both climbed into the truck and headed back toward town.

Rose made sure she moved over to the middle seat next to Gabriel.

Chapter Five

They pulled into the diner's parking lot to find it packed. Gabriel didn't get discouraged, though. He knew there had to be a spot somewhere. He circled the lot several times, then found an open spot at the rear.

"I think I'm going to text my friend with our order. What do you want? They pretty much have everything," Rose said.

Gabriel thought for a moment.

"I think I actually want some breakfast food, so tell her I'll take a stack of pancakes with a side of bacon and two fried eggs," Gabriel said.

"I thought you said you eat to conserve like you were going into the desert," Rose asked.

"Nope, I've come out the other side, and I've made it to paradise!" he said as he smiled at Rose.

She turned several shades of red before she could compose herself enough to text her friend.

She finally sent the text, then got a response a few seconds later.

"She said to come inside in about ten minutes, and she'll have it ready for us at the front counter," Rose said.

"Sounds good to me. I'll be ready for it," Gabriel said.

They talked until it was time to head in to pick up their food. While walking towards the front door, Gabriel's sniper senses kicked in, this time for real. He spotted a couple of men standing between two eighteen-wheelers. It didn't appear they were having a friendly conversation, but more like they were on the lookout.

Rose noticed Gabriel tense up.

"What's wrong?" she asked.

"Get inside, and I'll tell you," he answered quickly.

Rose shot him a worried glance as she quickened her pace.

After making it inside, Gabriel positioned himself where he could see out a window that faced where the two men were standing.

"What's going on?" Rose whispered.

"I think there is, or was, a kidnapping. I saw two guys standing between two trucks, and they weren't having a conversation that suggested they were friends," Gabriel said.

"You know this how?" Rose asked.

"I was in the military, remember? One of my missions was tracking down slavers and sex traffickers," Gavriel said quietly.

"Oh, my God! It *is* a thing," she replied with a horrified look.

"Yeah, but it happens over here too. As in right outside our doors," Gabriel replied.

He looked one more time out the window and then quickly turned back towards Rose.

"Go find your friend and tell her to call the cops. I'll be back," Gabriel ordered.

"You aren't going out there, are you?" Rose asked, worried.

"Yep, and with any luck, I'll be bringing some friends back with me for dinner," Gabriel said. "I'll be fine, I promise. I did survive that Middle Eastern diner, remember?"

"Come back to me," Rose said. She quickly kissed him, then ran to find her friend.

Gabriel headed out the front doors and stood just out of sight of the two men still standing between their two trucks. An eighteen-wheeler just happened to pass by, so Gabriel acted fast and ran behind it, then crossed between a few trucks that were over from where the men were standing.

He crept slowly towards the first truck and then placed his ear near the head of the trailer. He could hear the slight sound of what he thought was a muffled cry. He was correct. There was a kidnapping going on.

Gabriel knew there was no way to get whoever was in that trailer, or even the other one, to safety. He was going to have to do things the hard way.

He waited until another big truck rolled by and then quickly came up behind the two men, rendering them both unconscious by slamming their heads into the other. Knowing that the two men would be out for a few minutes, he quickly went to the back of the first truck and opened the back doors.

There was indeed someone inside. There were several people inside - several young females, to be exact. They were tied, gagged, and restrained to the trailer wall. They weren't going anywhere by the looks of it.

Gabriel quickly hopped inside the trailer and freed the girls. He told them to head towards the diner, and someone would be waiting for them; that someone was Rose and her friend. The girls were all in rough shape but moved as fast as they could.

Gabriel quickly hopped out of the trailer as the last of the girls made it out, then he went to the next trailer and opened it up. There was no one inside.

He made his way back to where the two men were lying and stood over them. One of them moaned a little and opened his eyes.

"Howdy. You wouldn't happen to be the owner of this truck here, would you?" Gabriel asked.

The man started to make a move, but Gabriel moved with a speed that only a U.S. military sniper could make and rendered him unconscious again. Satisfied that the men would be napping for a few still, he ran back to the first trailer, grabbed some straps out, and then headed back to the men and tied them up.

Gabriel then dragged both men to the diner's front door, where the cops were waiting.

"Officers, I'm assuming you have plans for these two?" Gabriel asked.

"We'll take it from here, thanks," one of the officers said.

The other officer pulled Gabriel aside to ask some questions.

"How did you know what was going on?"

"You don't spend as long as I did in the military and not learn a few things along the way," Gabriel answered.

"Like trafficking?" the officer asked.

"So much more than just that," Gabriel replied.

"Well, thank you for this. There are going to be some happy families tonight," the officer said as he shook Gabriel's hand.

Gabriel nodded, then found his way over to Rose, who was helping bandage up one of the girls. She turned as he got close, ran to him, and wrapped her arms around him. Tears stained her cheeks.

"Everything is fine, don't worry," he said as Rose sobbed in his arms.

She stopped crying after a minute and then pulled back and looked up at him.

"It's okay. All done," Gabriel said.

"I was worried something would happen," Rose said.

"I know, but I had to do something. I did what I was trained to do," Gabriel replied.

"Let's get our food and get out of here. Those girls have a long road ahead of them," Rose said.

Gabriel agreed. He had seen it too many times. It didn't always end this well, though, either.

Their food ended up being on the house. When the diner owner heard what happened, he thanked them both profusely.

They finally made their way back to Gabriel's truck and quickly got in. The news crews were starting to show up, and neither he nor Rose felt like talking to anyone but each other.

Gabriel could feel Rose trembling next to him. It was like the whole seat was vibrating. He pulled his truck over to the side of the road and turned a little so he could wrap his arms around her. She was clearly going through something.

"I know a lot just happened back there, but what else is going on?" Gabriel asked.

"You know when I said my ex was in the Army?" Rose asked.

"Yeah, why?" he asked.

"He was discharged for dishonorable conduct. I wasn't told all the details, but I found out through a friend of a friend that he and a couple of men had possibly raped some women while overseas. It couldn't be proven, but rather than have their actions tarnish the military, he was more or less kicked out. He wasn't home long before he started taking things out on me, so I ran," Rose explained.

"And here you are," Gabriel said.

"Here I am," Rose said.

"I had heard of stuff like that happening, but it always went away quietly. I'm really sorry that happened to you. So long as I am around, I won't let anyone hurt you," Gabriel said.

"I know you won't, and thank you," Rose said. She saw the clock on the radio and how late it was getting to be. "Do you want to just come back to my place? You still have a little bit of a drive, right?"

"Actually, I do, but that's okay," Gabriel said.

"I would feel better if you come back to my place. I promise everything will be okay," Rose reassured him.

"Okay. I mean, we do have all this food to eat," Gabriel said as he licked his lips.

"I almost forgot about all of this. I doubt I can eat all my stuff now," she said.

"There's always breakfast," Gabriel said.

"Very true," Rose said.

Gabriel got his truck back on the road and headed towards Rose's place. He knew tomorrow would bring about some interesting conversations, to say the least.

Chapter Six

They made it back to Rose's place. It was a small, one-bedroom apartment above a coffee shop in the downtown business district. It was quaint, and the decoration fit Rose's personality- soft shades of blues, pinks, and reds.

They were greeted by Rose's dog, Samson - a big, slobbery Chocolate Lab/Mastiff mix.

"Samson, we have company. Go lay down," Rose ordered.

Samson decided otherwise. There was a stranger in his house, and that stranger had food.

"He might need to check you out. He's cautious with new people, but he's never been aggressive except..." Rose didn't finish her sentence, but Gabriel probably could have guessed why - her ex.

Gabriel kneeled on one knee, although simply crouching would have sufficed. Samson was a big dog.

"Hi, boy. Do you mind if I come in and hang out with your mom for a while? I'll even share my bacon," Gabriel said.

Samson sucked in a large breath of air, then let out a giant bark, followed by a tail wag.

"Alright then, let's me and you see about some bacon," Gabriel said.

Samson thrust out his paw to signify to his new friend that he needed to seal the deal with a paw shake.

"Atta boy. Let's go," said Gabriel.

Both man and dog walked down the short hallway, then to the left, where the kitchen was.

"You two friends now?" Rose asked.

"Yeah, bacon might have been brought up, but it was worth it," Gabriel said.

"Samson is a sucker for some bacon, aren't ya, boy?" Rose asked.

Samson tilted his head to one side and sighed.

"It's coming, hold on," Gabriel said to the impatient dog.

"So, have you had much chance to think about your next chapter in life?" Rose asked.

"Actually, a couple of things. My folks have about twenty-five hundred acres, and I don't need that much. I was thinking about selling some of it to a wind farm company. The other thing I've been mulling over was to buy a couple hundred head of cattle and start a cattle ranch," Gabriel explained.

"Well, you sound as if you've got things pretty squared away," Rose replied, surprised by Gabriel's answer.

"I feel like I owe it to my parents to try and revive the ranch. Plus, I have Rex to help with things," Gabriel replied.

"Who's Rex?" Rose asked.

"Oh, he's the only ranch hand that stuck around after things fell apart when my parents went into debt and then when they both died. He's a third-generation rancher, so you might say that he's fully invested in the cause, too," Gabriel said.

"It's good that you have help," Rose said.

"I wouldn't say 'help.' He's getting up there in years, but I bet he's got a few years left in him," Gabriel replied.

Rose smiled.

"Something I said?" Gabriel asked.

"No, I just had a picture of what you might look like when you're old and gray," Rose said.

"Oh yeah, what do I look like?" Gabriel asked.

"Well, you still prefer to wear your suit and hat to church, and when you take your hat off as you enter the building, you have gray on the sides but the same dark color on top as you do now," Rose explained.

"What else? Do I have a limp or a cane? Any scars I need to know about?" Gabriel asked.

"Nope, you have a really good wife that keeps you healthy," Rose said, then smiled, not making eye contact.

"Ah, I see. Does this wife have a name?" Gabriel asked.

"I'm not sure, but I think she makes you happy. You always smile when she comes into the room," Rose said.

"Well, I guess I better keep my eyes out for her then," Gabriel said, looking down at Samson. "If you see my future wife, be sure and give her a big kiss for me, okay?"

Samson tilted his head and looked long and hard up at Gabriel, then stood up on all four legs, walked around the kitchen island, suddenly stood up on his hind legs, looked Rose square in the face, and licked her clean across the face.

Both Rose and Gabriel had shocked expressions on their faces.

Still standing on his hind legs, Samson looked at Rose, then over at Gabriel, and was panting. He lifted one paw and put it on Rose's hand, resting on the counter. It was as if he were giving his blessing for something that was yet to happen.

"Well, okay then. I guess I better give the man his bacon before he starts dancing in circles," Rose said.

"Me too. I mean, I better eat some of that bacon, too," Gabriel said, trying to correct himself.

"Or what, you'll start dancing in circles?" Rose said and then laughed.

"I only dance in circles if I have a partner to dance with," Gabriel said.

Rose turned around, turned the small radio on sitting on the windowsill, and then turned the kitchen lights off. She walked over to Gabriel and held out her hand.

"What were you saying about having a partner to dance with?" Rose asked quietly as she held out her hand.

Gabriel took her hand, stepped into her space, and placed his other hand around her waist until it was in the small of her back.

"I said I would only dance in circles if I had a partner. It looks like I found one," Gabriel said, pulling her in close.

A song by Brad Paisley was playing softly on the radio, lyrics that made Gabriel's and Rose's bodies slowly sway in rhythm.

The song eventually stopped, and a new one came on, but they continued to dance as if the original music was still playing.

A sudden clap of thunder exploded outside, causing both dance partners to flinch. The next sound was the sound of Samson helping himself to goodies in the diner bag that was now on the floor.

Gabriel was the first to notice and started to laugh.

"A man that knows what he wants. I like it."

"What do you want?" Rose asked, looking up into Gabriel's eyes.

"Well, clearly, breakfast is out of the question now, but…"

Rose grabbed Gabriel by the back of the head and pulled it down, guiding his face towards hers. A long emotional-laden kiss awaited his lips. There was a deeper meaning in there with some untethered emotion. Rose had reached her emotional breaking point, and the fire that she had kept hidden had broken forth from the tinder box she kept it in, and her heart was now on fire.

Gabriel saving those girls at the truck stop diner had only hastened the flames within her. She felt safe with him, and feeling the energy ripple down his arms into his hands as he lifted her up, then searching for a place to land in the living room only intensified.

Lightning crackled just outside, giving off a burst of light, casting shadows on the walls and the ceiling that told a story of an ensuing passion.

A warrior that had come home to claim the love of his princess.

~(-)~

The next morning told a much different story. Outside, the sky was gray and with a chill in the air. While inside, two lovers lay snuggled under mounds of blankets, wrapped in each other's arms.

Gabriel lay staring into Rose's eyes, neither wanting to move or even close their eyes again for fear that what they were experiencing was a dream.

"Thank you for last night," Gabriel said.

"You're welcome, and thank you," Rose said. "I don't know what happened in the kitchen, though. I mean, the last thing I remember is you and I slow dancing, and then thunder and lightning, then you lifting me up and-" Gabriel kissed Rose and smiled.

"I'm not going to deny what happened or even try to figure it all out. I will say this, though, I'm not much into the supernatural, but I believe there was a certain kind of energy last night, and I really hope it sticks around for a while," Gabriel explained.

"Me too," Rose said, giving Gabriel a return kiss.

There was a sudden pressure in between them that could only come from a large mammal standing on the bed.

"Good morning, Samson," Gabriel said as he pulled back the blankets.

"Hi, baby. I am so sorry. Mommy went to bed without saying goodnight," Rose said.

Samson looked at Rose, somehow able to see through her lie. He started to pant, which caused a vast amount of drool to roll out.

"I think he knows you didn't go to bed with the intention of saying good night, at least not to him," Gabriel said.

"Yeah, well, he ate our food, so there!" Rose bit back playfully.

"About that, how good are you at making an actual breakfast?" Gabriel asked.

"Better yet, why don't we go downstairs and get some coffee. My best friend owns the coffee shop. She'll make us anything we want," Rose said.

"Deal, but then I get to pick what we do next," Gabriel said.

"Is this going to turn out to be an all-day date?" Rose asked.

"Well, I know this all may be a little fast, especially last night, but I just spent the past twenty years doing what the government wanted. I think I owe it to myself to do what I want for a change," Gabriel said with a hint of vim and vigor in his voice.

"I second that. Let's go get something to eat and drink, then figure out the rest of our day," Rose said, flipped the covers off her, and jumped out of bed.

"Race you to the shower!" she said, taking off towards the bathroom.

Gabriel let her take the lead. He liked the view.

Chapter Seven

The coffee was good, but the food was even better. Rose's friend made a giant grilled cheese sandwich with bacon and a bowl of hot beef stew for each. While making the food, Rose's friend, Emelia, interrogated Gabriel with the usual questions that a protective friend would ask. Gabriel passed with flying colors.

As they devoured gooey cheese and the most sumptuous beef stew, Gabriel watched the interaction between Rose and Emelia. He hadn't known her for very long, but that was the most relaxed outside of her home that he had seen of her. There was a sense of safety between those two.

Rose wrapped her arm around his, interlacing her fingers with his. It was a strange but comforting feeling to Gabriel. The only thing he had interlaced his fingers with was the trigger of a gun, but he had never made love to his weapon. What happened the night before was a first for him on all accounts.

Eventually, all the food and drink had been consumed. Rose had given the non-verbal sign it was time to go, but Gabriel had missed it. Rose's friend did not, though.

"I'll be right back. I need to use the little girls' room before we go," Rose excused herself.

"Gabriel, can I give you a piece of advice?" Emelia asked.

"Sure, go ahead."

"When you were in the military, you had signals that were unspoken, correct?" Emelia asked.

"Of course. We didn't dare say a word if we were in a tight spot. Why do you ask?"

Emelia looked to make sure Rose wasn't hiding around the corner.

"Well, if you and my friend are going to be a thing, you might want to learn her cues when she is telling you it is time to go," Emelia said.

"Ah, is that why she looked at me and then tapped my leg with her leg?" Gabriel asked.

"Yep, and now you know. So, keep an eye out for those little signals," Emelia suggested.

"Thanks for the food. How much do I owe you?" Rose said, popping back from around the corner.

"Nothing. It's on the house. Consider it a congratulatory gift," Emelia replied.

"For what?" Rose asked.

"You know why," Emelia answered, giving another signal, but was caught this time by Gabriel.

"I'll call ya later, and we can talk about all of this," Rose said.

"Bye! Have fun, you two," Emelia said. "Oh, Gabriel, hold on a sec."

Gabriel stepped back to hear what Emelia had to say.

"Be careful with her. Her wounds run deep. If she's opening up to you already, that means she trusts you, and considering what her boyfriend did to her, you need to be all in or let her go now before she gets too close. Okay?" Emelia asked with eyes wide open.

"I understand. I won't let her, or you, down. We'll go nice and slow to make sure everything fits just right," Gabriel replied.

"Thank you."

Gabriel smiled and then caught up to Rose, waiting by the front door.

"What was that about?" she asked.

"She just wanted to give me one last piece of advice," Gabriel said.

"Oh, yeah? What was it?" Rose asked.

"To let you have the bathroom first in the morning. You tend to be a little gassy," Gabriel said with a serious look.

Rose stopped dead in her tracks and looked up at Gabriel.

"She did not say that," Rose said, appalled.

"That's what she said. You can go ask her yourself," Gabriel said, still trying to keep a straight face but failing.

Rose saw his lower lip quiver. He was trying to stifle laughter from erupting.

"You are so bad! She did not say that!" Rose said.

Gabriel couldn't contain himself anymore. He started laughing so hard that he grabbed his sides.

"I'm sorry! I'm sorry. I promise I won't do it again!" Gabriel said, still laughing.

Rose was red from head to toe with embarrassment.

"That's twice you got me now. I owe you big time!" Rose said.

"I know. I'm sorry. Come here. Let me make it up to you," Gabriel said, smiling.

"No way. You're in trouble," Rose said as she walked ahead of Gabriel.

He caught up to her in just a couple of quick strides, pulled her back into his arms, and held her tight. Rose had gone from being embarrassed to crying in a matter of seconds.

"Hey, it's okay. What's wrong?" he asked.

"You! You don't know how hard it is to be where I am right now. My ex used to publicly embarrass me to keep me down and control me. Then, when we would get back home, he would yell at me for embarrassing him; that's when things would get bad quickly. I got lucky this last time. Emelia happened to be in town and stopped by for a surprise visit. She heard the shouting and called the cops," Rose was trying to explain in between catching her breath.

The trauma she had been storing up was coming out of her like ink from a fountain pen, leaking all over, making a mess. This mess needed to happen, though. She needed to heal.

Gabriel held her tight. He was no stranger to trauma. He had killed countless people, and his day of reckoning would one day come as well. Rose needed her reckoning to come now, as it would no doubt come again, but hopefully less painfully next time.

"Rose, listen to me, okay? Just listen. Emelia's advice was to take the best care of you I could as long as I was interested. Otherwise, she said I should let you go."

"Are you?" Rose asked.

"What?" Gabriel asked.

"Going to let me go?" Rose asked.

"You know, the Bible doesn't speak much about destiny or fate, but I believe there was a reason I came back here besides taking back my parent's ranch. It was to meet you, and I intend to do things right. Emelia told me to take things slow, and I plan to do just that! I'm done doing things like Uncle Sam wanted me to. I'm going to reclaim what's left of my life and give it to one person and one person only; that is, if she'll take it," Gabriel said. He looked down at a still trembling Rose and wiped a stray tear.

"If you mean me, then yes. I'll take it. I want to do things right, too. And I know you probably have things to deal with, so how about we both take care of the baggage as it comes up?" Rose said.

"I agree. I did a lot of things people would be horrified by, and you were with a guy that did some horrifying things too. Let's both deal with our past so we can move forward," Gabriel said.

"Okay. I think we can do this," Rose said, then buried her head in his chest one last time.

"Hey, you guys," it was Pastor Nick.

Rose looked up with fear in her eyes.

Gabriel had his back partially towards Pastor Nick, thus being able to hide Rose from view.

"He can't see me like this. He'll think something is wrong."

Gabriel turned quickly to see Pastor Nick just a handshake away from him.

"Good morning! Rose and I just finished up a coffee date, unexpectedly, that is. Someone said she wasn't feeling very good," Gabriel said, trying to cover up what had just happened.

"Rose, you okay?" Nick asked.

"I'm fine. Probably female-related. Although that storm last night was pretty rough," Rose followed up, adding to the little white lie.

"Well, I trust Gabriel will get you home safe. I guess it's a good thing you live upstairs, huh?" Nick asked.

"For sure. Good seeing you, Pastor Nick. I'll be in tomorrow morning," Rose said, moving towards her front door.

"Sounds good. You two have a good rest of your day," Pastor Nick said and then headed down the sidewalk.

Neither Rose nor Gabriel spoke until they were back upstairs at her place. Rose shut and locked the door, leaned against it, and exhaled loudly.

"Wow, I'm pretty sure I'll be praying at church a lot more this Wednesday," she said.

"Why, you *were* dealing with some female stuff. You didn't lie about that," Gabriel said, trying to reassure Rose.

"Yeah, but there's female, and then there's *female* stuff. You know what I mean?" Rose asked.

"I know what you mean. I was just saying that you'll probably be fine. Besides, we're two grown adults doing adult things, and the last time I checked, Pastor Nick wasn't wearing a white collar and sitting on the other side of a privacy screen," Gabriel said.

"I know, and you're right. Our lives, our business," she replied.

"Good business, though, nothing bad," Gabriel added.

"You got that right!" Rose said.

"So, what do you want to do?" Gabriel asked.

"Well, I actually just realized you are in the same clothes that you went to church in yesterday. Do you need to go home to change?" Rose asked.

Gabriel looked down at himself and shook his head in disbelief.

"I guess you're right. You wanna come with me? I can change clothes, then show you around the ranch," Gabriel asked.

"I'd like that. Are you sure you're up for more time with me?" she asked.

"I did say all-day date, right?" he asked.

"Yep! So, should I bring some extra clothes? You know, in case I get dirty or whatever it is you do on the ranch," Rose said.

"Probably not a bad idea," he answered.

"Okay, let me get some clothes packed, and then we can head out," Rose said excitedly, then headed towards her bedroom. "Hey, can we bring Samson too? You know, in case our all-day date turns into an all-night date."

Gabriel laughed.

"Yeah, we better bring the big fella. It would be nice to have a dog wandering around the property again," Gabriel said.

"Good. Would you mind grabbing some dog food for me and putting some in a bag?" Rose asked.

"Why don't we just stop by the store, and I'll get some? Then we can have some here and at my place?" Gabriel asked.

"Really?" Rose asked as she popped her head around the corner.

"Yep, might as well do it right. Besides, I need more than just *guy* food at the house," Gabriel replied.

"What do you mean?" Rose asked.

"I went to the store the other day and literally just bought a shopping cart full of steaks. I was done with military food and went all out and loaded up on meat," Gabriel explained.

"Sounds good to me. Although maybe with some healthy stuff thrown in there, too," Rose said.

"Yeah, I need to," he said.

Rose appeared suddenly with a large bag.

"Ready to go!" she said.

"Me too. Are you ready to go, boy?" Gabriel said.

Samson looked up and wagged his tail across the floor.

"I guess he's ready," Gabriel said.

"Alright, let's get going. We got chores to do," Rose said, trying to sound like she lived on a ranch too.

Gabriel smiled. It was going to be a fun afternoon. The proverbial ice had been broken already, and he even passed the test of a friend. Gabriel was on the right track.

Chapter Eight

They made it back to the ranch to find Rex sitting on the front porch like a parent waiting for a child to get home from a night out. Gabriel couldn't help but feel a little anxious as Rex gave a partial scowl at the sight of Rose and the dog.

"Bring home some company, did ya?" Rex asked.

"Yep, Rex, this is Rose and her dog Samson. Guys, this is Rex," Gabriel said.

"Hi, Rex! Nice to meet you. Gabriel was telling me about you yesterday. He said you're a third-generation rancher. I can't even imagine how things have changed through the generations," Rose said, trying to engage Rex.

"Well, some things have, and some things haven't. One of the things, though, and I stick by it, is calling your ranch hand when you aren't going to make it back home when there are things to do around the ranch," Rex said, giving Gabriel the stink eye.

"Come on now, Rex, I went to church and then out to lunch with Rose here. I didn't realize it would turn into coffee the next morning. Besides, I can't call you if you don't have a cell phone," Gabriel said.

"I got a house phone, though," Rex fired back.

"Would you have answered it?" Gabriel asked.

"Maybe, maybe not. Depends on how I was feelin' at the time," Rex said stubbornly.

"Exactly, so are we done with this little parental chastising, or is there more?" Gabriel said, his patience wearing thin.

"Nope, I just wanted to throw out there that the next time you decide to go shack up at a woman's house that you ain't never been to, t'would be a nice idea if you'd let me know, so I can make other plans," Rex said and then tipped his hat and walked away.

Gabriel was shocked as he watched his friend/adopted father walk away.

"Um, I don't know why he said that. He's been around me my whole life and never acted that way. I'll be right back," Gabriel said, trying to apologize.

He leaned in and gave Rose a quick kiss on the cheek, then hurried after Rex.

"Hey!" Gabriel called out. "Rex!"

Rex stopped and turned around to face Gabriel.

"I don't know where that came from, but talking to Rose that way is not going to happen again!" Gabriel said, staring straight into Rex's eyes.

"I ain't too concerned about it. She ain't gonna stick around anyway. Girls like her are a dime a dozen. They see a man fresh out of the service, and they just wanna show him a good time," Rex said.

Gabriel didn't realize Rose was within earshot of them, but when she heard Rex say what he had just said, she took off running towards the truck and got in, calling Samson after her.

She started the truck and took off back down the long gravel driveway.

"Rose!" Gabriel called after her, but no luck. She was too far out of range.

He turned around and stared Rex down.

Rex knew he had done Gabriel and Rose wrong but wouldn't admit it.

"If you were anyone else, even my dad, I would lay you out where you stand," Gabriel fired off.

"So, what's stopping you?" Rex asked, staring back at Gabriel.

"Because I'm not interested and adding another death to the tally,"

"You'd be doing me a favor. I'm just happy your parents aren't here to see this," Rex said.

"My parents wouldn't have said what you just said, and my dad loved my mom more than anything," Gabriel yelled.

"And your dad wouldn't have been knock'n boots with her the first night they were together!" Rex yelled back.

Something snapped inside Gabriel. He wasn't the young soldier he used to be, but he moved fast enough that Rex didn't have time to prepare for what was coming.

In a matter of seconds, more like breaths, Gabriel had Rex firmly by the front of his shirt, hoisting him off his feet, then turned his whole body in the air and slammed him into the side of the house.

The windows in the old house rattled, and timbers creaked as the old man's body hit the outer wall.

The look on Rex's face was one of shock and horror. He knew Gabriel was a strong and dangerous man when he needed to be, but this was more than that.

"Son put me down," Rex whispered, then coughed. A red stain covered his lips.

Gabriel saw the blood coming from Rex's mouth and immediately dropped him. He thought he had broken his friend.

"Rex, I'm sorry. I didn't mean to-" Gabriel stopped talking as Rex went into a coughing fit. Blood rushed out, splattering the front of Gabriel.

Gabriel immediately pulled out his cell phone and dialed 9-1-1.

"9-1-1, what is your emergency?" said the operator.

"Yes, this is Gabriel Sterling at the Sterling Ranch. My friend is coughing up blood, and he can't catch his breath."

"Have him sit down so that he doesn't fall and cause worse damage. Can you tell me how old he is?" the operator said.

"Um, I dunno, maybe late sixties, early seventies," Gabriel answered.

"Okay. I'll get an ambulance dispatched. You said Sterling Ranch, correct?" the operator asked.

"Yes, please hurry!" Gabriel said.

"It looks like there is an ambulance ten minutes out. If you can get him calmed down, that would help until they get there," the operator instructed.

"I'm trying. There's a lot of blood coming out, though," Gabriel said. "Rex, I'm so sorry. Please don't die on me! I need more time with you. Please don't go anywhere."

It took a minute, but Rex could finally sit upright and take a more complete breath. There was only a slight gurgle when he breathed.

"What the hell was that?" Gabriel asked.

"Well, I wish I could say it was you and your brute strength just knocking the ignorant out of me, but I think I have something wrong on my insides," Rex said.

"Like what?" Gabriel asked.

"I dunno. I'm a ranch hand, not a doctor."

"I'm so sorry! I should have watched myself," Gabriel said.

"It's okay. I had it coming," Rex admitted.

"Maybe, but I didn't need to use you like a wrecking ball," Gabriel said.

"I'll admit, you're a lot stronger than I thought you were," Rex said.

"Twenty years in the military. They expected us to be in top shape, especially us snipers," Gabriel said.

"Well, Uncle Sam raised you to be a strong young man. And for the record, I'm seventy-four," Rex said.

Gabriel laughed. Rex always had to be the one to get the last word in.

~(-)~

Rose tore off down the gravel road in a truck that was not hers, but she didn't care. She was beyond hurt. No one had ever confused her for a whore or anything else of that nature. She may have been a little flirty over the years, but she had never, ever come across as a woman of ill repute.

Rose got to the highway that led back to town just in time to see an ambulance speed past.

She watched the ambulance in the rearview mirror when a knot formed in the pit of her stomach.

"Gabriel!" Rose shouted, then spun the truck around and followed the ambulance.

She was emotionally overloaded already. Seeing the ambulance made things worse. A couple of minutes later, she pulled up right behind the ambulance just in time to see what looked to be Rex loaded up into the ambulance.

She threw the truck into park and launched herself out of the driver's side door.

"Gabriel!"

"Rose!"

Gabriel met Rose by the ambulance. He scooped her up into his arms and held her tight.

"I'm so sorry, Rose. He should never have said that," Gabriel said, muffling his words into her shoulder.

"It's okay! What happened, though? Did something happen?" Rose asked.

Gabriel set Rose down. He now needed to confess, more like share how he defended her honor.

Before Gabriel could explain, he saw the EMT shut the back door and look his way.

"Sir, you can follow us up to the hospital if you want?" the EMT said.

"We'll be right behind you," Gabriel said. "Um, I can drop you off if you want?"

Rose looked at the EMT, then back at Gabriel.

"No, I want to go. You don't need to be up there alone, you know..." Rose didn't finish the sentence. Gabriel knew what she was trying to say.

"Okay, meet you there then," the EMT said.

Everyone got in their respective vehicles and headed out. The hospital was about thirty minutes from where they were now.

They spent the first couple of minutes in silence. Gabriel wasn't sure what to say, and neither did Rose. Both people's hearts ached.

"I shouldn't have left. I'm sorry." Rose said, breaking the silence. "And I took your truck too."

"It's okay. I'm sorry Rex said what he did. I think he's sick or something. He shouldn't have coughed blood like that," Gabriel said.

"What *did* happen?" Rose asked.

"As soon as you flew out of there like a bat out of Hell, the old man kept spouting off. I snapped. picked him up by the front of his shirt, and slammed him into the house. It knocked the wind out of him. He started coughing real bad, then blood started coming out, too, and he couldn't catch his breath. I immediately called 9-1-1. I knew that wasn't normal," Gabriel explained.

"No, you might have bruised his back and his pride pretty good, but what you did shouldn't have caused what happened, hopefully not anyway," Rose said, trying to comfort Gabriel.

"I know, but either way, I shouldn't have done what I did," Gabriel admitted.

"Neither should he. And for the record, I've never slept around, so I hope that puts things at ease. What we did last night was out of passion and being caught up in the moment," Rose said, trying to justify herself.

"Rose-"

She looked at Gabriel. His voice changed for a second, sounding different.

"You are the most beautiful woman I have ever seen. Believe me, I've traveled around a lot and seen many women, but none of them compare to you. Inside or out. I promise," Gabriel said, reaching out with his right hand and placing it on Rose's.

"Thank you. You can drop me off at my place if you need to be up there with him alone. I don't want to cause any problems," Rose said, then pulled her hand away from Gabriel's.

Gabriel looked over at Rose, then back at the road.

"I was going to ask you the same thing. More so if it was too hard for you being up there and all. Otherwise, I could use you being with me. Hospitals and I don't usually do well, you know, with me being in the military," Gabriel said.

Rose looked at Gabriel and could tell by the look on his face that hospitals truly were not a good place for him. She hadn't thought of that.

"There's a Bible verse that says something about "wherever you shall go, I shall follow." I believe this is one of those times I need to be here for you, even if it is about Rex. Chances are, it will end up being more about you, too," Rose said.

Gabriel raised an eyebrow. The depth of her genius was astounding.

"You sure you aren't a doctor or at least a psychologist?" Gabriel asked, then smirked.

"No, quite sure I would have remembered all those years of school. I do read a lot of books, though," Rose admitted.

"I believe there is a verse somewhere that mentions the counsel of a good woman and the teaching of her kindness or something of that nature," Gabriel said.

"Yes, Proverbs thirty-one, verse twenty-six, and you were close," Rose said with a smile. "Pastor Nick would be proud."

"He wouldn't be so proud if he knew what I had done to Rex," Gabriel said.

"Whatever happened is between you, Rex, and the Lord, and if Rex doesn't forgive you, God will," Rose said, trying to make Gabriel feel a little more at ease.

"I'll keep that in mind. Thank you," Gabriel said as he squeezed Rose's hand.

The hospital finally came into view. The ambulance had beaten them there. They were allowed to speed, but Gabriel was not. He still drove at an accelerated rate of speed for most of the drive.

Gabriel and Rose left the truck windows partway rolled down, so Samson wouldn't overheat. She would call Emelia as soon as she got inside to see if she could come to get Samson.

They hurried to the front desk, gave the hospital staff the name of whom they were there, then raced towards the elevator to get to the floor Rex would be on.

The desk person said that Rex was already up on the x-ray floor, having some films taken but would be down whenever the technician got what they needed.

"I guess we go sit and wait, huh?" Rose asked.

"Yeah, I guess so," Gabriel said, his eyes darting around.

Rose noticed what was happening and placed her hands on his face.

"Hey, look at me."

Gabriel looked down at Rose.

"You got this. Whatever happens, I'm here, no one else, just you and me, okay?" she said as she stared deep into Gabriel's eyes.

"I know. It's just that the last time I was at a hospital was when I had the body of a little girl in my arms. A roadside bomb went off, and shrapnel had ripped through her little body. I never did find out if she was okay," Gabriel said, trying to explain the best he could why he was triggered.

"Gabriel, look at me. Right now, Rex is having a procedure done that may or may not show something good or bad. We don't know the outcome, so we have to stay strong," Rose said.

"I know, and that memory is from ten years ago. I should be over it by now, but clearly, I'm not," Gabriel said.

"You needed closure, you didn't get it, but now, here you are. Rex will need something, too. Closure might not be the word for this, but you are the closest person to him, right?"

Gabriel nodded.

"Then give him the best you that you can. I'll be right here next to you. I promise," Rose said, pulling him in for a tight embrace.

Gabriel and Rose made it up to the floor where Rex would be moved to. They didn't have to wait too long before a nurse came out to find them.

Mr. Sterling?" the nurse called out.

Gabriel shot up out of his chair.

"That's me. How is he?"

"He's in surgery right now. They found a strange mass in his left lung. It looked like it had somehow come loose and was free floating in his lung," the nurse explained.

Gabriel looked at the nurse, then at Rose, then back at the nurse.

"Are you saying he had a tumor in his lungs, then it somehow broke loose and now is sitting in his left lung?" Gabriel asked.

"I can't confirm that, but it sounds about right. As soon as he is out of surgery, someone will come get you," the nurse said.

"Okay, thank you," Gabriel said, then sat back down.

Three hours later, a surgeon came out to talk to Gabriel.

"Mr. Sterling, I'm Doctor Haywood, the surgeon that just worked on your friend, Rex Dansbury."

Gabriel stood up and shook hands with Dr. Haywood.

"I have never had a more confusing surgery than the one I just performed," Dr. Haywood said.

"How so?" Gabriel asked.

"So, when I saw the x-ray, it looked like there was a mass in his left lung. When I opened him, it was just sitting there, like it had fallen off wherever it had come from. Strangest thing I've ever seen. Anyway, the tumor was removed, and any affected areas of concern were examined. We have him on some high-dose meds for pain. No doubt that thing caused some issues. Blood tests did reveal he had lung cancer, but it was contained to the lung with the tumor," the surgeon explained.

"So, what can we expect once he gets out of here?" Gabriel asked.

"He's going to need rest and lots of it. There will be a post-op follow-up, and then I want to see him in here in three months, so I can see if anything else has developed since removing the tumor," the doctor said.

"Is he okay for the most part?" Rose asked. She wasn't sure if Gabriel was going to ask that or not.

"I mean, the man just coughed up a tumor. There isn't much else wrong with him other than being older," the surgeon said.

"Whatever it takes to make him better," Gabriel said.

"We'll do our best. We'll get you when he's back in his room. Hang tight," the surgeon said, walking back towards the surgery suite.

"That's good news, right?" Gabriel asked.

"I think so," Rose replied.

"Do you think what I did caused the tumor to become unattached?" Gabriel asked.

"I don't think you can rule it out, and if that's the case, Rex is probably the luckiest man on Earth right now," Rose said.

"I just hope he's okay. He's never been to the hospital. There were a couple of times he should have gone, but you know how stubborn old men are," Gabriel said.

"I know how stubborn younger men are, too," Rose said, looking at Gabriel.

"I guess I can't really deny that, can I?" Gabriel asked, a small smile forming at the corners of his lips.

"No, you can't. I better text Emelia and make sure she got the other stubborn man in my life home okay," Rose said as she got out her cell phone to text her friend.

Did you get Samson home okay?

A minute or two went by, and a reply came back as a picture message. It was a picture of Samson stretched out on his floor pillow, fast asleep.

Gabriel looked down at Rose's screen and smiled.

"Lucky dog. I could use a nap right now."

"Well, as soon as we see Rex and make sure he's okay, maybe we just go back to my place and take a nap," Rose suggested.

Gabriel looked down at his legs and laughed.

"What's so funny?" Rose asked.

"I'm still wearing the same damn clothes from yesterday. I'm never going to get to change out of them, am I? I am doomed to wear my goin' to church clothes for all of eternity," Gabriel said.

"At least you'll look good!" Rose said, laughing.

"A nice hot shower would be nice, and I'll put the clothes back on, but I gotta change out of these at some point," Gabriel said.

Rose looked Gabriel up and down, then pulled her cell phone back out.

"What are you doing?" Gabriel asked.

"Nothing you need to worry about! Just keep a lookout while I text Emelia," Rose instructed.

"Yes, ma'am," Gabriel replied.

I need another favor! ASAP!

Anything for you! Emelia replied.

Can you run to that clothing store quick and pick up a shirt, pants, socks, and maybe some boxers? Rose texted back.

Do I want to know why? texted Emelia.

It's for Gabriel. It's a long story, but let's just say the poor guy hasn't been able to change out of his clothes since Sunday when he put them on! I'll text you the sizes and then send you some money. Just let me know how much to send, Rose texted back.

Okay, but this better be a good story! Emelia texted.

Rose texted back an image of a thumbs up and Gabriel's sizes. She didn't actually know them, but she was a pretty good guess at things like that.

"So, you gonna tell me what it is you and Emelia were texting about?" Gabriel asked.

"Nope, you'll just have to see," Rose said, putting away her cell phone with a huge smile on her face.

"Gabriel Sterling, you can come back now. Rex is awake and asking for you," a nurse said.

"About time!" Gabriel said and then shot up out of the chair.

He and Rose rushed to the room down the hall, but then Rose grabbed Gabriel's arm right before they got to Rex's room.

"What's wrong?" Gabriel asked.

"I think I should wait out here until you tell him I'm here. I don't want to assume it's okay to go in just because I'm with you," Rose said.

"It will be fine, but okay, just give me a minute to talk to him, then I'll come get you," Gabriel said.

Rose nodded her head, then reached up and kissed Gabriel.

"Good luck," she said.

Gabriel nodded and went into the room. To say he was a little nervous was an understatement.

Chapter Nine

Rex lay in the hospital bed with more tubes and wires than Gabriel had ever seen. He was shocked at first, but when he realized Rex was talking to him, he snapped out of it.

"At ease, soldier, get over here," croaked Rex.

"Yes, sir," Gabriel replied.

"They tell me that I had lung cancer. Is that right?" Rex asked.

"Yes," Gabriel answered.

"They also said there was a mass that had somehow got unattached from inside of my left lung," Rex said.

Gabriel nodded.

"I would say I owe ya one for savin' my life then," Rex said to Gabriel.

"Rex-"

"It's okay, son. It's okay. I shouldn't have said what I said, but on the other hand, if I hadn't said it, that cancer would still be in my lungs, and you'd still have a girlfriend," Rex said with a hint of an apology in his voice.

"I have a lot of things to fix within me, but I promise I will never do that again. You're all I have left of my family," Gabriel admitted.

"Well, maybe that sweet girl I offended will forgive you and me and take ya back?" Rex asked.

"I already have," came a voice from behind Gabriel.

"Shucks, she's sneaky too!" Rex said with a painful smile.

"No, just in love with this man, and if you'll allow me to stick around, I'll even love you too," Rose said.

"I reckon it's the least I could do. I'm sorry I said what I said, darlin'. It was a weird way to say to this big fella that I love him, but it's true. I ain't never had a family of my own, so when Gabriel's parents pulled me in and made me one of their own, I took a liking to Gabriel and eventually treated him more like a son," Rex explained.

"Ya did good, Rex, ya did good," Rose said.

"He tell ya about that time I caught him skinny dippin' in the pond?" Rex asked, trying to embarrass Gabriel.

"No, I'm afraid he hasn't told me that one yet. Should I be concerned?" Rose asked, then gave Gabriel a playful eye.

"Um, maybe we should skip that part of my life?" Gabriel asked, not wanting those memories to resurface.

"Oh, no, I wanna hear all about that!" Rose said, trying to act serious. Rex was trying not to laugh. He was in too much pain to let loose.

"We should probably let Rex rest. I'll meet you in the hall," Rose said to Gabriel.

She walked over to Rex and attempted to hug Rex. There were too many contraptions and wires to allow for a real embrace, but nonetheless, Rex knew all was well.

"I'll see when I get out, okay?" he asked Rose.

"I hope so. I'll be doing some mighty fine cookin' so you can recover faster!" Rose said.

"And she can cook? You better keep this one!" Rex said to Gabriel.

"I'll sure try," Gabriel said, wrapping his arm around Rose to hug her.

There was an awkward silence for a moment, and then it was broken by the nurse on shift coming in, letting the men know that visiting hours were almost over.

Gabriel said goodbye and headed out. He needed to clear his head and get some rest. He was half tempted to tell Rose that he would drop her off and then go back to his place, but when he saw her smile, it was all over.

"Let's get you back to my place so you can get cleaned up and maybe rest too. Does that sound okay?" Rose asked.

"Sounds good to me. Thank you," Gabriel replied.

They headed towards the elevator. Rose slid her hand into his as the elevator doors opened.

Feeling her hand in his was enough to make him relax a little. He now knew that he had a lot of work to do to really consider himself on the mend.

Maybe he needed a little more one-on-one time with God or at least someone with a better relationship with God than he did.

Maybe he'd start with Pastor Nick.

Chapter Ten

There wasn't much said on the way back to Rose's, at least not verbally. Once in the truck, Rose sat beside Gabriel back to her place. She laid her head against his shoulder, trying to comfort him, but also needing to close her eyes for a moment or two. Too much had gone on in two short days to file it away and deal with another day. She went from being single to feeling like she was in a serious relationship in just a short amount of time. She needed to seek the counsel of someone with more answers than she had.

"Thank you for being up there with me. I know that was a lot to ask," Gabriel said.

"I wouldn't have it any other way," Rose replied.

She felt a question on the tip of her tongue but decided to keep it to herself. Almost anyways.

"You know, being in the military and being a sniper gave me some superpowers," Gabriel said.

"Oh, yeah?" Rose asked. Curious now by the sudden admittance of having superpowers.

"Yep, sure did," he answered.

"Like what kind?" she asked.

"Like, I can tell when you have something on your mind. Your breathing changes, and you fidget a little," Gabriel answered.

"You can really tell all of that?" Rose asked, astonished.

"Yep. I had to use every bit of my sensory abilities when I was out in the field, and now that I'm out, they are still there," Gabriel said.

"So, basically, you're learning to read me?" she asked.

"I guess you could say that," Gabriel said.

"You can also just ask me what's wrong. I'll tell you," Rose said.

"Okay, so what's wrong?" Gabriel said, trying to get straight to the point.

"I'm worried," she answered.

"About what?" Gabriel asked.

"That I'm overstepping or overstaying my welcome, I dunno," Rose said as she looked out the passenger window.

Gabriel came to a stop and looked at Rose.

"If anyone is doing either of those things, it's me. I've never felt like this before. You gotta realize, and maybe you do from being with your ex, but being in the military forced me to shut certain things out, not to mention doing what I did for all those years. I would have been dead if I had given my position up just once. I spent a lot of time over the years by myself and a lot of time wishing I was somewhere else. Now that I *am* somewhere else, I'm not quite sure how to be," Gabriel explained.

"If it helps you any, my whole world has been turned upside down since I met you," Rose said.

"You mean a whole three days ago?" Gabriel asked, halfway smiling.

"Honestly, it feels like three years ago. I think some people are meant to cross into other people's lives. I think we are two of those people," Rose said.

"I do too. I just need to learn to deal with things better," Gabriel said.

"You and I both," Rose said.

"At some point, you're going to have to stop kidnapping me and let me get my stuff done," Gabriel said.

"Oh, yeah? Like what?" Rose asked, shocked that she was finding herself in the blame seat.

"Like getting my jobs done at the church. I'm sure Pastor Nick is a patient man, but that patience might not last long," Gabriel said.

"True, but considering what just happened, I think he'll let things slide a little. Besides, I'll help get things done. I am the one partially responsible for holding you up," Rose admitted.

"Well, maybe a little, but I would say what happened to Rex trumps anything you have distracted me with," Gabriel added.

"Really? Even more than this?" Rose asked, then leaned up and kissed his earlobe.

Gabriel wasn't expecting that, and his foot slipped off the gas pedal and onto the brake, nearly causing Rose to hit the dashboard. His reflexes were faster, though, and blocked her from becoming a human pinball.

"We really need to get to your place soon before something else happens," Gabriel said.

"I agree," Rose said.

They were in luck. The coffee shop that Rose lived above was right in front of them.

Gabriel parked his truck in the first spot he could find, then together, he and Rose headed upstairs to her apartment. They were greeted immediately by a hungry dog.

"I'll take care of Samson if you want to head to the shower. Just throw your clothes back into the hallway, and I'll get them in the washer," Rose said.

"You sure it's okay? I don't mind going home to get cleaned up," Gabriel said, giving himself the out he almost wanted. What he wanted more so was to take a shower, then crawl back into bed with Rose curled up with her.

"Of course, I'm sure. Now get going!" Rose said, then whipped the kitchen towel at him.

~(-)~

Hot water washed over Gabriel's tired body like a waterfall of pure pleasure. Stress had almost the same effect on a body as

97

being physically active. It was in this shower that Gabriel had a moment of clarity. It was as if a voice from somewhere just out of reach was calling to him - *You need to get your affairs in order before you lose focus and things spiral out of control.*

It was a moment of clarity that he needed, but he knew that if he listened to that voice and did what he thought it meant, it would mean slowing things down with Rose, even distancing himself from her a little.

"Hey, any chance you are hungry?" Rose asked from the bathroom doorway.

"Asking someone that used to ration his food if he is hungry is like looking outside and seeing storm clouds and wondering if it's going to rain. So yes, I'm hungry. What ya thinking?" Gabriel said.

"Thanks for the analogy. I was thinking of pancakes with a side of bacon. I have this recipe I've been wanting to try. Wanna be my guinea pig?" Rose asked.

"Pancakes in the afternoon? Absurd! I'll take them," Gabriel said.

"Okay, well, you better hurry up, or I'm eating without you!" Rose teased.

So much for getting my affairs in order. She wants to make pancakes. How am I supposed to pass that up?

Gabriel turned the shower water off, stepped out, and dried off. He wrapped the towel around his waist and walked back into the bedroom.

A new pair of jeans, a t-shirt, socks, and boxer shorts lay across the foot of Rose's bed. Gabriel was dumbfounded.

How the hell am I supposed to tell her I need a little space to get things in order when she does stuff like this?

"Everything okay? I took a guess at your sizes," Rose said from the bedroom doorway.

"Thank you. I would have been okay just wearing a towel until my clothes dried off," Gabriel answered.

"And what would have happened if your towel would have fallen off?" Rose asked with a coy smile forming at the corners of her lips.

Gabriel cocked an eyebrow and returned the smile that she was giving him.

"Well, I guess it would depend on whether or not anyone saw and, if they did, what they were planning on doing about it," Gabriel answered.

"Well, I usually turn to the Bible for a good many things, but this doesn't seem to be something that I would find an answer to there," Rose said.

"I can think of a couple of references," Gabriel said.

"Oh, yeah? Like what?" Rose asked, curious about what Gabriel was going to say.

"Matthew 6:13- the part where it talks about not being led to temptation. I believe there is also a verse that talks about women being modest and having self-control," Gabriel said, trying to plead his case.

"Okay, well, let's say the roles were reversed. I get out of the shower, and you walk into the bedroom without knowing I was in just a towel, then it suddenly falls to the floor. What would you do?" Rose asked.

"Pray for mercy," Gabriel said.

"That's not fair! Why do you get to cave in, and I don't?" Rose asked.

"No one said you had to. I was just answering your question," Gabriel said, then smiled.

"I see. Well, why don't we discuss this back in the kitchen over hot buttermilk pancakes and bacon?" Rose asked.

"Sounds good to me. Let me get dressed, and I'll be right out," Gabriel said.

"Nope!" Rose replied.

"Huh?" Gabriel asked, confused.

"Leave the towel on, and let's eat. I want to test your theory. As a matter of fact, I'll put on a towel myself so that we're even," Rose said, raising the stakes.

"Oh, I see how it is. Fine, the towel stays on. I'll meet you in the kitchen," Gabriel said, then strode his way out of the bedroom.

Rose smiled at Gabriel as he walked past. Then swatted him across the backside to see if he would jump and drop his towel, but he did not. He kept a firm grip on it and kept on walking.

Rose quickly stripped down and wrapped a towel around herself, so nothing showed.

She, too, strode out of the bedroom, smile and all.

"Alright, who's ready for the best pancakes ever?" she asked.

"Load me up!" Gabriel said as he licked his lips with anticipation.

Rose put a stack of four on a plate, then handed it to Gabriel with a side of bacon.

"That should be a good start, huh?" Rose asked.

"These look delicious, yes!" Gabriel answered.

He smeared butter across each pancake, then soaked them all with a copious amount of syrup.

"I don't suppose you have any milk, do you? You can't have pancakes without a glass of cold milk," he asked.

"Now, you're talking. Let me pour us some," Rose said.

She opened an overhead cupboard, and as she reached for a couple of glasses, her towel dropped to the floor.

"I win!" Gabriel shouted.

"That's not fair! I wasn't even trying to do that," she said.

"I guess we never talked about what happens if someone does have a towel that drops," Rose said.

"Well, all I can say is that you better eat up because you're gonna want to have some energy," Gabriel said,

"Oh, yeah? Why is that?" Rose asked.

Gabriel stood up and let his towel fall.

"Well, suddenly, those pancakes don't look as good as they did before," Rose said.

"We could always come back. I'm sure they'll still be good," Gabriel suggested.

"Good idea, but I'm putting the bacon in the fridge. A certain someone will definitely help himself to it," Rose said.

"Sounds good to me. Better hurry, though, or I might have to pull the towel back up!" Gabriel said as he slowly started reaching for the towel on the floor.

"Now, hold up! Let's be fair about this," Rose said.

"Oh, it's fair," Gabriel said and then turned slowly and headed towards the bedroom, walking slowly with each step.

"You better hurry! I'm right behind you," Rose said playfully.

The pancakes ended up being an afterthought, but a snack was definitely in order after Gabriel and Rose worked out their differences in the bedroom.

Chapter Eleven

The next morning, Gabriel and Rose woke to the sound of thunder. This made going back to his place harder, but he knew it needed to happen. It would be a simple matter of telling Rose what he needed.

"You know I have superpowers, too," Rose said, looking up at Gabriel.

"You too?" he asked.

"Yep. So, you wanna tell me what's on your mind?" Rose asked.

"I have stuff I need to get done, which means I need to go, which means I have to be without you," Gabriel said.

"I know you do. I was just hoping to make this dream last a little longer," Rose said.

"It can, but can we come back to it? Rex will be out any day, and I need to get things squared away with where he will be staying. I can't trust that he'll behave all by himself. Also, the windmill company and Pastor Nick were looking into buying some cattle," Gabriel explained.

"Oh, all of that stuff. Why didn't you say so?" Rose said with a hint of sarcasm in her voice.

"Because a certain someone took off with my heart, and now I don't know what to do," Gabriel replied.

"I do," Rose said,

"You do?" Gabriel said with actual surprise in his voice.

"Yep. It means that we have to be adults sometimes, even when we don't want to be. We have to promise each other that if this is what we want, then we have to come back," Rose said.

"Oh, I'll be back, that much I promise," Gabriel said, reassuring Rose.

"Me too, then. And I'll even make pancakes and not distract us from actually eating them when they are fresh," Rose said. Gabriel laughed. He knew what she meant.

"Okay, then. I guess I'll get dressed and head out. Are you okay with everything?" Gabriel asked.

"Yes, but will you call me later when you have time?" Rose asked.

"You got it," Gabriel said. He kissed Rose, then climbed out of bed.

With each article of clothing he put on, it was getting harder to leave, but he needed to. There were too many other things at stake that needed his attention.

"Okay, so I'll call you later, okay?" Gabriel asked.

"Okay. I'll be right here waiting for you. I'll probably be reading a book or something. I might get some coffee from downstairs first, though. Coffee and a good book go hand in hand," Rose said.

"I agree, which is why the next time it's thundering outside, we're both going to get some coffee, then grab a good book and curl up and read, or whatever else we feel like doing," Gabriel said.

"I'm going to hold you to that!" Rose said. She reached up and kissed Gabriel goodbye. She decided to stay in bed where it was warm. Seeing him out would not have been easy.

"See you soon, and I'll call you later," he said, then gave her one last kiss and headed out.

Gabriel got outside to what appeared to be a monsoon of a rainstorm. Temptation crept in, but he needed to get at it. If he went back upstairs, it would be all over. He needed to test the waters a bit and see how things felt after a little distance was put between him and her.

Rather than go home, he decided to grab a few things he needed for the job at the church. Today was a good day to knock a few things off the to-do list.

Pastor Nick was sitting in the front row at the church when Gabriel walked in.

"Howdy, Pastor, mind if I come in?" Gabriel asked. He didn't feel like he could barge in, even though it was a church. Somehow it had a very home-like feel, and he wanted to sit and relax, but he knew he needed to get some things off his chest before he could truly be comfortable in the Lord's house.

"Come on in. I was hoping you would stop by soon," Pastor Nick said.

"Well, I was in town and decided to stop by and see what I could get done before things got crazy back at the ranch," Gabriel said.

"Got some big plans, do ya?" the Pastor asked.

"Yeah, I have a couple of ventures I'd like to try out. Something my parents would never have been okay with, but like my old friend Rex reminded me of - my parents aren't around, so the ranch is mine to do whatever I want," Gabriel said.

"Rex sounds like a wise man," Pastor Nick said.

"Well, he is, but I'm hoping when he gets out of the hospital, he'll be even wiser," Gabriel replied.

"Hospital? I'm so sorry! What happened?" Pastor Nick asked.

"Well, short version..." Gabriel didn't want to divulge too much info, so he stuck to a less revealing story. "Rex and I got into a heated argument that led him to have a coughing fit, which led to him coughing up blood. I called 9-1-1, and they took him to the hospital," Gabriel explained.

"Wow, I'm assuming that because you said he was in the hospital, he is injured?" Pastor Nick asked.

"Yes, but it turned out to be a blessing in disguise. Apparently, he had some sort of mass in one of his lungs, and when he had one of his coughing fits, it dislodged the mass. He started coughing up blood. When we got to the hospital and found out what had happened, we were all relieved," Gabriel explained.

"Why do I sense a little bit of resentment?" Pastor Nick asked.

"Because I was hoping not to come that close to losing someone so soon," Gabriel said.

"Well, it sounds like what happened was a blessing in disguise. I would start with that and run with it," Pastor Nick said.

"Is that *your* official ruling or God's?" Gabriel asked.

"More mine at this point. Do you know about Samson of the Old Testament?" Pastor Nick asked.

"Yeah, why?" Gabriel asked, curious where the Pastor was going with this little lesson.

"He was blessed with a massive amount of strength, and in the end, he had to sacrifice himself to do away with some very bad people. In a way, he was freed from his shackles," Pastor Nick tried explaining.

"You don't expect me to pull the roof down on my head, do you?" Gabriel asked.

"No, but the Lord does expect you to come to terms with your own strengths and weaknesses and cast off the shackles that are holding you back. In your case, you have twenty years of deprogramming yourself from the military. It won't happen overnight, so don't be discouraged," Pastor Nick said.

"It's a good place to start, for sure. Will God forgive me though of my sins? I did a lot of things I can't undo while I was in the military," Gabriel said.

"For those sins as well, you need to have a conversation with God about them. A simple admittance isn't always the way to be free of our sins. You have to be vulnerable and open about things. You'll know once you get to the place in the road where you no longer feel your load is as heavy that things have been removed from you," Pastor Nick said.

"Kind of like the footprints in the sand parable?" Gabriel asked.

"Exactly like that. When you are ready to turn things over to the Master, he'll be ready to walk in your place for a while. He'll take the burden so you can walk with ease," Pastor Nick said.

Gabriel started feeling his chest tighten a little. He definitely had some things to get rid of, but ridding himself of certain things would require a hard conversation or two.

Pastor Nick could tell Gabriel was struggling with something but didn't want to pry, so he left the proverbial door open.

"If you ever really want to talk, let me know. My door is always open, and so is God's," said Pastor Nick.

"Thanks. I might take you up on it," Gabriel said.

"Is it okay if I start working on some of the smaller stuff around the church?" Gabriel asked.

"By all means. Go ahead. I'll be right here giving a few things up to God," Pastor Nick said.

"Thank you," Gabriel said.

He stood up and walked back out to his truck. The notepad was up on the dash, so he grabbed that and looked over the things he knew he could get done today. It looked like he was going to be able to knock out some of the items related to wall repair. Easy enough.

Gabriel grabbed a cloth tarp, a drywall compound container with some patching fiberglass, and a drywall trowel. Painting would have to be done another day.

It took him just a couple of hours from start to finish to get done with the messy parts of repairing drywall. After cleaning up, he headed out with the promise that he would return with the rest of the list of things to finish.

Gabriel was relieved he was able to salvage part of his day at least. He realized on his way home that he hadn't even thought about Rose until that very moment. What a ride that had been. He no sooner came home from the military, stopped by to ask about a handyman job at a church, found the girl of his dreams, and now he was just trying to survive. He needed to think seriously about how he might deconstruct some of the things the military built up within him. Maybe being with Rose was meant to be a part of the healing process.

Time would only tell.

Chapter Twelve

Gabriel pulled up to the ranch. He felt like he hadn't been there in ages. Really, it had only been since Rex was taken to the hospital and before that, when he left to go to church. He needed a moment to focus on whatever task was at hand. Too many needed his attention, so he tried to focus on one - himself.

Getting to where he didn't feel like he was just on leave would be a tough road. This was real. The ranch, Rex, settling down. Then, there was the matter of his newfound relationship. Where did that come from?

Having a relationship with a woman was foreign to him, yet it felt like an old hat, like a warm coat on a cold winter day.

He wasn't superstitious either, but on the other hand, he had been in a few situations over the years that led him to believe someone or something else had other plans for him. Kinda like when he went to the grocery store to get some food and then saw the handyman advertisement. He didn't need the job or the money. His military pension was enough for what he wanted to do in life.

Then there was the church and Rose. One meant his salvation. The other meant opening up to something he had never really experienced. He was on the fence about which one was which.

He felt his pocket vibrate. It was his cell phone going off.

"Hello?"

"Is this Gabriel Sterling?" asked a voice on the other end.

"Yes, who is this?"

"This is Dr. Haywood. I wanted to talk to you about Rex Dansbury if you have a moment."

"Sure, he was actually on my list of things to figure out today," Gabriel said.

"Well, I guess I called at a good time. Rex is doing pretty well, considering what was pulled out of him, but he will need a lot of time to recover from this. I'm guessing since he's a rancher, he lives there on your property?" asked Doctor Haywood.

"Sort of. He has his own portion of it. He lives by himself on a few acres he bought from my parents a while back," Gabriel answered.

"How feasible is it to have him stay at your house until he is back to normal?" Dr. Haywood asked.

"I'm okay with it, but Rex is more than likely going to say no. He worked hard to get where he's at, and if you take things away from him, he might give you a fight," Gabriel said.

"Well, I can arrange for a nurse to come out and visit. Do you think he'd be okay with that?" the doctor asked.

"As long as he gets to stay in his own house, I would say so. I'm sure he's going to joke about the nurse being cute. Plus, I can check on him throughout the day. It would just be if I'm in town or not," Gabriel said. The part about being in town was more directed at possibly being with Rose, but there were times when he needed things beyond just her.

"I'll speak to him about what you and I discussed. He should be ready to go by tomorrow. I'll draw up the orders for some meds to keep things on the up and up. Meanwhile, just do your best when you can. I think the healing part will be okay," the doctor said.

"Alright then. Tell him to give me a call when he's ready to go, and I'll be right up," Gabriel said.

"Sounds good, thank you," Doctor Haywood said, then hung up the phone.

Gabriel had no sooner set his cell phone down, and it rang again. It was the windmill company.

"Mr. Sterling?" came a voice on the other end.

"Yes?"

"This is Marcus Rogers. I'm sorry for the delay. I was out of the country. On the flight back, I did have a chance to look at your land and the possibility of a wind farm. Do you have a minute to talk?"

"Yep. You were also on my list of things to do today," Gabriel answered, thinking he was starting to sound like a broken record.

"So, if you were willing to sell, tell me again how many acres you were thinking?" Marcus asked.

"I can do up to six hundred acres. I have around twenty-five hundred. My ranch hand-" Gabriel paused for a quick second. Rex deserved more than to be just a ranch hand. He was going to be Gabriel's business partner. "Excuse me, I misspoke, business partner. The guy knows more about large animals than I do. He and I were thinking about buying some cattle and trying that instead of horses like my dad used to do. The difference in what my dad did and what we're going to do is actually try to make some money," Gabriel said.

"Well, if we buy all six hundred, we'd offer you one point two million for the land, and I'd like to bring you in on a little something - what if we put your house on turbine power instead of the national power grid. We'd really like to show proof to people in the area that wind power is truly better than your typical power that comes from power lines." Marcus said.

"Will it save me any money?" Gabriel asked.

"Save and make you money too. There is one more thing I'd like to try with you - can I add some solar panels to your house as well? Think about that part. It would be a good compliment to the wind power coming into your house. We can talk about that part later," Marcus said.

"I like what I'm hearing. One thing I learned while in the military is that you have to evolve, or you will get left behind. So, here is me evolving! I give you permission to do

113

whatever you are going to do, and as long as you don't burn any of my buildings down, you have my blessing to light the place up, so to speak," Gabriel replied.

"Great! So, the offer stands as is - one point two million, and we can have the money in your bank by the end of day tomorrow."

Marcus paused to let it all sink in, but Gabriel was already past that and had the money spent.

"Sold. Six hundred acres. I just need enough for the cattle I get to buy now," Gabriel said.

"That's great! I can meet you at your bank tomorrow if you want, and we can go over the paperwork," Marcus said.

"Sounds good to me. I'll see you then." Gabriel ended the call.

He had managed to knock three things off his list.

Just one more thing to do - find some cattle.

Auctions came up regularly enough. He just needed to find one. There was a side problem: if he and Rex purchased some cattle, they would need men to take care of the cattle, and then there were supplies.

He would need to have that conversation when Rex was home, but his to-do list was done for now.

"Well, now what?" Gabriel asked himself out loud.

He looked at his watch and saw it was close to five p.m.

"Dinner time, I guess."

Gabriel walked over to the refrigerator and saw that his selection was steak, which sounded good, but sharing a steak with someone sounded even better. Again, he had forgotten about Rose. Maybe he wasn't as attached to her as he first thought, then he mentally kicked himself. Images of her started flooding his mind.

He pulled out his cell phone and sent her a text.

I don't suppose you're free for dinner, are you?

Gabriel stared at his phone longer than he probably should have. Texting a woman wasn't new to him, but being in love with one was. Half of his life had been given in service to his country, and now that he had his life back, he wanted to make the other half of his life count.

His phone vibrated.

I was wondering if you had forgotten about me!

Was she setting a trap? She didn't need to know that he actually had forgotten about her or that he had forgotten she wanted him to call her when he was done.

Are you kidding me? I may have been able to mark almost everything off my list of things to do today, but I missed you like crazy, and I'd like to put you back on my list.

So, what are you waiting for then? Get over here! You might want to bring some clothes though! LOL!

Good point. Let me grab some things, and I'll be right over!

He grabbed a day's worth of clothes and headed towards the front door.

He left one light on, then shut and locked the front door.

Even though he had spent the amount of time with Rose that he had and had seen her without any clothes on and had some intimate moments with her, he was feeling nervous in the pit of his stomach. If you put a gun in his hands, there wouldn't have been such a thing, but he wasn't used to romantic muscle memory yet. This part of his life was new. It was raw, and there was bound to be pain, but he was hoping for more good stuff than anything.

Chapter Thirteen

Gabriel grabbed a couple of steaks and his clothes and headed out the door. As he drove up the gravel driveway towards the highway, he looked back in his rearview mirror. The look of his house, his land, all he owned was behind him. What lay in front of him was unknown. He knew that if he wanted Rose to be a part of his future, he would have to play his cards right.

Now, he wasn't much for being a gambler, but if there was one thing he learned while in the military, it was that you only took chances if you knew the outcome would be in your favor. Rose was in his favor, but the gamble was finding a way between her past and his.

Rex was going to be another. He was stubborn but had a good heart. He was strong but knew how to be soft. Heck, he spent more time with Gabriel being a fatherly role model than his own father.

He wasn't looking forward to the next few weeks of Rex's recovery, but Rex needed it, and so did Gabriel. Rose was thrown in there somewhere, too. If she was going to stick around, she and Rex would have to build their relationship. One that Gabriel couldn't interfere with. It had to grow and mature on its own.

Gabriel pulled up in front of Rose's building and got out of his truck with steak and the bag his clothes were packed in. Something was missing, though.

He looked up to the sky as if the clouds would provide answers. They did not, but in his peripheral, he saw a sign on a building that did - Florist. He hurried over to the store and walked in.

"Hello, what can I get you?" a woman from behind the counter asked.

"Well, I need some flowers that say way more than they should mean on our third date. At least, I think that's where we are," Gabriel said.

"Hm, well, you could go for the standard dozen roses, but then again, every guy gives that; you need something with some fire and soul!" the woman said.

"Whatever that is, I'll take it," Gabriel said.

"I just happen to have an assortment of roses. Would you like to see all the different colors?" she asked.

"Sure," Gabriel said.

"Give me one second, I'll go grab a few," the woman said and then disappeared.

A couple of moments later, she reappeared with an armful of roses, some of which he didn't even know existed in the colors he saw.

"Let's see, I have this rainbow rose, the purple variety, a couple of varieties of blue ones, the standard red ones..." she said as her voice trailed off. There were just too many to pick from.

"So many to choose from. I'll tell you what..." Gabriel said while contemplating what to get. "I'll take one of each rose you have."

The woman nearly lost her composure as her knees buckled momentarily.

"Um, would you like a baby's breath sprig with that?" she asked.

"Sure, might as well add that to it, too," he answered.

"Okay, give me just a minute to wrap these up for you. If you want to take a card there and write something to your sweetie while I get these ready, that would also be a nice addition," the lady suggested.

Gabriel set his stuff down and grabbed a card and a pen. He had no idea what to write. Romantic sentiments were new to him, but honestly, they had only been locked away in his heart, waiting for the right moment to emerge.

The florist noticed he was struggling. She smiled a little. She knew all the signs of a new love.

"It's been a while, hasn't it?" she asked.

"How about the first time? I've been in the military since high school. You might say squeezing the trigger of my sniper rifle felt more normal than this, but she means everything to me, and to be honest, it almost feels like something brought us together. I'm not superstitious or anything, but this feels different," Gabriel explained.

"Well, I hope it's all you've ever wanted. Can I give you a piece of advice?" she asked.

"Yes, please," Gabriel answered quickly.

"A woman doesn't always tell you with words what she wants or needs, so you kinda have to use your intuition and add in a little body language, too. Don't overthink it, though; just go with your heart and add in a little gut instinct, and I think you'll be fine," the woman said.

Gabriel listened to every word the woman said. It made sense and was not too difficult, but he knew things wouldn't be that easy.

"Thank you. I will try to keep what you said close by in case I ever get in a bind," Gabriel said.

"You'll be fine. Just keep what I said in mind," the woman replied.

She caught a glimpse of the name on the card and smiled.

"Can I ask a question?" she asked.

"Sure," Gabriel said.

"I notice the name you wrote down. Is that the same Rose that sang at church last Sunday?" she asked.

"Yep, the very one," Gabriel answered.

"Wow! I guess you weren't kidding when you said you felt like something had brought you together," the woman said.

"Do you know her outside of church?" Gabriel asked.

"No, and I don't mean this disrespectfully, but I've only heard others talking about her. More so about her past," she replied.

"What do you mean?' Gabriel asked.

"Well, I don't like to say things to other people that aren't true, but since I was actually there when I overheard the conversation, I feel like what I'm going to tell you is the truth," she paused to lean in a little closer. "I heard your Rose telling her friend that her ex used to abuse her bad. A lot of mental abuse, and I think Rose said there was just one time of physical abuse, and that's when things changed, and Rose went into hiding."

Gabriel stood listening to what was being shared with him, and while he knew a little of Rose's past, physical abuse was not mentioned. He knew former military soldiers who didn't come back home in one piece, whether physically or mentally, but her ex taking things out on her by means of physical violence was unacceptable on all levels, no matter what demons he still faced.

"She had mentioned some things to me, but never the physical stuff. I'll keep an eye on her, and I hope the ex doesn't ever come into the picture," Gabriel warned.

"Yes, please take care of our Rose. This community is better because she is in it," the woman said as she handed over the bouquet of flowers.

Gabriel inspected the assortment and then, with an approving nod, swiped his debit card into the card reader. The florist printed out the receipt, handed it to Gabriel, and thanked him for stopping by.

Now, he felt a little more like a romantic. He headed up to Rose's apartment via the entrance next to the coffee shop. As he was walking up the stairs, he could hear Samson's thunderous bark in the apartment at the top of the stairs.

Gabriel knocked on the door and heard a faint response, followed by a woman's voice that sounded slightly angry.

"For the last time, Sampson, will you please move out of the way so I can answer the door. I'm quite sure it's not for you anyway."

Rose opened the door to see the largest bouquet she had ever seen in her life. Behind it somewhere was Gabriel.

"Oh, my! I hope there is a man to go with all those flowers," Rose said.

"Yep!" Gabriel said and then turned sideways so she could see him.

"Ah, there you are!" Rose said and then leaned her head out of the doorway and kissed Gabriel.

"I'm assuming these are for me and not Samson?" she asked jokingly.

"Well, I did bring some steak, so if he wants that, I mean, steak *would* taste better than flowers," Gabriel said.

"Nope, he can't have either of those, just me, and that includes you!" Rose said, staking her claim.

"I'll take that. Sorry buddy, I guess you are just going to have to share," Gabriel said as he entered Rose's apartment.

Samson gave off a slight whine but conceded victory to Gabriel.

"Where would you like these?" he asked.

"Just put them in the sink for now. I'll find something to put them in later," Rose said.

Gabriel did as instructed with the flowers, then laid the packages of the steaks on the counter.

"So, how do you like your meat?" Gabriel asked with a smirk on his face.

"Um, did you say men or meat?" she asked, then tried to hide her snickering.

"Okay, well, I didn't bring dessert, just the main course, so maybe we can discuss things after we eat?" he asked, giving Rose a wink that suggested he was up to no good.

"Sounds good to me! So, do you want the cast iron skillet or the flat top?" Rose asked.

"Um, skillet. I want to try this thing with the steaks that I heard about. The chef cooked the meat, and then when almost done, he took the meat out and sauteed some garlic in butter, then added the meat back in and spooned the garlic butter mixture over the meat," Gabriel explained.

"That sounds amazing!" Rose said. "Do you want anything to drink while you're making me dinner?"

"Yeah, whatcha got?" Gabriel asked.

"Well, I have a bottle of white wine that won't go well with steak. Wait, I have a bottle of Cab and a bottle of Zin, which one?" she asked.

"Hm, I guess get them both out. I've never paired wine with food before, so this should be interesting," Gabriel said.

Rose pulled out both bottles and uncorked them, letting them breathe a little.

"Thank you for the roses, by the way. Did you get them from the flower store up the street?" she asked.

"Yep. I didn't feel like showing up with nothing to show for myself, so I got you those. I hope they are okay and not too cliche, considering your first name and all," Gabriel said.

"They are perfect, thank you. I bet Mrs. Connors was surprised," Rose said.

"You might say that. She picked up on the fact that I was new at picking out flowers, so she pulled out all the stops and sold me those," Gabriel said, pointing to the large bouquet in the sink.

"Well, you did just fine," Rose said, kissing Gabriel's cheek.

He suddenly found himself at a crossroads. Mrs. Connors telling Gabriel about what had happened to Rose was firmly planted in his mind and bothering Gabriel enough that Rose noticed a look on his face that suggested he was thinking about something.

"So, is now the time I use my superpowers to deduce what you're thinking?" Rose asked.

"You could, but I have a feeling you wouldn't like what I was thinking," Gabriel replied.

"Uh, oh, should I be worried?" she asked.

"No, but I might want to be," Gabriel replied.

It was too late. Rose had thrown up her wall and was on the defensive.

Gabriel turned the burner off and moved the skillet to the back burner. He then moved closer to Rose to look her in the eyes.

"When I was in the military, I saw a lot of things and did a lot of things that probably will never come up in a normal conversation," Gabriel started to explain.

"I'm assuming as much. I would never ask you to talk about any of that. I'm sure it was rough to deal with afterward," Rose said as she reached out and put a hand on Gabriel's forearm.

"Rose, I killed a kid. A damn kid!" Gabriel said.

Rose's eyes went wide. She left her hand on Gabriel's arm, but there was some tension between the two now.

"The last job that I did, I was sent in to take out a terrorist leader, but no one had ever seen what he looked like until someone slipped, and our guys on comms heard it, then everything got real busy, real quick. When I took up position and found my target, I almost lost my nerve. My target had just become real. It was a kid no older than sixteen or seventeen, but the intel had proved correct, so I took the shot," Gabriel explained.

"You did what you were told. You took out a terrorist, Rose said, trying to confirm back to Gabriel what he already knew to be true.

"You're missing the point. I killed a kid. This kid, even though he was a terrorist, was *just* a kid. He didn't know the rest of the world saw him as a bad guy. He was just going off what he was told growing up," Gabriel said.

"So, what are you saying, that you should have refused orders and not killed the terrorist?" Rose asked.

"No, I'm saying that sometimes we understand what we need to do, but our heart doesn't quite comprehend what is being asked of us. I went through a fair amount of counseling at my exit interview with the military, but I still have that kid's face burned in my brain," Gabriel said.

"My ex went through something similar, but something must have been missed when he got out. He was not a nice person when I left him, which tells me he either went through some really hard stuff, or he was just the way he was to begin with, and no amount of counseling was going to fix him," Rose said.

"Is that why he hurt you?" Gabriel asked, point blank.

All color drained from Rose's face. She retreated into her own safe space mentally.

"Who told you? Did Emelia say something?" Rose asked.

"It doesn't matter who told me. I just wanted to tell you that you never have to worry about that stuff with me. I want to be your safe space," Gabriel said.

Rose was getting angry. Someone had violated her trust, and now she felt exposed. A switch had been flipped.

What about Rex's safe space?" Rose asked. She knew she had just crossed a line, but someone had spilled the beans on what had happened to her, and she was going to find out who.

"That's not fair," Gabriel said softly, keeping himself in check. He knew Rose was in defense mode. He needed to recover somehow.

"It wasn't fair when my ex did the things to me that he did either, but you don't see me picking grown men up off the ground and slamming them into the sides of houses!" Rose yelled.

Gabriel turned and walked out of the kitchen. He grabbed his bag on the floor and walked out the front door.

"Wait! Where are you going?" Rose asked.

"Somewhere that doesn't make me feel like I'm on trial," Gabriel said.

"I'm sorry. I shouldn't have said that," Rose admitted.

"All I was trying to do was open up to you about how I was feeling and what I had been through and somehow make you feel like you could trust me enough to let me in the rest of the way. And yes, I do know about what your ex did to you, and it's not okay, just like it wasn't okay that I nearly broke in half the only man that ever was a father to me," Gabriel said, yelling back. His voice reverberated off the walls of the stairway. If things didn't quiet down soon, anyone within earshot might come running to see what was happening.

"Please come back inside. We'll talk about this and fix it. I didn't mean to upset you," Rose said.

"And yet here we are. Like I said - all I wanted was to share with you that you could trust me, unlike your ex who clearly had issues that weren't dealt with, and yet I get blamed for things," Gabriel said.

"I'm not blaming you for anything," Rose said.

By now, panic had set in. She knew she was a second or two from losing the only man she had ever felt close to in such a short amount of time, and there wasn't anything she could do except watch as he walked away.

"Unlike your ex, who clearly had some issues and couldn't see you for the beautiful woman you are, I do see that, but maybe I should go see someone for the issues I still have. Otherwise, someone else is bound to spread rumors about how I killed children for a living," Gabriel said, firing back another jab of insult. The situation was escalating fast. Someone needed to walk away.

Rose knew what Gabriel had just said was meant for her. She was in shock, but her only reaction was to turn and go back inside, slamming the door as she went.

Gabriel's reaction was a little different. He reached down with the other hand, grabbed the handrail, and pulled hard, yanking the handrail, wall anchors and all, clean out of the wall.

He launched it up the stairs like a javelin, causing it to puncture the wall at the top of the stairs. Then he turned and left.

Too much had been said. Too much anger had been felt. He had hoped that he was past all of that, but clearly, he was not.

Neither was Rose, though, but then again, she wasn't haunted by killing a child, just that of her abusive ex, which did not excuse his actions either. Either way, some trauma had to be dealt with before more people got hurt.

He threw open the door to his truck, climbed in, and then slammed the door shut. He knew he needed to calm down, but the blood coursing through his veins felt hot, making it harder for him to relax.

He looked through his windshield, tears forming at the edges of his eyes. To say he was at a breaking point wasn't quite saying enough.

"I can't do this by myself anymore. I need help. I've hurt too many people," Gabriel said, pleading to anyone listening.

Suddenly, the church at the end of the street came into view - Mount Hope. It was turning out to be the place of refuge for him, more so, God's salvation.

Surely, there would be someone he could talk to. Maybe Pastor Nick would be there.

Either way, he was going to be getting some things off his chest.

Chapter Fourteen

Gabriel was nearly at the top of the stairs when Nick came out of the church. He almost didn't see Gabriel and came to a screeching halt when he turned around and came nose-to-nose with Gabriel.

"Gabriel! Hi. I almost didn't see you. Is everything okay?" Nick asked.

"Well, no, not really. I had a blow-up over at Rose's over something stupid, and I may have said some things I shouldn't have," Gabriel said.

"Did it also include a handrail being thrown through the wall?' Nick asked.

"Yep, that too," Gabriel replied.

"She just called and asked if I could come over. She needed someone to talk to. Now, I know why," Nick replied.

"I'll give you the quick version - I need help. I guess thinking I could handle things on my own just isn't going to speed the healing up," Gabriel admitted.

"You can't speed the healing, my friend; otherwise, you won't learn the lessons you were meant to learn. If we try to speed up the recovery or learn the lessons faster, we may miss the true impact of their meaning," Nick said.

"What am I supposed to learn from my memory of killing a terrorist kid?" Gabriel asked.

The color in Pastor Nick's face drained. He wasn't expecting that kind of answer from Gabriel.

"Do you know who Socrates is?" Nick asked.

"The philosopher, sure, but what does that have to do with me?" Gabriel asked.

"Well, he is quoted as saying something about knowing thyself. Now, you can look at that any way you want, but let me just say this - to understand the version of you from back then, you must get to know the version of you right now. The world is in turmoil. Always has been and always will be. Men like you are called upon to be the world's peacekeepers, and no one said it would be easy. As a matter of fact, it's going to be more difficult than you ever will know, but maybe, just maybe, you will find some peace in knowing what you did may have saved some lives," Pastor Nick said.

"I guess my head is still stuck in that moment I realized it was a kid I saw through my scope," Gabriel said.

"Your heart saw a kid, but your mind saw a terrorist. Who knows what he would have gone on to do if you hadn't taken him out. He could have been the next Twin Tower bomber," Nick said.

Hearing that puts things in a better perspective. It didn't make it any easier, but it helped a little.

"You have a good thing going for you, especially now that you are out of the military. I have no doubt that the baggage you carry is a lot, but remember, God won't give you any more than you can carry, even if it doesn't seem like it," Nick said.

"It sure feels like it," Gabriel said.

"The sooner you forgive yourself, the sooner you can get back to living and maybe make things right with Rose," Nick said.

"You're right. I need to start with Rose, though, and work my way backward," Gabriel said.

"Why don't you come with me? I'm heading there now to talk her off the ledge, so to speak, and when I give you the all-clear, you come in and start things over. Don't worry, I'll make sure I work you into the conversation, too," Pastor Nick said.

"As long as you are okay with it. I also bought her a large bouquet of flowers. I'm hoping that counts for something," Gabriel said.

"I'm sure it did. Let's go find out," Nick said.

"If this works out, you can have the steak I left at her place," Gabriel said.

"What kind?' Nick asked, curious.

"Ribeye. Is there any other kind of cut?" Gabriel answered.

"I'm right there with ya. The right amount of seasoning..." Nick didn't finish his sentence. He was already devouring the steak in his mind.

~(-)~

Pastor Nick and Gabriel headed back to Rose's apartment, but not before getting coffee from Emelia's. While paying, Emelia gave Gabriel the stink eye, and he knew word had spread.

"She told you, I'm assuming?" he asked.

"You mean that you added an extra coat hanger that she didn't need? No, I saw that for myself after you stormed out. I did see Rose all piled up on the kitchen floor saying something about how she messed things up, and now she'll never get you back," Emelia said with a tone that suggested some serious forgiveness was going to need to happen.

"I shouldn't have said anything, but she saw the look on my face when she said what she did, and then I knew things weren't going to end well," Gabriel said.

"Well, said or not said, you have more than a wall to patch," Emelia said.

"I know, with her and within myself," Gabriel said.

"Can I ask a question?" she asked.

"Yeah?" Gabriel said, tilting his head.

"You were in the military, right? You saw some pretty bad things, too. Rose was not in the military, but somehow, her ex played games with her that made her feel like she was. Be the guy that saves her; don't be the next guy that destroys her," Emelia said, and to drive home her point, she added - "In other words, figure out how to piece your own life back together

134

before you try to piece your life with hers. The puzzle will look much better that way."

"You sure you aren't a minister? You just made more sense than Pastor Nick did," Gabriel said.

"Nope, no minister here. I just serve the truth one cup at a time," Emelia said.

Gabriel stood staring at Rose's friend, shocked by the truth that had just been served him. She was correct. No matter what Rose had said, he needed to be the bigger person. He had trauma, of course, and Pastor Nick was right - he needed to know his current version of himself and all his scars to forgive his former self.

He felt his cell phone vibrate. It was Pastor Nick telling him he could come up now. He thanked Emelia for the coffee and the hot dish of 'Know Thyself' she'd just served.

He slowly walked up the stairs, worried about what was to come. As he looked up from staring down at his feet, he saw the handrail sticking out of the wall like a missile sticking out of an intended target, but failing to go off, only he did go off.

He knocked on the door, but before he could prepare himself, the door flew open, and out came Rose.

"I'm so sorry, Gabriel. I had no right to say what I said," Rose started to say.

"I had no right to add a coat hanger to your wall and possibly the inside of your apartment. I need to get a better handle on things. Pastor Nick and Emelia both now know the ugly side to me and gave me some really good advice that I will be following from here on out, but you need to hear something first before anything else gets said," Gabriel said. He could see her whole body tense. She was preparing for the next grenade tossed in her direction.

"We both have had a *lot* of trauma in our lives, but to survive the trauma, we have to understand it, even relive it first. I promise you that as I learn to recover from my past, the past that the military allowed me to go through and even support, I will do a better job at learning to help you with yours. I will never walk out on you like I did earlier. I can do better than that. I just hope you will let me show you I can," Gabriel explained.

Rose stood, bracing for impact from something that never came. She wasn't sure what she was expecting to hear, but Gabriel humbling himself in front of her was not it.

Pastor Nick had tried to run interference for Gabriel, but hearing Gabriel plead his case made Rose break apart a little more inside. All he had ever done was be a gentleman and treat her with love. She even witnessed Gabriel rescuing kidnapped girls who were going to be sold as sex slaves. Gabriel had atoned for his sins as far as she was concerned.

She opened her arms, pulled him in, and held him tight. It was Gabriel who started to cry. He felt the weight of his transgressions come crashing down on him and now was when his walls needed to be torn down completely.

Nick joined the embrace. He was now in the inner circle of both people's worlds and had become integral to their healing process. It was his calling. It was his responsibility because they were a part of God's flock, which meant they were a part of his flock, too.

Chapter Fifteen

A couple of hours later, all three sat around the dinner table. Having just finished the best steak of their lives, their bellies and hearts were a little fuller now. The repair process had begun, but time would be the real healer of their wounds, with a little bit of grace and love added in.

"Thank you so much for allowing me to stay for dinner. Gabriel, are you sure you didn't also go to chef school? I've never eaten better steak in my life," Pastor Nick mentioned.

"Well, once you understand how things work when it comes to meat and seasoning, everything else just comes together on its own," Gabriel replied.

"I guess. I don't know if God is a vegetarian or not, but I think even he would like that steak!" Pastor Nick said.

"I think that is probably the best compliment I've ever been given. Thank you," Gabriel said.

"Well deserved," Pastor Nick said.

"Anyone want some dessert? I have some cheesecake in the fridge," Rose said.

Both men sighed at hearing there was cheesecake.

"As much as I want to, I better say no. I need to get going and hope somewhere along the way I have enough energy to write next Sunday's sermon," Pastor Nick said.

"I'll take a small piece. Someone has to make the sacrifice," Gabriel said, as if he were taking on a great burden.

"How about I send home a piece with you?" Rose asked Pastor Nick.

"Now that sounds like a deal and a great snack for later," he said with a big smile on his face.

Rose got out a container for the dessert while Gabriel cleaned things up.

A few minutes later, Pastor Nick was gone, which meant Rose and Gabriel could officially start the healing process. They sat back down at the table, reaching for each other.

"So, are we going to make it?" Gabriel asked. He needed the official verdict.

"I needed to fall apart before I could move forward. I was wrong to act the way I did," Rose said.

"All I can say is things needed to happen to move forward, and I'm willing to be where I'm needed. If you'll have me still?" Gabriel said with some reassurance in his voice.

He knew things had gotten out of hand earlier, and from recent experiences, he needed to have kept himself in check better. A *lot* better, even if that meant regular meetings with Pastor Nick.

Lesson learned.

"I need to learn to let go of my past, too. I guess the only thing I'm worried about is one day running into my ex," Rose admitted.

"Well, if you do, I hope I'm there with you," Gabriel said.

"I hope so, too. I need to be stronger than I am now but also prepared if I do see him and he thinks I'm still his property, what he might do," Rose said.

"Hopefully, nothing. I don't mean to escalate this when we're trying to put things to rest, but if you and I are going to move toward a future together, I will do my best to not let anything happen to you, which means protecting you at all costs. I also don't want you to think you have something to prove by standing up to him. If he hurts you again, there will be a reckoning," Gabriel said.

He was not trying to get things stirred up. Clearly, enough of that had been done, but his main intent was to let Rose know he wanted to be with her and for her to feel safe. Clearly, the ex didn't do his job at that part.

"Thank you for that. To be honest, I don't think I would handle things very well. It wasn't all that long ago when I was with him, and I'm sure if he saw me, he might snap," Rose said.

"Well, let's hope things stay kosher then," Gabriel said.

"I hope so, too. The good part is that he has no idea where I am. Emelia and I made sure to cover our tracks when we left," Rose said.

Gabriel could tell Rose was mostly confident in covering her tracks, but she didn't know military training like he did. Depending on the unit and training, soldiers stuck to their mission even if it took time. He needed to do some digging without her knowing it. The only way things would truly get better for Rose was to know where her ex was so he could decide the next steps.

"You up for some TV? I haven't watched anything good for a long time," Rose asked.

"Sure, as long as it involves you and being under the covers!" Gabriel said.

A change in scenery and activity was a wise choice at this point.

Enough damage had been caused that day. He needed a break from all thoughts that revolved around violence, except her ex, that is. If he ever showed his face around there, he would gladly show him what happens when you are on a Marine sniper's radar.

Chapter Sixteen

The next morning came with a text message to Gabriel's phone. He opened his eyes to see who it was and nearly knocked everything off the bedside table when he saw who sent the message.

"Crap, I gotta go!" Gabriel said as he launched himself out of bed.

"What's wrong?" Rose asked.

"Rex is home already. I should have been there to pick him up," Gabriel said.

"Wasn't he supposed to call you first to let you know he was ready?" Rose asked.

"Uh, yeah, that didn't happen. Let me call him quick," Gabriel said.

He dialed Rex's cell number, and not even a full ring, a strange voice answered.

"Hello?" said the voice.

"Who is this?" Gabriel asked.

"Rex. Gabriel, why are you asking me who is on the phone?"

"Um, you just sound different," Gabriel answered.

"Well, you might say I had a rude awakening, and had it not been for you doing what you did, I might be dead," Rex said.

"Rex-" Gabriel started to speak but was cut off.

"Son, let me finish," Rex said.

Gabriel had not been called that in a long time. It caught him off guard.

"I know you didn't mean to do what you did, but honestly, had you not, the doctors said I would have died a miserable death. I know I'm just a dumb ranch hand to most people, but I've probably learned the biggest lesson a person could ever learn - live each day as a blessing," Rex said.

"Either way, I'm sorry for the way I handled things. I'm going to start going to counseling to get my life back in order," Gabriel admitted.

"That's a good idea. I'm home, by the way. My home. I should have called you this morning to come get me, but I needed to see things through. I called a cab and got myself home. A nurse will be coming over every day to check on me and make sure everything is okay. The doctor said I have to take things easy for a while, but I should be good to go in a couple of weeks," Rex said.

"Well, it's a good thing you have some time to heal from home now. I need help with allocating some cattle," Gabriel said.

"Well, I have some time now, so I better make the best of it. I'll check with the usual cattle auctions and see what kind are being sold," Rex said.

"Do you need me to come over?" Gabriel asked.

"No, but if you wouldn't mind putting Rose on, I need to talk to her for a minute," Rex said.

"Um, okay. Text or call if you change your mind," Gabriel said, then handed his cell phone to Rose.

"Hello?" Rose said.

"Hello Darlin'. I need a favor from you," Rex said.

"Sure! What can I do?" Rose asked.

"I need you to look after Gabriel for me. He's been a trained killer for so long now, he's going to need some help learning how to be everything but that. You know what I mean?" Rex asked.

"Yeah, I do know, but yes, I will do more than look after him. I will give him my full attention," Rose replied.

"Good enough then. You two take care, and I'll see the both of you soon. Give that big lug a hug and tell him it's from me," Rex said, then ended the call.

Rose handed the cell phone back to Gabriel with a confused look on her face.

"Strangest phone call I've ever had," she said.

"I agree. He must still be on some pretty good painkillers. I better get dressed and see if he's okay," Gabriel said.

"Um, I wouldn't, not yet anyway. Let's see where this goes. Like you said, he's gotten this far in life. Let's see how the next day or two plays out," Rose said.

"Good point," Gabriel said.

His phone went off again. This time, it was Marcus. He wanted to let Gabriel know that his plane had just landed and that he would be in town within the next hour or so.

"Well, how do you feel about going out for some coffee with a millionaire?" Gabriel asked.

"Huh?" Rose asked.

"The guy I am selling some of my land to is coming into town to write me a check for a million dollars and some change. He wants to meet so we can make everything official," Gabriel explained.

Rose nearly choked on her own saliva when she heard the amount Gabriel was being paid. She quickly got out of bed and hurried to the kitchen for a glass of water.

"Are you okay? Gabriel asked.

"Yep, just trying to keep my composure," Rose said, shocked.

"It's not *that* big a deal. Besides, it's all going in the bank. I'm sure some things will need to be taken care of in terms of what my dad owes. I'll give Rex a day or two, then he and I will have to start talking business," Gabriel said.

"True, you both are entering a new chapter in your lives. You'll want to do things right, and what better time to start than with an awesome cup of coffee," Rose said.

"Good idea. I think I need a third business partner. You can be my executive coffee purveyor!" Gabriel said with a smile.

"Funny! I was thinking I could maybe be your accountant or something. At least your secretary," Rose said.

"Accountant?" Gabriel asked, somewhat stunned.

"Yes! Did I not tell you once upon a time I was an accountant?" Rose asked.

"Uh, no! You did not. Why aren't you still?' Gabriel asked, curious.

"The company I worked for was doing some shady dealings, and when I found out, I left before they had a chance to realize that I had found out what they were up to," Rose said.

"Good idea. Well, Ms. Callahan, let's go celebrate your new appointment!" Gabriel said, then scooped Rose up in his arms, spun her around, and kissed her like he had just come home from a long deployment.

"Wow! Do that too many more times, and we'll be ordering a lot more coffee from home, just so we don't have to leave!" Rose said.

"I can put off meeting my guy at the bank if you want?" Gabriel said.

"No way! I want to find out what a million-dollar coffee tastes like!" Rose said.

"Good point. Maybe we'll eat steak *and* lobster tonight?' Gabriel suggested.

"I know a place that serves the exact thing. We have to dress up a little, though. Think you can handle that?" Rose asked.

"I think I can. Let's go get things taken care of and see where we end up. I'm sure I can afford a fancy meal every once in a while," Gabriel said.

"If I'm really going to be your accountant, I'll make sure there is always money in the budget for steak and lobster!" Rose said, then kissed Gabriel hard enough to make him blink like a deer staring straight into oncoming headlights.

Chapter Seventeen

Gabriel sat across from Marcus, trying to pay attention, but his mind was elsewhere. There were too many things and moving parts that he needed to keep track of, and they were starting to add up.

"Well, Gabriel, thank you for this opportunity to help my company grow even more. The next step will be to have a team come out and start marking out where the first few wind towers will be. How do you feel about helicopters?" Marcus asked.

"I've been in a few. Usually, they were under fire from the enemy, but we got out of there pretty quick," Gabriel said.

Marcus was at a loss for words but quickly regained his composure.

"I can assure you there will be no enemies shooting at us. The placement of the first few wind towers will be important, plus, after we get everything mapped out, it will be easier to put in the rest as each phase of construction is complete," Marcus said.

"Well, I look forward to seeing how things turn out," Gabriel said.

"Here's the contact info for my head guy in charge of the first phase. I'll have him call you when he gets up here and can get things moving. Thanks again for everything!" Marcus said and then reached out to shake hands.

"Thanks again. I look forward to seeing you again," Gabriel said.

He waited until Marcus was out of earshot before he did a victory dance that included picking Rose up and spinning her around again.

"Got any plans?' he asked, smiling.

"Nope, why?" Rose asked.

"Because we're going out for dinner. Where's that place you said had steak and lobster? Gabriel asked.

"It's in the next town over. We better call now if we're going to go," Rose said.

"Alright, give them a call while I drive us over to the other end of town so we can shop at those overpriced clothing stores," Gabriel said.

"What? Are you sure?" Rose asked.

"Yes! My dad nearly drove the land they lived on right back into the arms of the bank that owned the land. He was old school and stuck in his ways. My mom tried telling him that ever since I was a kid, and you know what? I now fully own the land, and guess what? My mom should be here to celebrate, so we're going to eat a nice dinner and have a few drinks, and when this is all said and done, people from all over will know that Sterling Ranch is here to stay!" Gabriel said with tenacity.

"Alright! Let's go celebrate in your mom's honor! Should we bring back something for Rex?" Rose asked.

"Oh, yeah! He gets the biggest piece of steak!" Gabriel replied.

Gabriel headed towards the center of town, where he had seen several clothing stores, and found a spot to park near both. He didn't want to spend time walking around, having to dodge this person or that person. He was on a mission.

When Rose looked up and saw the clothing stores, she did a double take and glanced sideways at Gabriel.

"You sure you want to go here? The clothes in here are super expensive," Rose said.

"I want my executive assistant to look good!" Gabriel said. "Let's go!"

Rose was a little slower getting out. She was a little nervous about what was about to happen.

They walked into the store with Rose trailing behind.

"Hi there! How can I help you?" asked a friendly store associate.

"Well, here's the thing: We're celebrating a very important occasion, and I want my girlfriend to look and feel like she's the prettiest girl in town. Think you can make that happen?" Gabriel asked.

"I think we can handle that," said the store associate, smiling.

Gabriel turned to see Rose looking more worried than ever. He needed to pump the breaks for a second and reassure her that everything was okay.

"Rose, this is okay. I'm not trying to pressure you, but I want to celebrate with you. I've never once in my life been anything other than thrifty with my money or been able to spend it, so for once, I'd like to spend it on someone I care about, which is you! I'm giving you permission to have fun, go wild, and get whatever you want here. I'm going to go next door and do the same. Meet me at the truck when you are done, okay?" Gabriel said.

A lone tear ran down Rose's cheek. Gabriel wiped it away and pulled Rose into his chest.

"He never made me feel like I was beautiful or even worthwhile. How is it that you have managed to steal my heart and repair it at the same time?" Rose asked, voice muffled from having her head buried in Gabriel's chest.

"Well, despite my failed attempt at remodeling the outside of your apartment, I care a lot about you, and I'm going to step way outside of my comfort zone and probably yours, but I want to see where things go with you and I. I have a lot of things to work through, but I think between your love and Pastor Nick's biblical wisdom, I can work through some things and come out the victor in the end," Gabriel explained.

"I feel the same way. I have a few things to deal with, too. I just hope you'll be patient with me as I try to heal from everything," Rose replied.

"I'm not going anywhere, I promise," Gabriel said.

Rose reached up with one hand, caressed Gabriel's cheek, and kissed him softly.

"Okay, are you sure about this? Because I've been in here before window shopping, and I've seen some clothes that will stop traffic if on the right woman," Rose said.

"Then you better pick out something that will stop a train!" Gabriel replied.

"You got it! Meet you back at your truck soon!" Rose said with a smile that he hadn't seen in a while.

He left the store feeling like he had just won the lottery. His 'winnings,' if held onto tight enough, would last him a lifetime. He just needed to make the right investments.

Gabriel walked into the men's clothing store right next door. He was out of his element now, for sure. Luckily, a store employee spotted the deer in the headlights look from across the room.

"How can I help you?" asked an older gentleman.

"Well, I've just spent the past 20 years of my life in the military only to retire and then win the lottery," Gabriel answered.

"What's her name?" the man asked.

"Her name is Rose, and she happens to be next door buying some clothes that will probably cause a few heads to turn. So, I need a little help picking out something that will match her, but I have no idea yet what she'll be picking out," Gabriel explained.

"Hm, well, black is a safe option, and considering your build, I think I have a really good option for you. Without being too forward, mind if I ask what you had in mind spending?" the man asked.

"Between you and I, I just made a million and a quarter selling off some of my dad's land, so I think I can afford whatever you're going to put me in," Gabriel replied.

The man nearly choked, but he ushered Gabriel to the sports coat section after he recovered. The gentleman headed straight for one particular jacket. It was a western, tux-style, paisley-lined sport coat. He quickly eyed Gabriel's top half and flipped through a couple on the rack. Smiling, he handed it to Gabriel with satisfaction, feeling quite sure it would fit, and it did.

"I also have a cowboy hat to match as well as pants and boots if you would like those as too?" the man asked.

"I would, and then I would also like to pay for them and put them on. I need to be at my truck before she comes out so I can be ready for the main show," Gabriel said.

"Alright, then, let's speed things up. If you want to head to the changing room, I'll get the other clothing items and meet you there in five minutes. I promise everything will fit precisely!" the man said with a little extra confidence.

"See you in five," Gabriel said, walking towards the changing room.

The man was true to his word. He was there as promised with everything that Gabriel would need to turn Rose's world upside down.

It took Gabriel a few minutes to put everything on, but he gave a satisfactory whistle when he was done.

The man was waiting back at the counter and was thoroughly surprised when Gabriel stepped up to the counter.

"If you ever need a job modeling men's western wear, there will be a job waiting for you!" the man said, his jaw partly hanging open.

"I'll keep that in mind. Thank you again for your help. I'll be back for something to get married in at some point, "Gabriel said.

"I look forward to seeing you again! Be sure and bring in the future Mrs. Sterling!" the man said as he waved goodbye to Gabriel.

Gabriel made it to his truck in time, or so he thought. As he was putting the bag with his clothes in the back seat of his truck, he turned around to see Rose standing behind him. Gabriel nearly fell off the curb.

Rose had indeed picked out the right clothing. She was wearing a long black dress with a slit up the side, high heels, and a diamond necklace that hung just perfectly in the right spot on her chest. She'd somehow managed to curl her long blonde hair and have it pulled to one side of her head.

"I'm pretty sure more than one train is gonna stop for you tonight," Gabriel said with a look of awe.

"Is it okay? I can go back and put on something else?" Rose said.

"Please don't. I'm pretty sure half the hosts in heaven are giving you a standing ovation. You look so beautiful," Gabriel said.

"I can't believe you let me get all of this," Rose said as she turned slowly in a circle so that Gabriel could see the whole picture.

People nearby stopped to watch, and cars driving by slowed to catch a glimpse.

"I did it because you make me happy, and I want to take you out for a night on the town," Gabriel said.

"Thank you for this. I'll find a way to pay you back," Rose said.

"No, that's not what I want. I just want you, and you're right. I didn't need to buy you all of that or buy myself all of this, but I wanted to just for a moment, show you how beautiful you are and to step out of the normal part of life and enjoy tonight," Gabriel said.

"Thank you. By the way, you look really good in that," Rose said softly.

"Thank you. We better get out of here before people start thinking we're royalty," Gabriel said, then helped Rose get into his truck.

Chapter Eighteen

Gabriel pulled up to the restaurant, noticing the mile-long line of cars pulling into the parking lot. Worry started to creep in as he wondered if their date would be cut short.

"Did they give you any problems when you made a reservation?" Gabriel asked.

"No, I gave them your name, and they said there would be plenty of seating," Rose answered.

"I sure hope so. This line has me worried," Gabriel said.

"Want me to get out and start moving cars so you can get through?" Rose said jokingly.

"I'm starting to wonder if that isn't such a bad idea," Gabriel said.

"Seriously?" Rose asked, shocked that Gabriel might have meant what he said.

"No, I'm kidding. I don't want to take the chance of hitting you," Gabriel replied.

He kept his patience in check and stayed the course. He even turned on the radio, which helped things even more.

"Tonight, out at the Ranch, country band Prairie Land will be playing, so stop by and see them and enter to win a meet and greet with the band!" announced the radio DJ.

"So, that's why the traffic is as bad as it is. Ranch is next door," Rose said.

"Well, good. Maybe the restaurant won't be as busy," Gabriel said, but his wishful thinking was cut short when he saw yet another long line of cars.

Out of the corner of his eye, a parking spot suddenly became available. He quickly pulled around the car in front of him, made a sharp left turn into the next row, and pulled into the spot.

"Ah, much better! Let's go before a plane or something falls out of the sky and lands on us," Gabriel said.

"Well, that went dark fast," Rose said, shocked by Gabriel's sudden doom and gloom comment. "Would it help if I admitted I may have forgotten to tell you that I know the owners, and we have a special table waiting for us out back overlooking the lake?" Rose said shyly as she smiled at Gabriel.

Gabriel's face lit up as his expression went from disappointment to happiness in a matter of seconds.

"That's it, you're never leaving my side!" Gabriel said as he leaned over in the truck bench seat and kissed Rose.

"Promise?" she asked with a hint of seriousness.

"If I have any say in it, yes," Gabriel answered with a serious look. Before Rose could respond, he was out of the truck and over to her door in seconds.

"Your door, ma'am," he said as he opened the passenger door.

"Why, thank you! Rose said.

Gabriel shut the truck door, then held out his arm as he escorted Rose inside.

Once inside, there were indeed a lot of people, but that's not what got Gabriel and Rose's attention. It was the vaulted ceilings and timber columns that caught their eye. Antler chandeliers were hanging from the cross beams, and on what appeared to be a feature wall, a giant floor-to-ceiling fireplace with an ambient fire burning inside.

"This place is amazing," Gabriel said as his gaze moved from one feature to the next.

"Rose Callahan, is that you?" came a voice from somewhere in the crowd.

Rose turned to see a man and a woman coming towards them. Her face lit up excitedly as she was pulled into a dual embrace.

"Is this the man you were telling us on the phone?" the woman asked.

"Yes! John and Martha meet Gabriel Sterling. He just retired from the military and took over his parent's ranch," Rose said, introducing Gabriel.

Gabriel shook hands with the couple, exchanging pleasantries.

"It's so good to see you out and about. When I heard what had happened, I was so worried for you," Martha said.

"Well, I found a good place to move to and an even better person to be with," Rose replied.

Martha smiled back at Gabriel, then whispered in Rose's ear. "They sure grow them big out at the Sterling Ranch, don't they?"

Rose's mouth hung agape, then giggled after hearing what Martha whispered, but she one hundred percent agreed.

As the ladies took the lead to where the table was waiting, the two men hung back to guard the rear.

"So, military, huh?" John asked.

"Marines. Sniper. Twenty years," replied Gabriel. "You in?"

"Navy Seal. Fifteen years. Were you around when the Vulture was taken out?" John asked.

Gabriel stopped for a brief second. The intel that mentioned the terrorist's name, the Vulture, was top secret.

"I was the one who took him out," Gabriel replied, looking John dead in the eyes.

"Well done, soldier. My squad was on standby if your mission failed. I'm glad we didn't have to go in. Intel reported a whole other terrorist cell was a short way away to rendezvous with the Vulture and his group the same time you took him out," John said.

"I wasn't aware there were more tied to that particular cell," Gabriel said.

"Yeah, but you cut off the head of the snake, and the body withered away. We managed to clean everyone else out a short time later," John replied.

"I'm glad I could do my part," Gabriel replied in his most humble soldier's voice.

"Spoken like a true soldier," John said.

Finally making it to their table, John and Martha parted ways, but not before John pulled out a business card and quickly wrote something on the back, then handed it to Gabriel.

Gabriel waited until John and Martha were out of visual range, then flipped the card over and read: *Take care of Rose! She means the world to us. Dinner is on the house tonight. Enjoy!*

He handed it to Rose, who was shocked as she held the card.

"Something wrong?" Gabriel asked.

"No, not anymore," Rose answered.

"What do you mean?' Gabriel asked.

"John and Martha are Emelia's parents. They were home that night when Emelia dropped me off. They took care of me while I was down. John must have a good feeling about you. Otherwise, he would have gone his separate way after introductions," Rose said.

"Well, he knew that I was military, and when I told him what I did, he might have relaxed a little afterward," Gabriel explained.

"I don't blame him. I know I relax when I am around you," Rose said, then briefly leaned her head on his shoulder.

Gabriel and Rose picked up their menus and nearly dropped them on the floor when they saw the prices of some menu items.

"I'm by no means poor, but holy smokes!" Gabriel said as he saw the price of one particular menu item. It was a sixteen-ounce porterhouse steak with Maine lobster.

"I knew they served good food, and their prices were up there a bit, just not sky high," Rose said.

"Well, we pretty much have been told to eat up, so I say let's eat up!" Gabriel said. "Respectfully, of course."

Gabriel stuck to the plans and did, in fact, order steak and lobster. Rose ordered steak as well, but with a salad on the side.

Their orders were collected by a waiter, and in less than thirty minutes, their food was brought to them on a cart containing several large plates and platters.

"Wow! Look at all of this!" Rose said as her eyes darted from one delicacy to another.

"Is there a hotel nearby? I think I might need to stop and digest after eating all this," Gabriel said.

"I don't have a problem with that, even if you didn't need to stop and digest," Rose said, looking at Gabriel with a hint of mischief.

"I guess we could get dessert to go," Gabriel suggested.

"Oh, there will be dessert," Rose said, picking up her knife and cutting her steak.

Gabriel and Rose ate and talked somewhat, but each bite of meat, whether steak or lobster, led to one blissful moment after another. Of course, a proper meal of that level of taste and preparation should be paired with only the best drinks as well.

As equally as long as it took their food to reach them, it took that long for Gabriel and Rose to eat it. They both knew a meal of that quality was not to be devoured, so when they were finally finished and the last bit of steak juice was wiped from their lips, they sat back in their chairs and sighed.

"I may have to go in on a second location near the ranch just so I can eat this more often," Gabriel said as he leaned his head back and closed his eyes.

"I don't think that would be a good idea," Rose said, but wasn't in complete disagreement.

"Yeah, a guy can dream, though, right?" he asked.

"Now, about that dessert," Rose said, implying it was time to leave.

Gabriel immediately opened his eyes and smiled.

"Indeed. How do you feel about cheesecake? I saw some on the dessert menu and thought it looked good," Gabriel said, but also not missing the hint that was dropped.

"I've heard about the cheesecake here. It's a meal in and of itself. We better get it to go," Rose said, hinting again.

As if on cue, the waiter appeared out of thin air.

"Will there be any dessert?"

"I think I will take the chocolate cheesecake," Rose said.

"And for you, sir?" the waiter asked.

"I will have the New York cherry cheesecake, and both are to go, please," Gabriel said.

"I'll get them ready for you. It will just be a couple of minutes," the waiter said, then disappeared as fast as he appeared.

Gabriel looked around the room and saw many similar faces that probably said the same thing as his - satisfied. While gazing around the room, he felt Rose place her hand on his and then turned his attention toward her.

"Are you okay?" he asked.

"Better than ever. You don't know how much this has meant to me, especially bringing me here and being able to meet John and Martha," Rose said.

"Well, I would say it's been a perfect night, but it isn't over yet," Gabriel added.

"I was hoping you would say that," Rose said while squeezing Gabriel's hand.

The waiter returned to their table with two rather large dessert boxes and set them down.

"Here ya go. Thanks for dining with us," the waiter said and then turned and walked away.

Gabriel pulled out his wallet and pulled out a hundred-dollar bill.   Rose caught a glimpse of what he had pulled out and made a faint gasp.

"I know, but in this kind of place, you don't leave a small tip, even if you are getting your meal for free," Gabriel replied.

He tucked the money under the basket of bread but still left enough that the waiter would see it sticking out. Gabriel grabbed both boxes of cheesecake in one hand and Rose's hand in the other and headed toward the entrance.

They saw John and Martha from across the room and waved. Gabriel smiled and tipped his hat at John. There needed to be a special acknowledgment given.

Many vehicles were still coming and going from the restaurant and the venue next door, but not so much that it made it impossible to go anywhere. However, walking comfortably seems nearly impossible when you are full from eating the best meal ever.

About a row away from his truck, Gabriel spotted what looked like two men, possibly three, tailing them. Now was not the time to pick a fight with him.

Gabriel gave Rose's hand a harder-than-normal squeeze, which suddenly caused her to look up at Gabriel.

"Keep walking like you don't know that three men are coming up from behind. As soon we get to the truck, I want you to hop in, lock the doors, and immediately call the police and tell them that three bodies will be waiting for them at the restaurant," Gabriel said quietly.

"What are you going to do?" Rose asked.

"Burn off some calories," he replied. "Now, walk a little faster. We're almost there."

Just as they passed the front end of his truck, Gabriel threw the cheesecake boxes in the truck's bed and spun around in time for Rose to hop in and slide to the middle of the front seat.

The first assailant was right on their heels, but not before Gabriel could throw the big truck door open, causing the first man to run headlong into it and then fall unconscious.

"One down, two to go," Gabriel said.

The two other men stood one to each side of Gabriel. Both had rather sharp-looking knives pointed right at him.

"Look, fellas. Ya caught me at a disadvantage," he started to say.

"Oh yeah, what's that?' the man to his left asked.

"I just had the best meal of my life, so I'm running a little slow. At least let me take off my coat," Gabriel said, trying to stall. He could hear Rose on her cell phone talking to the police.

He whipped off his jacket in time for the man on his right to come at him with a thrust of his knife. Gabriel was anything but slow. Gabriel sidestepped and grabbed the man by the wrist. He grabbed the knife from the man's hand in that same motion, then turned away from the assailant. He pulled the arm over his shoulder and rolled his right side forward, causing the attacker to fly over Gabriel and land hard on the pavement.

There was a loud thump as the man hit the ground, also rendering him unconscious.

"That's two," Gabriel said as he looked up from attacker number two and straight into the eyes of his third attacker.

"Your odds of survival are going down with every second you stand there. I suggest you decide how you are going to try and come at me," Gabriel said.

The remaining attacker didn't see that Gabriel now had a weapon of his own, and it was in the hand that he had almost behind him and out of sight of the other man.

Gabriel noticed the gun holster on the man's hip and the hand itching to go for the gun resting inside.

Rose was inside the truck, watching the whole thing play out. She had just witnessed two attackers hit the ground, and now the third was sizing up Gabriel. She had not seen the gun in the holster on the hip of the man in front of Gabriel.

She decided to throw confusion into the mix and reached over and started honking the truck horn. This was just enough distraction for the remaining attacker to look at Rose, taking his sight off Gabriel, who in turn was on the man in a split second, giving him a quick hook to the jaw.

"And that's number three," Gabriel said.

"The police are on their way," Rose said.

"Good. I don't think these three will put up much of a fight," Gabriel said, removing the handgun from the third man.

The police arrived shortly to find all three men tied at their hands and feet. There would not be a round two for any of them, at least not until they were behind bars.

"Mr. Sterling, thank you for apprehending these men. I'm glad the both of you are safe," one of the police officers said.

"I'm just glad they came after me and not someone that didn't know how to protect themselves," Gabriel replied.

"Did you serve?" the policeman asked.

"Twenty years in the Marines. I just retired and decided to move back home," Gabriel said.

"Well, we're glad you decided to come back home, and thank you for your service," The police officer said, then snapped to attention and saluted Gabriel as a show of respect.

Gabriel returned the show of respect and then shook hands with the police officer.

Once the scene was clear, Gabriel got in the truck and left the area as quickly as he could safely do so. He drove just a short way down the road when he decided to pull over.

He turned to Rose to check on her.

"Are you okay?"

"Yeah, I'm fine. I just don't understand why those men came after us," Rose said.

"I do, well, sort of," Gabriel said.

"You do?" Rose asked, shocked.

"I think so. The last guy that came at me had a sidearm and didn't pull it out. Have you ever seen a bad guy not use his gun if he was holding up someone?" Gabriel asked.

"No, and I didn't see that either. You could have gotten shot," Rose said, scared.

"Nah, he wasn't going to shoot me. He was testing me, or, should I say, John was testing me," Gabriel said.

"What do you mean John was testing you?" Rose asked.

"Well, John is a former military man like myself and happened to be on standby on the same mission I had when I took out that terrorist I was telling you not too long ago. I got the kill, and his team didn't. There was a little bit of a rivalry between branches when it came to certain missions," Gabriel explained.

"That's ridiculous. John would never do that. He knows that my ex is former military and is crazy," Rose said.

"You'd have to be a little crazy to come after a Marine sniper. But now that John knows I passed his test, I think he and I will get along okay," Gabriel said.

"I'm not okay with it, though! He sent guys after you," Rose said. She was getting visibly upset now, and Gabriel needed to diffuse things.

"Here, let me prove to you it was him. I'll text him," Gabriel said.

Gabriel pulled out the card that John had given him and texted the number on the front.

I met your friends. Thank you for the workout! Gabriel pushed send, and the message was off. It was only a couple of minutes later that his phone went off.

I needed to know you would keep Rose safe. Her last boyfriend nearly cost Rose her life.

Gabriel showed his phone to Rose as proof that John really had sent the men after them, more so Gabriel.

"I can't believe he would do that," Rose said in disbelief.

"I promise you it's okay, and to be honest, it's the other three that are going to have issues with John, not me," Gabriel said.

"Why is that?" Rose asked.

"I don't think concussions were a part of the deal," Gabriel said.

"Well, I still don't like it," Rose said.

"Well, the good part is that I'm hungry again. Speaking of which, where is the cheesecake?" Gabriel asked as he suddenly realized something very important was missing.

He scanned the truck's cab, then looked out the back window and saw the dessert boxes in the bed of his truck.

"Ah, found them," he said, opening his door and hopping out to retrieve the boxes.

"Here, ya go, dessert," Gabriel said, smiling at Rose.

It was hard to resist Gabriel Sterling, which is why falling in love with him was so easy.

Rose knew then that he would be her protector, lover, friend, and maybe one day husband, but there was a lot of ground to cover before that last one could happen.

For now, she would be happy with the version of Gabriel that sat next to her.

Chapter Nineteen

The next day, after Gabriel and Rose were back home at her place, Gabriel's cell phone went off. It was Rex. He was caught in a jam and needed some help. He wouldn't say exactly what was wrong, but he asked if Gabriel could come over and help with something personal.

Without hesitation, Gabriel and Rose, with Samson trailing behind, hopped in his truck, and headed towards the ranch. When Gabriel's dad gave Rex the option of anywhere he wanted, he took him up on the deal and laid down a claim to a plot on the opposite side of the ranch. When asked why he chose so far out to go, Rex said it was because that was where he felt most at peace. There just happened to be a stream-fed lake there, too.

Gabriel pulled up outside of Rex's cottage; from outside, he could hear Rex swearing up a storm.

"Rex, It's Gabriel, I'm here. Rose is with me, too."

"I ain't decent, so Rose needs to stay outside, but you can come in. And hurry up about it, would ya?!" Rex said.

Gabriel went inside, leaving Rose on the front porch. Before he even started to speak, he could hear why Rex might have needed him. Rex stood bracing himself against the bathroom door with a shotgun in one hand and a cell phone in the other.

"Do I want to know what you're doing with a shotgun outside your bathroom?" Gabriel asked.

"I think he wore himself out. Listen," Rex said, hitting the door with the heel of his boot. A loud scream mixed with a growl came from the other side of the bathroom door.

"Is that a mountain lion trapped in your bathroom?" Gabriel asked, suddenly alarmed.

"Sure is! I fell asleep on the front porch in my chair, and this critter snuck in and started going through the pantry. I grabbed my shotgun and some buckshot and pelted his hide. Now he's in there crying about it," Rex explained.

"I should've just had you stay at my place," Gabriel said as he shook his head.

"Nonsense. I'm not intruding on you and your little miss's privacy. How is she, by the way?" Rex asked.

"She's fine. Can we just focus on getting the big cat out of your bathroom?" Gabriel asked, trying to focus on the task at hand. Then a lightbulb went off. "Do you have any tranquilizer darts?"

"Yeah, but they are probably expired," Rex answered.

"I don't care. I just need them to be strong enough to put him out, even just for a few minutes," Gabriel said.

"I think they are in the red toolbox over by the gun case," Rex said as he nodded toward the far corner of the room.

Gabriel ran over and opened the toolbox, and sure enough, there were darts and just two of them. There was even a pistol used to shoot them, which would help immensely. He ran back to the front door and opened it. Rose was standing right where he left her.

"I need you and Samson to get back in the truck. Rex decided to invite a cougar over for the night and apparently didn't end things well," Gabriel said, trying to explain what was going on, adding a bit of humor.

"I heard that!" shouted Rex from inside.

Gabriel smiled.

"Anyway, get back in the truck and lock the doors. I'm going to try and tranquilize the kitty cat and drag him outside and into the bed of the truck so we can take him up into the mountains," Gabriel said.

"Are you sure that's a good idea? I mean, can't fish and wildlife come out?" Rose asked.

"No, he'll have that door ripped to shreds by the time they get here. I'll be out in a few, so stay put until I tell you to come out," Gabriel instructed.

He slammed the door and went back to where Rex was standing.

"Okay, so here's what I think I might try - I'm going back and open the front door, then move back over here with a tranquilizer gun loaded and ready to go. On my mark, as soon as you open the door, I'll fire the first and second rounds at the cat and see what happens. If he runs out, you run into the bathroom and shut the door. He'll have a better chance of getting me out here than you in there," Gabriel said.

"You sure about all of that?" Rex asked.

"Unless you have a better plan, yes, this is the best I can come up with besides outright shooting it, which I believe will cause a bigger mess than either of us wants to clean up," Gabriel said.

"Okay, well, let's get going. I got stuff to do," Rex said.

"On the count of three, ready?" Gabriel asked.

Rex nodded, and then Gabriel gave the tranquilizer gun one last look over and counted down.

"1...2...3... Open!" Gabriel shouted.

There was indeed a mountain lion inside. The cat was surprised by the sudden opening of the door. Gabriel got off both shots before the cat could realize it had a way out. It took two steps out of the bathroom door, then crumpled to the floor. Gabriel gave it a minute, then rushed over to the cat and checked to make sure it was alive and breathing. It was indeed doing both, but just barely.

Gabriel gently picked up the cat, hoisted him over his shoulders, and hurried the best he could outside to his truck. Rose was inside watching as she witnessed her first mountain lion being carried by a human. Sampson was behaving well for a dog that was usually on guard.

He slid the big cat down off his shoulder and into the truck bed, then carefully shut the tailgate. He ran over to his side of the truck and climbed in, then started the truck and took off.

"How long do you think we have?" Rose asked.

"I'm not sure. Go ahead and call fish and wildlife and tell them we are on our way up to the mountains. We'll meet them there," Gabriel said.

"Good idea," Rose said.

She pulled out her cell phone and called the local fish and wildlife number. After finally getting a hold of someone, she explained what was happening and ended the call.

"What did they say?" Gabriel asked.

"Well, there was a swear word in there, but then they said they would meet us, and then they will take it from there," Rose said.

"Okay, well, the sooner we can get our sleeping guest back there out of my truck and into their hands, the better I'll feel. I think Rex would have preferred to shoot it, but I think he realized that it would have been him to also take care of the mess," Gabriel said.

"Kinda hard to finish recovery if you end up getting hurt again and possibly worse than the first time," Rose said.

"Yeah, well, he doesn't need to ever get hurt like the first time, and he certainly doesn't need to get attacked by a mountain lion. He's tough, but not that tough," Gabriel said.

The drive didn't take too long. When they arrived at their destination, the fish and wildlife officer was waiting.

Gabriel pulled up a little way away from the other vehicle for safety reasons and then got out and left the driver's side door open.

"How did you manage to survive this thing?" the officer asked.

"Well, my ranch hand actually trapped him in the bathroom and kept him in there. I showed up in time to shoot it twice with tranquilizer darts," Gabriel explained.

"Well, we'll get him secured in the kennel we brought, then give him a wake-up cocktail and see how things go. Thanks for your help," the officer said.

"I hope it all works out," Gabriel said, then got back in his truck and headed back to Rex's place.

They pulled up a short time later and saw Rex sitting on his front porch. All seemed to be well.

"Well, let's hope nothing else is hiding anywhere," Gabriel said as he put his truck into park.

"Yeah, two times of nearly being attacked is good enough," Rose said.

Samson barked in acknowledgment.

"You get that big cat taken care of?" Rex asked.

"Yep, we met an officer from fish and wildlife up near the mountains, and he took it from there," Gabriel said.

"Good riddance to ya! Well, since you are both here, do you want to get something to eat? I ain't had time to eat yet," Rex said.

Yep, that's fine. I just need to stop by the house and get a change of clothes, and then we should be okay," Gabriel said.

"Did you two have a late night last night?" Rex asked, then smiled.

"Sort of. We went out for dinner after meeting with the guy from the wind farm company," Gabriel said.

"Don't forget the part where three guys jumped us," Rose chimed in.

"What? What happened?" Rex asked.

"Nothing much. It's a long story that involves an overprotective father figure and three guys who were more than likely paid to check out Gabriel.

"Well, you're still standing, so you must have whooped 'em?" Rex asked.

"You might say that. It all worked out in the end," Gabriel said.

"So, what's that make it since you've been back and gotten into a fight? Twice?" Rex asked, half joking.

"Sounds about right, except the first one was because I stopped a sex traffic ring from doing more bad things," Gabriel said, trying to justify himself.

"You did a good thing there, son. We need to protect our women folk, and don't you think either that I'm so old school that I think women are only good for a couple things," Rex said, looking directly at Rose. "No, ma'am. I know the chain of command, especially after working for your mom and dad for so long. They were perfect for each other in every way," Rex said.

"Yeah, they kinda were. I just wish I could have gotten back sooner," Gabriel said regretfully.

"You were on a mission. What were you supposed to do? Tell the United States Marines to go screw themselves?" Rex asked. "No. Your parents knew what was involved when you signed up, but I do think they were kinda hoping after a couple of tours, you would have come home."

"I wanted to, believe me, but after a while, the team you are with kinda becomes your family. I don't mean to sound like I didn't love the family I had, but when someone is covering your back while you take out a target, you kinda form a bond," Gabriel explained.

"I understand, believe me. I was in Vietnam, remember?" Rex asked.

"Yep, I do, and I'm very much glad you made it out okay, well, the best you could anyway," Gabriel replied.

"Hey, um, you two war heroes going to be done reminiscing anytime soon? We'll be looking for breakfast at this point," Rose said, trying to light a proverbial fire under the men's butts.

"Read ya loud and clear base command," Gabriel said, teasing Rose. "So, where we going, ol' timer?"

"Well, I could go for a juicy cheeseburger and an ice-cold beer. How's that sound?" Rex asked.

Gabriel and Rose looked at each other, then nodded in agreement.

"Well, let's go then. Do I need to drive separately, or will big boy be okay with me riding next to him?" Rex asked, trying to test the water.

"Let's ask. Samson, is it okay if Rex rides in the back with you?" Rose asked her dog, pointing at Rex, then Gabriel's truck.

There was a resounding bark, which sealed the deal.

Samson moseyed over to Rex and nudged his hand as if to say, "Come on, let's go!"

The drive to town was uneventful. Rex did take notice of Gabriel and Rose's interaction. He smiled when he saw Gabriel look at Rose and wink. Gabriel might not have been his son, but he sure made Rex proud, despite the accidental lung tumor extraction episode.

Chapter Twenty

Dinner went by quickly. In between bites, Gabriel and Rex talked mainly about the ranch and the changes happening over the next few months. They both agreed that having a wind farm would be different, especially having something other than cattle. They both agreed that Gabriel's dad would roll over in his grave if he knew there would be something other than horses grazing out in the pasture.

"We still need to get to an auction and check out some cattle breeds, don't we?" Rex asked.

"Yes, but I was looking at an auction with Highland cows," Gabriel said.

"Highland cows? Ain't them those shaggy lookin' fellas?"

Both Gabriel and Rose laughed when Rex asked about the cows. He was definitely in for a treat when he purchased some.

"Ha, yes! I've seen them in person once when I was en route from overseas and got delayed in Scotland. They are some beautiful creatures. They are supposed to be a docile breed, so easy for us and pretty easy to feed," Gabriel said.

"Good. I'm too old to be fightin' with a two-thousand-pound bull. I think I'll let you handle those if we end up with any," Rex informed Gabriel.

"How about we hire some help and let them decide who's going to be going toe to toe with a bull?" Gabriel asked.

"I'm just sayin' I have some fight left in me, but not enough to withstand being thrown out of a pen," Rex said.

"I'm right there with ya. I'll help out, but getting in there and splitting up the troublemakers can be someone else's job. Although, if they are docile like I read, worrying about them at this point wouldn't serve much purpose," Gabriel said.

I just want both my men to be safe," said Rose as she draped her arms around the necks of Rex and Gabriel.

"We'll do everything we can do, that's for sure. Anytime you are doing something new, there is always that risk of something backfiring. I can't tell you how many missions the plans had changed at the last minute or even while in the field. Being prepared for anything is a top priority," Gabriel said.

Rex swallowed his last bit of beer, then slammed his glass down, satisfied. Gabriel and Rose were a couple of bites and swallows behind Rex, but both finished with a satisfactory smile and an arm stretch up to the ceiling.

"Well, I'm ready to go when you two love birds are. There might just be enough sunlight left to do a little fishin' still," Rex said with a smile.

"Well, you heard it, let's get goin'. We don't want gramps late to the fishin' hole!" Gabriel with a hint of mischief in his voice.

"I'll show you gramps when my size 12 boot finds your man parts and rearranges them!" Rex said in a very matter-of-fact tone despite the half-cocked smile.

"Boys, no one's man parts are going anywhere. Let's get going before someone overhears and thinks you two are gonna start fighting," Rose said, with a mama bear look.

Both men got up from the circular booth and escorted Rose out of the restaurant, a man on each arm.

~(-)~

After dropping Rex off at his place, Gabriel and Rose headed back to his. Staying there instead of crashing at Rose's seemed like the better choice. While Gabiel was checking the voicemail on the house phone, Rose took the opportunity to wander around the house. She was curious about how things looked and knew that Gabriel hadn't been there long enough to change things. Maybe he would let her help with that decision.

"Rose? Where'd ya go?" asked Gabriel. Don't go in the room with the closed..."

It was too late. Gabriel saw the bedroom door open and stopped dead in his tracks.

"I'm in the back bedroom," she answered, not realizing he was standing in the doorway.

"Did you get lost?' Gabriel asked as he entered the room.

"No, I was just looking around while you were checking the voicemail, and something caught hold of me when I walked past this room," Rose answered.

Gabriel remained silent as he looked around the room. It was as if time had frozen in this room. A bed was centered on one wall with a dust-covered nightstand next to it. On the opposite wall was a desk with a single picture frame that looked to have a couple of military medals on it and what looked to be a folded United States flag in front of it.

"Who's room is this?" Rose asked.

"This was my brother's room. He and I joined at the same time, but for whatever reason, we got separated after boot camp. He made it through his first tour, but when he was at the start of his second, he was killed," Gabriel explained, his voice barely audible.

Rose watched as Gabriel clenched his fists. His expression changed to that of sadness. A deep sadness that swallowed a person whole if you didn't have the strength to pull yourself out of it.

She wrapped her arms around his waist, pulled him close, and held him tight. Suddenly, the shoulder area of her shirt felt wet. It was then that she knew Gabriel had allowed an old wound to open, whether on purpose or by accident, but the door that was once sealed tight had been cracked open.

Gabriel began to sob harder and harder, and his body weight began to weigh more and more on Rose. She had to sustain his weight by trying to hold him up, but he finally became too much for her small body, so she slowly worked them down to the floor, where she pulled his head onto her chest as he continued to sob.

"I should have stayed by his side, Rose. I should have been there. He only joined the military because he didn't want to be stuck at home with mom and dad, so he followed me," Gabriel said in between sobs, trying to catch his breath.

"It's not your fault, baby, it's not. He made that decision because of other factors. Ones that you couldn't have made better, no matter what. It's not your fault, I promise," Rose said, trying to console Gabriel.

How long had he been carrying this weight, and why had he not told her he had a brother before now? Questions that would be answered later.

She heard the front door open suddenly and Rex calling out.

"Hey, where's everyone at? You should see this monster of a fish I just caught!"

He suddenly appeared in the doorway and saw them lying on the floor. Rex's facial expression changed from a child-like happiness to one of sudden worry.

Gabriel didn't try to hide the fact that he was upset. Either that, or he just didn't care. Upon receiving word of Gabriel's brother's death, Rex had been the one to get stopped in the driveway by the servicemen who were there to relay the information about the Sterling's baby boy dying in the line of duty; that was really when things changed between the family members.

Rex knelt on the floor, every joint in his body popping and creaking on the way down. He put a hand on Gabriel's chest to let him know he was there and that it was okay.

"Son, listen to me. Your brother had decided long before you did that he wanted to join up. It was the only way to get out from under your mom and dad's pressure they had been putting on him to stay and work the horses. When he told them one last time that he was joining the Marines with you, that was the last straw for your parents, and that's when things started to change," Rex explained.

Gabriel sat up and tried wiping the tears from his face, but they kept falling.

"He had a different kind of fire in him that working the horses with your dad wouldn't have helped. It would have made it worse," Rex said.

"Do you know how he died?" Gabriel asked, finally able to speak.

"Yes, actually. This was the one and only time I had heard your dad say how proud of you and your brother he was. I had overheard the servicemen say that your brother died when terrorists converged on their convoy. A little boy was walking alongside the road when their platoon came under fire. Your brother jumped out of his vehicle and pulled the boy to safety, but not before he took two shots to the back. Your brother wasn't the only one who died either. Two other soldiers lost their lives while trying to pull him to safety," Rex explained.

"He died a hero then. At least he saved a kid. I only managed to kill one," Gabriel said with bitterness behind his words.

This didn't sit well with Rex. He had experienced much worse during his time in Vietnam. He witnessed firsthand what happened when people started calling those soldiers baby killers and much worse.

"Hey, listen, your orders were correct, right?' Rex asked Gabriel.

"As far as I knew. I mean, they kept that kid at the very center to keep him protected," Gabriel answered.

"And you did what you were ordered to do- shoot that little bastard, so he didn't have the opportunity to kill others or at least give the orders to kill anyone. Am I right?" Rex asked, trying to get Gabriel's head back in the game, but he had been there once when he was younger, so he understood where Gabriel was coming from.

"Yeah, it's just that kid never had the opportunity to know anything different. Be anything different than what they told him he had to be," Gabriel said, trying to justify the young terrorist and what he might have been one day.

"And that's the point- he didn't *know* any different. So, what exactly was he missing out on? I'm not saying the kid would have been a different person had someone pulled him out of that terrorist group, but that way of life was literally all he knew. They probably filled him so full of hatred, he didn't know any other way," Rex said.

"So, you're saying that the kill shot I took was a righteous kill?" Gabriel asked.

"I believe you did the right thing. You have to let that go. The young man whose life you were ordered to take might possibly have gone on to order someone else's life to be taken. Someone who might have been innocent. He was not, so you are justified in what you did. I promise; from one soldier to another," Rex said, then patted Gabriel on the chest just above his heart.

Gabriel got up to his feet and helped both Rose and Rex to theirs. He wrapped his arms around both and pulled them in tight.

"I love you guys. Rex, thank you for being the dad I never had," Gabriel whispered. Tears were falling again, but this time, they were happier tears.

"I wouldn't have wanted it any other way, son," Rex replied.

After another moment or two, Gabriel put his arms back down as he and Rex turned to head out, but he noticed Rose wasn't right with him.

"You okay?" he asked.

"Did you mean what you just said? That you love me?" she asked.

Gabriel stepped back over to Rose, placed his hands around hers, pulled them to his chest, and then looked her in the eyes.

"I don't need a lifetime to know what direction I need to go in or where my life is supposed to go next. I only know that I want you with me and me with you every step we take from here on out. It took me to see my brother's uniform and medals to realize that I could have easily been the one killed over there. Snipers were even less popular in the Middle East than regular troops were," Gabriel said.

At that moment, life had come full circle for all of them. They lived their lives running from one fire to the next, only to find their safe haven in the last place they thought they would find it - in the arms of someone just as battered and bruised as they were.

Gabriel and Rose knew true healing could begin as old wounds closed, leaving behind a tiny scar.

A scar that was meant as a reminder that the time they had together was precious.

Chapter Twenty-One

Usually, waking up to a thunderstorm was comforting, but when she realized she was the only one in bed, Rose sat up and looked around the room. Gabriel was not in the room. She got out of bed, put on a pair of shorts and a T-shirt, and headed toward the kitchen. Gabriel wasn't there either, but a warm pot of coffee and a coffee cup were there instead.

"Well, at least I have that to wake up to," she muttered, disappointed that Gabriel was not there to share it.

Rose poured some coffee, added the necessary additives, then stirred and sipped. Perfect.

It wasn't until she looked outside that she saw Gabriel sitting on the front porch in a rocker. She set her cup of coffee down on the counter and stepped outside. Gabriel looked over at her and smiled.

"Good morning, beautiful," he said.

"Good morning to you, too. How long have you been out here?" Rose asked.

"Since about four thirty this morning. I couldn't sleep, so I came outside for some cool air. The mountain storm that rolled in during the night brought one heck of a lightning show," Gabriel said.

"It would have been okay if you woke me up too. I wouldn't have minded. Unless you needed some air to yourself?"

"No, not all. I have moments where I wake up wired and ready to go," Gabriel said.

"Is it okay to join you now?" Rose asked, making sure he really wanted company.

"Definitely. Come join me. I'll even share my blanket with you," Gabriel said, unfolding the blanket across his lap. "There's a rocker on the other side of me here," he said, nodding to his right.

Rose stopped in front of him and kissed him on the lips.

"Good morning," she said softly.

Gabriel reached up, placed a hand on the small of her back, and returned the kiss with a little more force.

"Good morning," he replied.

"That's more like it!" she said.

"I'm sorry about leaving you in bed. I had some things I couldn't shake after last night," Gabriel said.

"I need to apologize for wandering through your house. It's not mine to do that, and I should have stayed put," Rose admitted.

"No, this house is yours too, now. I meant what I said last night. I love you. I've never said those words except to one other woman, my mom, and obviously those words have a different meaning with you, but..." Gabriel paused. He was getting a little more touchy-feely than he was used to, but he knew he needed to open himself up to that part.

"So, what are you saying?" Rose asked.

"I'm saying that I want to wake up with you every morning for the rest of my life. I want to watch every sunrise and every sunset with you beside me," Gabriel had the sudden thought that he better slow down for a moment to make sure she was on the same page as him.

He looked at Rose, who was looking down into her coffee cup.

"Did I say too much?" he asked.

"No. It was perfect," Rose said.

"Is there a but in there?" he asked.

"No, no but. I was actually just replaying in my head this same moment when we were in church, and I was sitting behind you. I had been praying for some time, asking if God would bring into my life someone who would make me whole again. Make me feel loved. When I woke up that morning for church, I heard this voice in my head that said if I truly wanted to be with someone again, I would have to accept the other person for all their scars and wounds. When I said that I needed someone who would also love me for all my wounds and scars, the voice told me that if I looked to the light, it was there that I would find the one I was supposed to be with," Rose explained. Gabriel was hanging onto every word she was saying.

"That morning when I sang up front, and I looked and saw you, the light from the stained-glass window was shining through and surrounding you so much that I almost didn't recognize you, but when you smiled at me, I just knew it was you that was being given to me."

It was Gabriel's turn to look down into his coffee.

"I'm not religious, but as I'm listening to what you are saying to me right now, I feel like there is some other force at work. When I saw the listing for help needed at the church, well, I clearly don't need the money, but something was pushing me towards that church," Gabriel explained.

"Mt. Hope has a way of making things happen in people's lives that maybe wouldn't have before had certain things not happened. Besides, you're a beautiful mess, and I'll take it!" Rose said, squeezing his hand.

"Does that mean I'll be watching the sunrise with you?" Gabriel asked.

"That means I'm not stopping at the sunrise or sunset. I want it all with you," Rose said, then leaned over and kissed Gabriel.

"I do," Rose said.

"I do, too," Gabriel said.

The hair on both of their arms stood on end as a sudden lightning bolt hit a nearby tree, reducing it to cinder and ash with a sudden downpour to follow. The clap of thunder to follow was instantaneous and caused Gabriel and Rose to nearly jump off the front porch.

There was no need to put the fire out as the rain became Mother Nature's fire extinguisher.

"Should we consider that lightning bolt God's blessing on our union?" Rose asked.

"Well, I'm not asking for a second one!" Gabriel answered, then started laughing.

"What do you say we go back inside and have some breakfast. I'll even cook," Rose asked.

"Well, Mrs. Sterling, I would say you got yourself a deal, but on one condition," Gabriel said.

"Oh, yeah? You got a better plan?" Rose asked.

"Yes, actually. Let's make breakfast, then take it back to the bedroom and eat in bed," Gabriel said.

"Oh, that sounds fantastic! I'm game. Let's go," Rose said, then got up out of the rocker, grabbed Gabriel's hand, and led the way inside.

~(-)~

Several hours and a few flapjacks with bacon later, Gabriel and Rose resurfaced from the bedroom to find Rex sitting at the kitchen table drinking a cup of coffee.

"Good afternoon, you two. I was wondering when you would be coming out for air," Rex said.

"We were actually up earlier, sitting on the front porch," Gabriel said.

"Before or after that tree out there exploded?" Rex asked.

"Before, during, and after. Once it started downpouring, we came inside, made breakfast, then went back to bed," Gabriel replied.

"Well, that had to have been some lightning strike," Rex said.

Gabriel looked at Rose and smiled.

"Oh, it was pretty intense," Gabriel said with a smile.

Rex squinted at Gabriel and then at Rose.

"Why do I get the feeling that you aren't thinking about the same thing as me?" Rex asked.

"Who says we're not?" Gabriel asked innocently.

"I'll never understand you kids these days. Anyway, I came over to ask if you wanted to go to Bozeman tomorrow for a cattle auction. I saw an ad in the paper for an auction that they were selling the Highland cows you were talking about," Rex said.

This got Gabriel's attention.

"How much per head, and are they auctioning bulls off, too?" he asked, quickly sitting down.

"Ad said the minimum bid was five hundred for cows and a thousand for the bulls," Rex said.

"How do you feel about going to an auction?" Gabriel asked.

"Do I get to dress like a real cowgirl?" Rose asked, smiling like a kid on Christmas morning.

"I think it's required," answered Gabriel, returning the smile. There wasn't such a rule. He just liked the way Rose smiled and the happiness that beamed from her.

"Alright, see the both of you tomorrow morning before sunrise. We got a little bit of a drive. I'll go ahead and get the trailer hitched up and make a few calls for some feed. Looks like we're back in the business," Rex said, then smiled. "It's good to have you back, son. Your dad would be proud."

Rex closed the door and headed towards the cattle trailer that was down by the barn.

Life might not have always gone the way he wanted it, but it was going his way more and more every day.

Chapter Twenty-Two

Gabriel and Rose were up, coffee in hand, and in the truck waiting for Rex by the time he pulled up in front of the house. Surprised to see them, he hobbled over and climbed into the back of the quad cab pickup truck.

"You still know how to drive this thing, or do you need an expert to drive it?" Rex said sarcastically.

"I did drive a few bigger vehicles in the military. I think I can handle this," Gabriel answered.

"Yes, but did you keep them on the road?" Rex asked, digging in a little deeper.

"Don't you have a nap or something to take?" Gabriel asked.

"Nope, too much coffee in me. Besides, I need to make sure you stay on the road. Remember, we could be hauling some cattle back with us, so don't wreck the truck before we get there," Rex said.

"I know. I got this. So, speaking of cattle, should we get a bull and a few cows?"

"At least. If the stock is good, we ought to be loading the trailer up. I did give old Doc Samuels a call to see if he would meet us down there. It sounded like he would," Rex said.

"Doc is still alive and practicing?" Gabriel asked, surprised.

"Yep, alive and kicking. His son and grandson are a part of the practice, too, so it looks like they aren't the only family business that will be around for a while," Rex said confidently.

"Well, it will be good to see them. I assume there will be a charge for having them come down?" Gabriel asked.

"Nope. He said he would be there anyway, so if we find what we are looking for and need him to check things out, let him know, and he'll come over," Rex said.

"Sounds like we're covered then. I just hope we find what we're looking for. There's usually a lot of big spenders at cattle auctions, and they don't mind letting you know who has the money," Gabriel said.

"Meaning there could be some competition?" Rose asked.

"Meaning, we need to steer clear of the high rollers. They don't play nice when they lose," Gabriel answered.

"Yep, your dad and I nearly got ourselves caught up in one of those exact situations. Luckily, the guy causing the problems backed himself into a pen with a bull in it. The bull kicked the guy, and he went flying. I'm pretty sure there was more broken than not after that," Rex said.

"I think I remember that. Didn't Dad actually get into a fight?" Gabriel asked.

"Yep. Your dad wasn't a hothead most times, but when he was, lookout! The only thing that saved your dad that day was your mom, and by saved, I mean didn't go to jail," Rex explained.

"Was it that bad?" Gabriel asked.

"Let's just say that when a man auctions off something, you better give the buyer the correct animal. There was a cattleman that had brought some special breed of horse that your mom had her eye on, and well, when your dad made the purchase and then got something other than what he paid for..."

" What ended up happening?" Rose asked.

"Well, four policemen and a bullwhip later, your dad had them all on the ground and said he was gonna whip every one of them until he got the horse he paid for. Luckily, your mom had enough sense to get the police. When they arrived, and the details were explained, the cattleman gave your dad the horse and was taken to jail for falsifying records and a couple of other charges. Your dad meant business. I mean, your mom ran the show back at the ranch, but your dad was not one to mess with or cheat out of a good horse," Rex explained.

"Well, let's hope that the auction goes smoothly. I don't want to see how far from the tree this apple fell," Gabriel said.

"Me either, but if you get cheated out of a horse *or* cow, I'll help ya whip 'em!" Rose said.

"Dang! I like this one more and more all the time. When you gonna make it official. Or are you two just gonna keep beatin' 'round the bush?" Rex asked.

Gabriel and Rose looked at each other briefly and smiled.

"You two got something up your sleeves?" Rex asked.

"Should we?" Rose asked.

"Go ahead. He's safe," Gabriel replied.

"Safe for what?' Rex asked, worried.

"Gabriel more or less proposed to me this morning during the thunderstorm," Rose answered.

"Well, shoot! I got me a daughter-in-law?" Rex asked, with a look of surprised shock showing on his face.

"Yep, I just need to buy a ring and make it official," Gabriel said.

"Man alive. Things are gonna work out after all," Rex said with a sigh. He reached up, patted Gabriel on the shoulder, and squeezed Rose's hand.

~(-)~

When the trio finally arrived at the auction, there were trucks and trailers as far as the eye could see, but Gabriel was determined to find a spot to park so they could get inside and start looking around.

The specific auction for the Highland bulls and cows Gabriel was interested in wasn't for a couple of hours, so they had time to check other things out.

There were all kinds of ranch animals on display, big and small. Vendors were trying to sell their products and everything in between. Gabriel realized he hadn't eaten when his stomach growled loud enough to be heard over the top of the animals around them. Rose giggled and then dragged him to the nearest food vendor. She made him get something to eat and reminded him he needed to stay on top of his game if he planned on winning the bid for one of the Scottish Highland bulls.

"Did I hear that you wanted in on the Highland bull bid?" the food vendor asked.

"Yes, why?" Gabriel asked, curious whether a food vendor would have any useful information.

"Well, I just heard a few minutes ago that only one bull made it. The other two were sold outside of the auction, and now only one will be up for bidding. You know what that means, don't ya," asked the vendor.

"Yeah, it means that I'll be spending more to get what I want, and I also need to watch my back," Gabriel said.

"Good luck to ya. It's going to be a long day," the food vendor said.

Gabriel and Rose made a beeline to Rex after they had their food in hand. The fact that there was only one bull instead of three might cause a problem for Gabriel.

They found Rex talking to a couple of guys that looked like they had seen their fair share of auctions.

"Hey, we just heard something about the Highland Bulls that are supposed to be auctioned off," Gabriel said, leaning in so only Rex could hear.

"Say what?" Rex shouted. Gabriel had to quiet him down while pulling him to a better place to talk.

"What'd you just tell me?" Rex asked.

"One of the food vendors told us that he had heard that two out of three of the bulls had already been sold in a private sale before the owners even got here," Gabriel said.

"Well, it's not great news, but it ain't the worst I've ever heard. We just need to bid high, so we make sure we end up with that last bull," Rex said.

"Don't you think that's what the other bidders are going to do?" asked Gabriel.

"Yes, but as long as the remaining bull looks good, we ought to start the bid on the high side; that way, some of the other bidders are scared off," Rex said.

"Good idea. Let's go see if we can get a look at the bull, then decide if we need Doc Samuelson to come over," Gabriel said.

Rex nodded, then took the lead in finding the one remaining Scottish Highland bull. It took a few minutes, between pushing through the throngs of onlookers and chit-chatters, but they made it over to the bull. There was a small crowd of admirers, but Rex, Gabriel, and Rose managed to make it to the front. They stood and watched as the bull glanced at the new onlookers sideways but then went back to hanging his head down and bellowing.

"I did some reading on these; they don't like to be alone for too long, or they get stressed," Gabriel said.

"Poor guy. I wonder how long he's been by himself?" Rose asked.

Gabriel squatted down to get a better look at the bull. He and the bull made eye contact, and the bull lifted his head and bellowed louder than before.

"I feel your pain, my friend. I'm here to help," Gabriel said under his breath.

As if the bull heard every word Gabriel had said, the bull started walking towards Gabriel and then stopped. He stood within a couple of feet of him. The bull made eye contact with Gabriel, then lowered his head and bellowed again, but not quite as loud.

"Hi. I'm here to take you home with me and maybe a couple of your lady friends, if that's okay?" Gabriel said to the bull.

The bull snorted as if trying to convey its own feelings, then took a couple steps closer to Gabriel.

"I think he likes you," Rose said.

"It appears that way," Gabriel said. He stood up, draped his hands down over the waist-high bar, and looked over at Rose to say something when he felt something nudge his hands. He looked down and saw the bull standing in front of him, looking up.

"I think you have a new friend," Rose said as she reached out to rub the top of the Highland bull's head.

"It appears that way," Gabriel said, reaching out to pet his head.

"I think we're drawing some unnecessary attention," Rex leaned in toward Gabriel and said.

"Who?" he asked.

"The two fellas on the other side of the pen staring right at us," Rex said.

"Well, let them stare. It's not like I'm trying to steal their bull. I might steal it from other bidders but not the owner," Gabriel replied.

"Still, we better start making our way to the arena. You know how much you're planning on bidding on?" Rex asked.

"I was thinking of opening with five thousand," Gabriel said.

Rex choked on his coffee, spewing it everywhere, then looked up at Gabriel like he was speaking in tongues.

"I know you have money in the bank, but do you really want to come out that strong?" Rex asked.

"I want that bull, so let's start with that, and we'll go from there," Gabriel said.

"Okay, well, let's roll the dice and see what happens," Rex said, shaking his head in dismay.

They made it to the arena just in time to register themselves and the ranch name under which any potential animals would be purchased under. Finding three seats together proved to be a chore, but eventually, they found three up in front, straight across from the auctioneers.

"Welcome, ladies and gentlemen, to this special auction. We have a very special breed of cattle coming out on auction for you this afternoon. This is a red Scottish Highland bull. He's three years old and ready to go, if you know what I mean?" the auctioneer said, with an added quick laugh. "Let's open the bid at one thousand dollars, shall we? One thousand dollars."

A couple of hands shot up, holding signs. Gabriel looked around quickly, then held his sign up with one hand and signaled five with the other hand.

"I'm sorry, are you telling me you are saying five thousand?" the auctioneer asked, looking straight at Gabriel.

Gabriel tipped his hat at the man and smiled.

"Alrighty folks, who will give me five and a half, five and a half going once…"

On the other side of the arena, a lone hand went up with a sign, signaling they'd pay the five and half thousand for the bull.

"Alrighty, five and a half it is. Can I get six thousand for the red Scottish Highland bull?" the auctioneer asked.

Gabriel held up his sign, then held up five fingers, then two more to represent he was offering seven thousand dollars for the bull. The room grew silent.

q "It looks like we have a bit of a competition, folks. I now have seven thousand for the bull; that is seven times the asking amount. Am I going any higher? Can I get seven and a half? Seven and a half going once. Seven and a half going twice..." the auctioneer paused.

Gabriel and the other person bidding stared at each other. Neither wanted to make another bid, but at the same time, both were prepared to go higher.

"Can I get seven and a half thousand going three times?" the auctioneer asked.

Gabriel's competitor shot up again and then held up the equivalent of eight thousand. Gabriel countered but put up both hands and all his fingers to signify ten thousand.

The auctioneer dropped the microphone accidentally as he was shocked by what had just transpired. He quickly recovered the microphone and looked back at both bidders.

"I have ten thousand dollars. Am I going up to ten and a half?" he asked.

The other bidder looked at Gabriel and touched the tip of his hat to signify he was out. Gabriel had won the bid at nearly ten thousand dollars.

"It looks like the bidder from Triple J Ranch is giving up on the bid. Win goes to Sterling Ranch. Please head to sales to collect your bill of sale," the auctioneer said, then started shuffling around paperwork to get ready for the next bidding war.

Rose got excited and jumped up and down, then wrapped her arms around Gabriel's neck, kissing him on the cheek.

"Come on, ya big spender, we better go get our boy before someone steals him," Rex said.

All three made their way to where they needed to pay the money so they could receive their bill of sale. They would need it in order to retrieve their new purchase from the chute.

A few minutes later, bill of sale in hand, Gabriel, Rose, and Rex were headed toward the chute to show proof of purchase. As they approached the area, three unhappy men started their approach towards Gabriel.

"You outbid our employer. He isn't very happy," one of the men said.

Rex stepped up next to Gabriel and smiled.

"Maybe your employer should bring more money or send some people that know how to play the game," Rex said.

"You letting senior citizens speak for you?" another man asked.

"I came to collect my bull. The three of you are in my way, and unless you want to take this outside, you'll move out of the way," Gabriel warned.

"Or what? One of us is leaving with the bull," the man standing in front of Gabriel said.

The man was a whole head shorter, but that didn't stop him from thinking he was bigger than Gabriel.

He reached up to put a hand on Gabriel's chest to dissuade him from going any farther. Gabriel looked down with a disappointed look, then into the eyes of the man blocking his path.

Gabriel grabbed the man by the wrist, spun him around, and shoved him towards the other two behind him. They stuck out their arms to catch their compatriot, and then the man turned back around and stared at Gabriel.

"I'm not in the mood for dancing, so if the three of you want to bow out, now's your chance," Gabriel warned them.

"I think we'll stick around and see how things play out. Who knows, maybe your girl will want to dance too?" the lead man.

"I don't think so. She's a one-man kinda guy. Now, last chance before the bidding opens back up again," Gabriel said.

"Oh, yeah, what are you bidding on?" the main guy asked.

"Your lives!" Gabriel said. With a lightning-fast swing of the arm, the frontman hit the ground with a loud smack as his face hit first.

"Now, there are still two of you. You could do the right thing by picking your friend up off the ground, or you could try your luck with me and see what happens," Gabriel said, almost taunting the other two. He was done playing around. He was there to collect his bull and leave. No one was going to stop him.

The other two started to charge at Gabriel, but Gabriel was a split second faster and lunged forward with both arms extended, clothes lining the two men, flipping them backward and headfirst onto the floor. Both men hit the ground hard, landing flat on their backs.

Gabriel was the first to step forward, followed by Rex and Rose.

"Next time, bring more money, and don't be such sore losers!" Gabriel said as he stepped over the three men.

Once all three were at a safe distance, Rose and Rex took an audible deep breath.

"Here I was hoping for an easy day," Gabriel said.

They finally made it to where their bull was waiting for them. The bull stood, swishing its tail, and bellowing loudly once he saw Gabriel.

"I'm here, my friend. Let's get you to your new home, shall we?" Gabriel said.

The bull snorted and shook his head, then pawed at the ground as if to communicate in agreement.

"Alright, off we go!" Gabriel said.

They backed the trailer up to the loading area, and the bull loaded up without so much as a fuss.

"You know we need to find some females, now, don't ya?" Rex asked.

"Yep. They are on my to-do list. I'll look for another auction or a ranch with some and maybe just outright pay for them. In the meantime, I want to enjoy our new friend back there and make sure he's taken care of. We'll probably want to have Doc Samuels over or his son to take a look and write him up a clean bill of health."

"I'll give him a call as soon as we get home. I'm sure he's probably running all over the arena right now," Rex said.

"Good idea. We should still buy a couple of horses. Especially if we end up with a herd and have to move them around at all," Gabriel said.

"Three," Rose said.

"Three what?" Gabriel asked.

"Three horses. You think you two get to be the only ones out there having fun? I want a horse, too!" Rose said.

"Alright, the lady wants a horse," Gabriel said, then smiled.

"Looks like our ranch will be up in no time," Rex said with a satisfactory smile.

"Yep, just a couple more things that need to be done, then we'll all be good.

The future was starting to present itself more and more every day, taking Gabriel that much closer to where his heart was leading him.

~ Mt. Hope ~

Chapter Twenty-Three

When they arrived back at Sterling Ranch, the Highland bull, aptly named "Red," pretty much walked out of the trailer, sauntered over to the water trough, and then helped himself to a mouthful of hay.

"Ya did good, but Christ Almighty, he's a hairy beast!" Rex commented.

Red must have come with super hearing because he reared his head back and bellowed after Rex had made his comment.

"I think he heard you," Gabriel said.

"Good! I hope he did. First time in my entire life I have livestock that came with a sense of humor. Don't expect your lady friends to think you're funny, and speaking of lady friends, you better put out, or you're going to get the shock of a lifetime!" Rex said, firing back a zinger.

"You keep talking to him like that, he isn't going to let you near him," Gabriel cautioned.

"I know. I'm just giving the big fellow a hard time," Rex said.

Red tossed his head back as if laughing and started walking towards them.

"Well, I guess he's coming to give you a piece of his mind," Gabriel said.

"Don't worry, I got my eyes on him, "Rex said.

Rex was preparing for the worst. He stood his ground, and when Red made it over, the pair stared straight into each other's eyes. Rex had worked as a ranch hand most of his adult life, minus being in the military, and had seen just about everything that could happen between man and beast, but he was not expecting Red to do what he was about to do.

"You got somethin' to say to me, fella?" Rex asked, not breaking his eye contact.

Rex had no sooner finished his sentence before Red's tongue darted out and licked the entire surface area of Rex's face, then let out a bellow that could only be considered the animal equivalent of a laugh. Red took off in a flash of red fur and headed to the far side of the pen.

"Did he just..." Rex couldn't finish his sentence as more cow saliva dripped onto his lips and into his mouth.

Gabriel and Rose laughed so hard that they had to lean against the fence to keep from falling over.

"I can't work with an animal that don't respect me! We're taking him back!" Rex said as he continued to wipe excess cow saliva from his face.

"It...it...could have been worse," Gabriel said, still laughing. "He could have turned and kicked you."

"I would have preferred that over this!" Rex said and then raised his fist in the air. "You just wait! Payback is a bitch, you four-legged tumbleweed!" Rex said, continuing to hurl insults.

"Come on, we better go see if his feelings are hurt," Gabriel said to Rose.

"Ya, we better. We don't want him to feel unloved," Rose said, looking at Rex and continuing to laugh.

"You laugh now, but just wait 'til he licks you up one side and down the other," Rex said.

"Ah, come on. He was just telling you he loves you!" Gabriel said, poking the hive one more time.

Gabriel and Rose watched as Rex stormed off to sulk. They both knew that Rex was a big softy and probably liked the attention from the Highland coo, but in the end, how the two formed their own bond was up to them.

Red found a patch of grass in the pen and was happily munching. Gabriel knelt in front of him but from the safety of the fence between them.

"I gotta hand it to you. You sure got Rex all worked up," Gabriel said to the bull.

Red raised his head and tilted it to one side as if contemplating what Gabriel had just said.

"Anyway, you might try a different way to express yourself with him. He's weird that way," Gabriel said.

"Yeah, and I'll take all the kisses you can spare!" Rose said.

Red snorted, then took a couple of steps forward, coming within an inch or two of the fence. He bobbed his head up and down a couple of times as if to signify he wanted something.

Gabriel and Rose exchanged looks and then held out their hands, palms facing up.

Red sniffed both hands, then swung his head between both hands, giving them yet another sign.

"I think he's trying to tell us something," Rose said.

Gabriel reached up, placed his hand on Red's head between his eyes, and started scratching. The bull immediately closed his eyes and made a low rumble in his throat.

"I think he likes that!" Rose said, shocked. She placed her hand on the side of his face just under his left eye and started scratching as well.

Red continued to make the low rumble sound in his throat. It was becoming very clear that Red was no ordinary Highland bull.

"I'm going to try something. Stay here for a minute," Gabriel said.

"What are you doing?" Rose asked.

"I just want to see something," Gabriel said.

"Please be careful. Just because he licked Rex's face and nudged our hands does not make him the family dog," Rose said.

"I know. I just want to see how he adapts to a human actually being near him," Gabriel explained.

Rose continued to scratch the side of Red's face while Gabriel slowly climbed over the fence. Red watched out of his right eye and didn't seem to mind that Gabriel was getting closer.

"Hi, boy. You don't mind if I join you, do you?" Gabriel asked, speaking in soft tones.

Red snorted. Whether it be a yes or something else, Red didn't seem to mind Gabriel being close.

Gabriel took a couple of steps back and then sat down. Red turned his head, looked at Gabriel, and swished his tail. It was the equivalent of a dog's tail wagging.

"Are you sure you-" Rose started to speak when she saw Red move over next to Gabriel, then lay down and place his head on his lap.

Gabriel and Rose looked at each other with their mouths wide open.

"No way!" Rose mouthed.

"You wanna try?" Gabriel asked.

"Oh, I don't, uh, no. I think that is a bad idea," Rose said.

"Nah, he would have let me know if I was invading his space," Gabriel said. "Climb over but stay in his eyesight. I think you'll be fine," Gabriel said.

"If he hurts me, I'm done for," Rose said.

"I know. I'm watching, so just be careful," Gabriel instructed.

"Here goes nothing," Rose said as she stood up and slowly climbed the fence.

Red's left eye tracked Rose as she climbed down, then stood close by. He kicked out slightly with both front and rear left legs.

"Is he telling me to sit down between his legs?" Rose asked.

"Maybe. Try sitting down next to his side and leaning against him," Gabriel said.

"What if he jumps up or something frightens him?" Rose asked, worried.

"Just be on guard, and don't get too comfortable," Gabriel said.

"This is the craziest thing I have ever done," Rose said apprehensively.

She lowered herself slowly to the ground and leaned against Red's side again.

Red started making that low rumbling sound in his throat.

"Gabriel, I don't think this is normal," Rose said.

"I know. Highland cows are supposed to be friendlier than most other livestock, but this beats anything I have ever heard of," Gabriel answered.

"So, how long do you think he'll stay like this?" Rose asked.

"I have no idea, but I'm in it for the long haul," Gabriel said.

The fact that this mighty creature would allow humans to get close but also allow them to snuggle up close was beyond belief. Gabriel and Rose soaked up the love from Red for as long as they could.

~(-)~

Red let Gabriel and Rose know when he was done lying down by bellowing loudly. Rose climbed out fast and then watched as Red eased himself up and off the ground, all the while staying clear of Gabriel.

"I don't understand what just happened. We literally just spent the better part of thirty minutes laying with an animal that should have either taken off or gored us to death, but instead, he chose to love us," Gabriel said.

"What's that tell you then?" Rose asked.

"It tells me that animals are smarter than humans are, and we don't give them nearly enough credit," Gabriel said.

"I agree.

"We better go see what old man grumpy pants is up to," Gabriel said.

"Yeah, plus it's probably time for supper," Rose said.

"You know, I didn't even realize it was as late as it was. I'd fire up the grill if I didn't think we could get something delivered faster," Gabriel said as he glanced at his watch.

"What did ya have in mind?" Rose asked.

"Well, there's that Tex-Mex place we could try?" Gabriel mentioned.

"You sure you don't want to just head into town? The delivery fee alone would be enough to feed a village," Rose said.

"True. Okay, let's go ask Rex if he wants to tag along," Gabriel said as he dusted himself off.

They went inside to see Rex sitting at Gabriel's laptop computer. Ordinarily, this would have been almost uncharacteristic of Rex. Still, he did like to remind everyone that he was tech-savvy enough to carry a cell phone, but then people reminded him that carrying a flip phone wasn't exactly something to brag about.

"Um, did I walk into the wrong house, or are you on my laptop surfing the web?" Gabriel asked.

"Well, I decided if you and I were to expand our business ventures, I better expand my computer knowledge," Rex said as he looked through his glasses and down his nose at the computer screen.

"So, Mister Tech Savvy, what exactly are you looking at?" Gabriel asked.

"I found a ranch about three hours away that has Highland cows for sale and at a pretty good price," Rex said.

"How good are we talking about?" Gabriel asked, curious.

"About seven and a half a head," Rex answered.

"Seriously?" Gabriel asked.

"Yup, and I may be able to get them cheaper," Rex said smugly.

"How so?" Gabriel asked.

"You remember the guy everyone called Snake McClane?" Rex asked.

"Sure, the guy with the giant snake tattoo on his upper body," Gabriel answered.

"Yeah, that's not why that was his name," Rex said, nearly turning red from embarrassment as he avoided eye contact with Rose.

"Huh?" Gabriel asked.

"Honey, it means he is well endowed," Rose said.

"Seriously?" Gabriel asked.

"Proportionally, he would put your bull out there to shame," Rex replied.

"Hm, well, good for him," Gabriel said.

Rex looked up at Gabriel and shook his head in dismay.

"There's something wrong with you, you know that?" Rex asked.

"What? I'm secure enough with my manhood to say that," Gabriel said.

"Maybe keep that to yourself if we are ever in town or at a rodeo," Rex said.

"I'm just sayin'," Gabriel said.

Rex continued to look at the computer screen but shook his head in disbelief.

"Want me to give the ranch a call and see if we can come out and take a look?" Rex asked.

"Sure. Then you wanna go out to dinner with me and Rose? We were going to try that new Tex-Mex place in town."

"They got steak?" Rex asked.

"I'm sure they do," Gabriel said.

"You buyin'?" Rex asked.

"Sure. Anything for my head bull whisperer," Gabriel said, then started laughing.

"That's not funny. I still have the taste of bull spit in my mouth," Rex said.

"Fine, I'll buy you a beer too. Happy?" Gabriel asked.

"Two, and you got yourself a deal," Rex said as he held out his right hand.

"Deal. Go ahead and give them a call. I need to change clothes. I just spent the past thirty minutes with an eighteen-hundred-pound bull's head on my lap," Gabriel said.

"Fine, but don't take too long. Save the bedroom business for later," Rex said, hinting that Gabriel and Rose had ulterior motives.

"Don't worry, I'll be quick," Gabriel said.

"Yeah, I bet Rose has heard that a time or two," Rex replied. This time, it was his turn for the comebacks.

"No, you didn't just make a joke!" Gabriel said, shocked that Rex would even joke like that. Even Rex could appreciate humor, but cracking a joke like that was next level.

"I blame it on the internet," Rex said, making a second comeback.

"Wow, I think someone better buy *me* a beer," Gabriel replied.

"I'll buy the both of you a beer if you both quit talking, so we can go get something to eat," Rose said with a hint of impatience.

"Yes, ma'am," said Gabriel and Rex simultaneously.

Rose nudged Gabriel towards the bedroom in hopes he would take the hint. Like cattle, even men needed prodding in the right direction from time to time.

Chapter Twenty-Four

A couple of days later, Gabriel, Rose, and Rex headed toward the ranch with the Highland cows up for sale. Gabriel was anxious to purchase some so he could get moving on things back at home. It wasn't enough to have the land, the animals, or to be able to take care of them. He had to draw attention to his ranch. He needed to get back into making an income.

The time on the road gave the three of them an opportunity to talk and plan a little bit, and even though Rose wasn't directly a part of the ranch in an official capacity, Gabriel and Rex still valued her input.

"As long as we end up with cows being shipped back home, we should be sitting pretty good, which means we better get some help lined up," Rex said.

"I agree. We ought to be able to make use of the different job posting sites and even spread word in town to get potential help, don't you think?" Gabriel asked.

"I think so. I'll even ask around when we get to where we're going. I'd be surprised if 'ol Snake doesn't give me a couple of names," Rex said.

"That would be good if he did, and they worked out," Gabriel said.

"Things have played out good so far. Let's see how the rest goes," Rex added.

The ranch they were headed to came within view. It was named Sky View Ranch. A tall man in blue jeans and a button-up shirt with a cowboy hat was waiting by a pair of wrought iron gates.

"Howdy, folks. Can I help? Wait, are you Rex Dansbury?" asked the man.

"It is. Who might you be?" Rex asked.

"My name is Alex McClane. I believe you know my dad?"

"Well, if you're talking about Snake McClane, then yes," Rex answered.

"He hasn't gone by that name in a long time, so you definitely go way back," Alex said.

"Yep, he and I started at the Sterling ranch just after we got out of the military, back in the late seventies," Rex said.

"Wow, okay. So, a *long* time ago. Well, he's up at the main house. If you want to head that way, you guys can catch up and look around. I'm assuming you're here for the Highland cows?" Alex asked.

"Yep. Depending on how good they look, we are looking to buy around 25 head or so. I have a bull back home looking for friends," Gabriel said.

"Well, you came to the right place. Head on up, and I'll text my dad and let him know you'll be there in a minute or two," Alex said.

"Sounds good, thank you," Gabriel said and proceeded down the long gravel drive.

As they approached what appeared to be a giant log cabin, a tall, older man who looked like Alex stood on the top stair.

Gabriel pulled the truck to a stop and hadn't even had a chance to unbuckle when he realized Rex was already out the door and headed up the stairs.

"Snake McClane! You old cattle-drivin' dog," Rex said with his right hand outstretched for a handshake.

"Rex Dansbury! You old saddle sore, how ya been? What's it been twenty, twenty-five years?" Snake asked.

"At least. How ya been?' Rex asked.

"Well, not too bad. I run the show around here. Rumor floating around says your ranch is startin' up again," Snake said.

"Well, now, here's the thing, it's under new management, and we already have money in the bank. But we ain't even got but one bull, so we thought we would come to the second-best ranch and by some cows for our stud back home to sow his wild oats," Rex said.

"Well, you came to the right place," Snake said, leaning closer to Rex. "Is that the Sterling kid?"

"Yep. He just got out of the Marines a while back and came back home to revamp the ranch and give things a go," Rex said.

"The Marines build 'em big, don't they?" Snake asked.

"They have to. Gabriel there took out the world's most wanted terrorist as his last kill order. Now, he's just trying to make up for the bad decisions his dad made," Rex said.

"Well, let's see about some cows for an old friend," Snake said.

"Hey, speaking of that, you wouldn't happen to know of ranch hands that are looking for work, would ya?" Rex asked.

"As a matter of fact, there was a neighboring ranch up for auction. The owners had to take the hit on everything, including saying goodbye to their staff. One of them is an old friend of yours," Snake said.

"Who might that be?' Rex asked.

A smile started forming at the corners of Snake's mouth. Rex knew that smile to be the foretelling of nothing good.

"You remember Millie Stafford, the camp cook from back in the day? She was sister to the wife of the guy that owned the Lucky Horseshoe Ranch over in the next county," Snake explained.

Rex had a look of concentration on his face and didn't seem to have much luck remembering who Snake was talking about.

"What did she look like?" Rex asked.

"Well, she had braided blonde hair and the prettiest big-" Snake was cut off.

"Millie Stafford! I know her. We met up at the bar in town a few times. She still wears tight jeans that could make a man forget his name?" Rex asked.

"Yep, and most men still do. She's actually out back. The owners are having a feast tonight. A bunch of rich city slickers are in town and wanted to know what it's like to drive cattle, so we rolled out the red carpet for 'em, and we're gonna feed them and then show 'em how we get things done," Snake said.

Rex started getting a little fidgety. He and Millie had a history together back in the day.

"What's a guy gotta do to buy some cows around here?' Gabriel said as he walked up behind Rex.

Rex was caught off guard and took off like his pants were on fire. He wasn't normally scared easily but seeing Snake and hearing about Millie completely put his mind elsewhere.

"Where's the fire? Hold on, let me get a bucket!" Snake said. Gabriel and Rose were three shades of red, they were laughing so hard.

"I hate it when you do that! It's bad enough you put me in the hospital for knockin' a lung out of my chest, but now you wanna give me a heart attack?" Rex said, panting as he walked back over to the others.

"Hi, I'm Gabriel Sterling, and this is my…" Gabriel stopped for a second. He had never officially told anyone that Rose and he were together. This would be the first time saying it out loud. "This is my girlfriend, Rose Callahan."

"Pleased to meet ya, Rose and Mr. Sterling. I remember you when you were just a little hot-headed kid runnin' 'round your daddy's ranch stirrin' up all kinds of trouble. Matter fact, I still remember hearin' about that time you were skinny dippin'-" Snake was cut short, more like saved by the bell, when a woman stepped outside of the main door to the house.

"Did I hear there was a Rex Dansbury on the property? Because if so, I don't recall this being a good idea. He has a habit of walking out on you," the woman said.

Everyone's expression went from laughter and smiles to concern and curse words in a matter of seconds.

Rex took off his cowboy hat and tucked it under his arm. Snake, Gabriel, and Rose cleared the path for the lover's quarrel that was about to ensue.

"I thought I told you I never wanted to see you again?" Millie asked, staring hard enough to bore holes through Rex.

"You know the real story, but if you need to be told the truth one more time, we can step aside and let Gabriel Sterling and his girlfriend do what they came for," Rex said.

"Did you say Gabriel Sterling? *Little* Gabriel? The last time I saw you, I was probably changing your diapers with your mom back at the ranch," Millie said, looking Gabriel up and down in disbelief.

"Yep, this is him. His parents are both gone now, and he's retired from the military. He's trying to put some lifeblood back into the ranch, which is why we are here- to buy some of your Highland cows so our bull, Red, can have a little fun out in the back pasture," Rex said.

"You'd know all about having fun in the back pasture, wouldn't ya?" Millie said, looking straight at Rex.

"I can see this is going to be a tough sale. Is there somewhere you and I can go to clear the air?" Rex asked Millie.

"Sure, why don't we go over to my cabin. It's just over there," Millie said as she looked in the direction of where her place was.

"Fine, let's go. Gabriel, don't let this two-timin' horse thief rob ya blind. I'll be back when I'm done sortin' out this mess," Rex said.

"I gotta handle on things. Go do what you gotta do," Gabriel said. He knew Rex wasn't really going to work anything out. Rex was many things, but a big talker, he was not. He'd tell you how it is, and that's all there was to it. Now, with Millie, he had some making up to do. There was a little bit of a love history between them, but Rex knew how to set things straight. Especially when it came to telling the truth. He may have been a crotchety old ranch hand, but he was an honorable one.

~(-)~

Snake McClane led Gabriel and Rose to the small fenced-in pasture out back. It was where they usually kept livestock for special reasons. In this case, it was showing them off to potential buyers.

"Well, here's the herd of Highland cows. We have a bull, too, if you're interested. He's kept separate due to mishandling from the previous ranch," Snake said.

"How many cows do you have here?" Gabriel asked.

"About five hundred head. My boss has been trying to sell them off so he can bring on different beef cattle. There's a ranch a couple of counties over to the east that has Angus cattle for sale and are going for above asking price, and that's before they go to auction," Snake said.

"Wow, I should have thought about this a little more," Gabriel said.

"Nah, you're in the right market. You just have to have the right connections and patience," Snake said.

"Do you know where I can find either of those?" Gabriel said, half joking.

"I'll tell you what, if I remember right, you have quite a bit of land, right?" Snake asked.

"Yeah, I just sold about five hundred acres to a wind farm company, which left me about two thousand acres," Gabriel replied.

"You should have enough land to keep things moving. I'll tell you what. You give me about seventy thousand, and I'll not only ship them to you, but I'll also throw in some ranch hands to get you started and a contact or two to help you get started, too. Highland cows can be tricky as far as selling them off for beef and let me tell you something. I've had Highland beef, and it is some of the tastiest beef I've ever had. I would take it over regular beef any day of the week," Snake said.

"Then why is your boss trying to get rid of all of his herd?" Gabriel asked.

Snake stepped closer so that only Gabriel could hear what he was about to say.

"He's trying to liquidate some of his riskier assets, which is why we are now what's called a working ranch," Snake said.

"Makes sense. Well, I came here wanting to buy about twenty-five head, and now I'm buying five hundred. Rex is gonna kill me," Gabriel said.

"I have a feeling that Millie is doing a little sweet talkin'," Snake said.

"So, what you're saying is, he'll be okay with this transaction?" Gabriel asked.

"Rex and I go back a long way, and I have never steered him or anyone else wrong. Call it my code of cowboy ethics, I guess," Snake said.

"Good to know," Gabriel said. "You know what, though, it just dawned on me. I was only planning on 25 head, so I only have that much hay and grain. Where can I get enough feed for the cattle you are sending me?" Gabriel asked, now worried.

"I can help you with that, too. Add on an extra five thousand, and I'll send a train car full of hay and grain enough to get you through the next month or so," Snake said, but then was distracted by his cell phone going off. "I need a second. It's my boss."

Snake excused himself and walked a few feet away, but Gabriel could still hear the conversation. It was thanks to his sniper's hearing.

"Yeah, boss, I'm in the middle of selling your Highland cows to Gabriel Sterling. Yeah, that's what I said, Gabriel Sterling. Why?" The expression on Snake's face went from mild annoyance to pure shock and awe. As he tucked his cell phone back in his pocket, he stared at the ground for a brief second in disbelief.

"Everything okay?" Gabriel asked.

"Um, yeah. Strangest thing, my boss just told me that he doesn't profit from selling to family," Snake said.

"What does that mean?" Gabriel asked.

Suddenly, a big, black Dodge pickup with dark-tinted windows pulled up. After coming to a full stop, the driver's side door opened, and a tall, middle-aged man got out and started walking towards Gabriel.

Everyone within visual distance who saw the man get out of the truck stopped in their tracks and stared at the man and Gabriel.

"Honey, he looks just like you. Are you sure you only had one brother?" Rose asked in a hushed tone.

"Well, I always thought so anyway," Gabriel answered, shocked.

Chapter Twenty-Five

A million thoughts swirled around Gabriel's head by the time the tall man got within shaking hand range. He had seen a lot in the world, but nothing like this. No one had ever come close to looking like him. At least not this close.

"Hello, I'm Malcolm Grant, and I'm guessing you have some questions for me?"

Gabriel extended his hand and shook the man's hand. It felt familiar. It felt strong and sure.

"Well, a few, but let's start with what Snake just said. 'Doesn't profit off of selling to family.' What exactly does that mean?" Gabriel asked.

"Well, there is a short answer and a long answer. If you want the short answer, the bill of sale to your new cows, and whatever else around here you would like, you can have it and then leave. Or, if you would like the full story, one that you might want to actually hear, we can all head inside for a cool place to sit and maybe a bite to eat. It's your choice, though," Malcolm said.

Gabriel had a look of contemplation on his face. He then looked at Rose for guidance. Rose tipped her head towards the house.

"Well, I'm grateful for the cattle, but there seems to be a general consensus that you and I look alike," Gabriel said as he pointed to the onlookers. "My vote is for inside and a bite to eat, if you're sure that's okay?"

"More than okay, and this isn't your average story, I promise. As a matter of fact, it has a happy ending. Come on, let's go inside. I'll have something made up for us to eat. I'm going to go out on a ledge here, but do you like ribeye steak?" Malcolm asked.

"Best cut on a cow," Gabriel replied.

"Words to live by," Malcolm said. "Hop in. I'll pull around back so we can go in through a less formal entrance."

Gabriel and Rose got in Malcolm's pickup truck, looked out the window, and stared in awe as they saw what looked to be a garden with a fountain and a terrace, which sat in front of what appeared to be a castle.

"Welcome to Grant Castle. This is part of the story that you would never have heard of had you not shown up today," Malcolm said.

"Meaning?" Gabriel asked, not sure where the story was headed.

"Do you believe in Fate? I do, well, sort of. Let me explain why I think Fate is a factor here- your father's name was Maxwell Sterling, was it not? Well, so was mine," Malcolm said. He let it sink in for a moment. "Any thoughts to add?"

"At least one. Either there was more than one Maxwell Sterling, or you are saying we might share the same father,"

Gabriel said, making it sound like he was guessing, but not really. It didn't take a genius to put the pieces together.

"So, what I'm officially saying is, yes, we are related. I am your older brother, but only by four years. Our father was in the military towards the end of the Vietnam War. Our father met my mother when he was overseas, stationed in England in the Navy. He kept hearing of this wild place called Scotland where these bonnie lasses ran free. So, he took a weekend pass and went exploring with some friends. The story I was told is that he met a Scottish woman the first night he was there, and they fell in love. After their weekend together, they continued seeing each other as often as possible and ended up getting married. Ten months later, I came into the picture, but without a mom. She died in childbirth. From what I was told, our father was so distraught that he resigned from his military commission, returned to the States, and carried on with his family business- horse ranching." Malcolm explained.

Gabriel sat in silence as he stared at a picture of who appeared to be a young version of his dad and a beautiful red-haired woman.

"I don't know what to make of all of this. Why wasn't I told about you? About this?" Gabriel asked.

"Because he made your mom promise not to tell you. Our dad wanted to keep it secret. From what my grandfather said, our dad was a good man, but the night my mom died, a piece of our dad did, too. I think he dealt with things the best he could," Malcolm said.

"So, how did all of this come to fruition?" Gabriel asked.

"When my grandfather died suddenly about six months ago, I became his sole heir. So, in my struggle to deal with one loss, I moved to the States hoping to find my father and get to know him, but that was before I knew he had passed. I met your mom, though. She was able to fill in some gaps for me, which included you. She made me promise not to seek you out just yet, and before anyone knew anything was wrong, your mom passed away, too. I was never able to get your information from her, so I left things the way they were," Malcolm said.

"There were a lot of things I learned in the military, especially being a sniper for as long as I was. We were trained to pack things away and do our job. There would be time to sort things out later. All of this is way different in terms of packing it all up and dealing with it later," Gabriel said.

"Do you mind if I say something?" Malcolm asked.

Gabriel nodded.

"If it helps, I grew up without parents, just my grandfather and grandmother. My family had some money, but it never meant as much to me as their love. I was in the military as well. The Royal Regiment of Scots, which was a part of the

British military, to be more precise. I did my time and got out. I had other aspirations, let's just say," Malcolm said.

"So, what exactly are you saying?" Gabriel asked.

"What I'm saying is that family is first, all else is second, which is why I said what I said to Mr. McClane about not profiting off of family," Malcolm said. "Side question. Why is his nickname Snake? Is it because of the tattoo?"

Gabriel nearly choked. He looked at Rose for help.

"Apparently, it has something to do with his manhood, and that's all I'm saying," Rose said.

"Rex and Mr. McClane were in the military back in the day, so you can see where all of that stemmed from," Gabriel said.

"Och. Christ Almighty!" Malcolm said with a Scottish brogue.

Rose gasped when she heard it.

"What's the matter? Haven't you ever heard a Scotsman speak?" Malcolm asked.

"Clearly, I don't get out enough," Rose said.

"I hide it pretty well. I quickly learned that to be taken seriously over here in the States, you need to fit in, so I learned to hide the accent," Malcolm explained.

"Well, don't hide it on my account. I think it's beautiful!" Rose said.

"A-hem!" Gabriel said, clearing his throat to get her attention.

"What? I happen to like his accent but don't worry. He doesn't hold a candle to you," Rose said as she wrapped her arm under his and grasped his hand.

Malcolm laughed. He was caught off guard by this.

"If it's any consolation, I'm married and have children of my own. They are back home in Scotland with their mom and her family. I live over here part-time to keep an eye on things, and then I go back home to be with my family," Malcolm said.

"My turn for a question," Gabriel said, more so to break things up a little. "McClane said you were trying to sell off some equity. What did that mean, and are things not okay here at Grant Castle?"

"Ah, well, to be honest, things are fine, but I am trying to sell off some things. The market isn't as strong as it used to be, so I'm downsizing. No, I'm not out of money, not even close. The thing I haven't said yet is that after I got out of the military, I went to university and majored in business finance. Then, when I was out of school, I went to work for my grandfather and ended up making the old man more money than he knew was even possible," Malcolm said.

"What kind of business was it you and he were in?" Rose asked.

"Locomotive technology. My grandfather had a thing for trains when he was a kid, so when he came into money himself, he bought stock in the European railway market, then eventually bought into some American railway stock. The American stock was my idea, though. I told him he needed to think bigger, and so he did. He bought a handful of shares that skyrocketed," Malcolm said. "Unfortunately, he passed away before he could enjoy the fruits of his labor."

"I'm sorry to hear about all of that. Our dad was definitely not the financial genius of the family; that was my mom. Our dad had a bad habit of buying things without consulting her first," Gabriel said.

"Sounds like we both could learn what it is to lean on another family member. Look, all of this must be a little much to digest, but it is out on the table now. I don't want our story to be done with, but that's not completely up to me. It's on you now. What did McClane quote as far as the price on my cows?" Malcolm asked.

"Seventy thousand, which included transport and a trailer full of grain and feed for the next month. I hadn't planned on buying that many head of cattle, so I only bought enough food for twenty-five head," Gabriel said.

Malcolm got up from the table and walked to a window overlooking the garden.

Rose and Gabriel exchanged a sideways glance and shrugged their shoulders.

"I'll tell you what, I want to change the agreement up a little, if that is okay? Let's go with the twenty-five you planned on. I'll ship them out to you and get you anything you need on your end, and I will keep the rest of the herd here. No need to stress out the poor beasts if we don't have to," Malcolm said, then gave Gabriel a moment to digest all of what was just said. "I want to make this a joint venture, if you'll take me up on it. Consider me a silent partner. As far as the money part, give me twenty-five percent of what McClane told you, and I will invest it on my end and have it doubled in profit in less than a month. Then we can talk about expansion on your end. How much land do you have?"

"Um, two thousand acres. I actually just sold off five hundred to a wind farm company," Gabriel said.

"Good idea, but the problem with that is, the profit from that is slow. They are selling the energy off to the national energy grid and getting pennies on the dollar, depending on the market at the time. So, here's my thought on all of that- you did good by selling off part of your family's land, but we're going to be buying more of it. I happen to know that the neighboring ranch on the west side of your land is going up for sale, and I want to buy it. This is where turning your money into profit will come into play," Malcolm explained, but he could tell he was losing Gabriel. "I'm going to stop there for now. I get excited about stuff like this, but I don't want to overwhelm you. There's been enough excitement for one day. I'll make a few calls and then get back to you, but in the meantime, I want you to have time to sit on all of what we talked about and think about it."

"I'm not a business genius, but I do know how to handle things in terms of money, which is why I sold off part of my family land. Our dad had dug such a hole financially that my mom must have gone crazy just trying to keep them afloat. So, when I started going through things, it made sense to accept the offer made by the wind farm rep. I ended up paying off the debt owed, and now the ranch is free and clear," Gabriel said.

"It sounds like you know what you are doing, which means I won't be surprised when I get a phone call saying you're accepting this joint venture," Malcolm said. "Anyway, enough dreaming for one day. Let's eat! All this talk about money and cattle has made me hungry."

~(-)~

Gabriel and Rose met Rex back up at their pickup truck. They had been standing there a few minutes when Rex came strutting over and was having a hard time concealing the smile on his face, but then again, so was Gabriel and Rose.

After goodbyes were given and a few hugs, Gabriel, Rose, and Rex got in the pickup and drove back home.

The first few minutes on the road were quiet, but then Rex started suspecting something was happening.

"Why do I have the feeling like I missed something really big?" asked Rex.

"Why don't you tell us your story first. It might take less time," Gabriel said, looking at Rex in the rearview mirror.

"Well, there ain't much to tell. I patched things up with Millie. As a matter of fact, we patched things up so much, she's coming to stay with me as soon as them city slickers get done acting like part-time ranchers," Rex said.

Gabriel nearly lost his footing on the gas pedal, causing the back end of the pickup to swerve for a brief second.

"So, what you're really telling me is that you and Millie-" Gabriel was cut off.

"Yes, son, I blew the dust off the old bottle and gave it a go. Are ya happy?" Rex asked.

"Are you?" Gabriel asked, shocked.

"Hell yes, I'm happy!" Rex said, smiling from ear to ear.

"Good for you!" Gabriel said.

"So, let's hear your story. Who was that fella that could have passed for your twin?" Rex asked.

"Well, I guess there was another woman before my mom was in the picture," Gabriel said.

"Now that's news to me. When did that all take place?" Rex asked.

"Apparently, my dad was in the Navy and was stationed in England. He ended up meeting a Scottish girl while on leave, and they fell in love and had a baby, but she died in childbirth," Gabriel was trying to recall what was said.

"So, let me get this straight. That man that was back there is what, your older brother?" Rex asked, putting two and two together.

"Sounds like it," Gabriel said.

"And he ain't disputing your claim on the land?" Rex asked.

"You saw where we were just at, right?" Gabriel asked.

"Yeah, sort of. Was there more?" Rex asked.

Gabriel and Rose exchanged looks again.

"What I miss?" Rex asked.

"Well, so not only is he my half-brother, but his side of the family has more money than they know what to do with. Not only is he selling us the cows we were there for, but four hundred and seventy-five more cows that he is going to keep there. He wants to go in on a joint venture with us," Gabriel finished explaining, then paused on the rest to let it sink in for Rex.

"So, what you're saying is that we are going to end up being a full-functioning cattle ranch?" Rex asked.

"It looks that way. Hope you didn't have any plans of retiring anytime soon?" Gabriel said with a hint of sarcasm.

"I wouldn't know what that is, but I would like to take a vacation, if that's possible? Maybe I'll even take Millie," Rex said.

"How's Scotland sound? I hear the weather's nice this time of year," Gabriel said, then looked at Rose for a final approval.

"I got no complaints. I'd like to hear more of their accent," Rose said.

"Well, we most definitely aren't going now," Gabriel teased.

Rex sat in the backseat watching Gabriel and Rose exchanging looks that meant there was more than what they were saying. One day, it would all make sense.

Chapter Twenty-Six

Gabriel took a couple of days to process everything that was shared with him. After Rose had found her way into his deceased brother's room, which stirred up some not-so-great memories, Gabriel decided that life was too short. He had already lost the chance to grow old with one brother. He wasn't going to pass up on the chance to do the same with his newly found brother.

Staring at the inside of his coffee cup, watching the cloud swirl of the creamer, he was lost in thought, and Rose could tell something was on his mind.

"I hope it's me you're thinking so hard about?" Rose asked, trying to snap Gabriel out of his dream state.

"Well, I have to apologize, but it's not you. Sorry. I'm still thinking about Malcolm and everything he said," Gabriel answered.

"Is there any part that seems off?" Rose asked.

"No, not really. Although the whole cattle thing and what he said about not profiting off family threw me off a little," Gabriel said.

"You and he look an awful lot like each other, though, and he had a picture of your dad when he was younger," Rose said.

"Yeah, I know. I guess a part of me is having a hard time believing there was someone before my mom," Gabriel said.

"Well, I mean, it was a long time ago, and he was in the Navy. It's not like every man in the military was upstanding and didn't go out and sleep around," Rose said.

"What do you mean by that?" Gabriel asked in a rather shocked, snarky tone.

"Honey, I mean that your dad had a bit of an adventurous soul and wanted to get out for a while and explore. I mean, think about it- it's the Vietnam era. You're stuck on a ship, unsure if you are even coming home. You are granted leave, *and* you're in Scotland," Rose said, trying to explain herself.

"I guess you're right. I would have, too. I mean, that part of Europe *is* on my travel bucket list," Gabriel admitted.

"Are you tired of traveling? You did do a bit of it while you were in the military," Rose asked.

"Nope, I'm not tired of traveling. I went where the government told me to go for twenty years. For once, I want to go where I want to go and not have to worry about what orders I've been given," Gabriel said. "I *would* like to go somewhere with less heat and sand, if that helps?"

"It does, actually," Rose replied.

"How does it help?" Gabriel asked, confused.

"Um, hello? The whole thing you tried passing off as a joke about going to Scotland. I'm all for it," Rose said, trying to get her point across.

"Oh, I forgot about that. I didn't think Rex was that serious about taking a vacation," Gabriel said.

"He's over seventy. The man deserves a rest. Plus, he's trying to rekindle something with Millie," Rose said.

"True. I guess we all need to get away. Once we get the new cows set up and the new ranch hands, then we ought to be able to go away for a week or two," Gabriel said.

"Who's going out of town for a week or two?" asked Rex as he and Millie suddenly appeared in the kitchen doorway.

"Rose has been trying to convince me that we should get out of town for a while," Gabriel said.

"So, what's wrong with that?" Rex asked.

"Nothing. We just have a lot going on around here, and I don't know that taking off would be a good idea," Gabriel said. In his head, he was kicking himself as the thoughts were pouring out of his mouth.

"Well, it just so happens I have a sweet deal for you!" Rex said, grinning like a schoolboy with a secret he knows he shouldn't tell.

"Why does this sound like the start of a bad infomercial?" Gabriel asked, afraid of what Rex was about to reveal.

"Millie, would you like to tell my boy Gabriel here what you, me, and Snake worked out?" Rex asked.

"Absolutely! So, you made a really big impression on Malcolm the other day. As a matter of fact, he hasn't stopped talking about you since you left. I think he was going to ask you, but I might reveal our little secret..." Millie took a pause.

"Son, your life has changed in so many ways since you've been home. You need to get your head screwed on straight. Malcolm wants to take you and Rose back home to Scotland to see where it all began. To see where your dad's journey started. To see where your cattle are coming from. That part alone is smart business. The rest of that is just pure enjoyment," Rex explained.

"Now that you say it that way, I guess going over wouldn't be a bad thing," Gabriel admitted.

"Plus, Snake and I worked things out as far as ranches and cattle management. He's going to send some of his guys over to help. Combining ranches is a really good idea. If you want to go down this path, let Malcolm do the money part, and you do the cattle ranching part. You've been around it your whole life, plus with being in the military, you have leadership skills that will come in handy," Rex said.

"True. Well, as Malcolm said it- Fate brought this together. Let's step up the game," Gabriel said, then looked at Rose. "Are you still in this with me? I guess I shouldn't assume you're in the game too."

"I'm in this for the long haul, and that means wherever life takes you, I want to be there with you. Every step of the way," Rose answered.

"Okay then, I guess we're going overseas. We better get our passports quickly," Gabriel said.

"Have you given Malcolm your official answer as far as joining forces?" Rex asked.

"No. I need to call him. I've been stuck in my own head trying to process stuff when, really, the truth is right in front of me. I'll give him a call now," Gabriel said.

Rex and Millie said goodbye and headed out so that Gabriel could make his phone call. The decision to do so should have been easier, but Gabriel was pacing the floors like a trapped animal.

"Are you still having a hard time with all of this?" Rose asked.

"No, I'm just rehearsing what I'm going to say," Gabriel said.

He looked down at the table as the screen on his cell phone flashed. Rose noticed it, too.

"It looks like your brother beat you to the call," Rose said.

"Well, I guess so. I better answer it," Gabriel said, reaching for his cell phone.

"This is Gabriel."

"Howdy! It's Malcolm. I just wanted to let you know that I have the cattle coming your way and should be there in a couple of hours. I loaded them up on a couple of my trucks and shipped them off. I also have some of my ranch hands coming your way too. I took a poll and asked if anyone wanted a change in scenery and said they could help out at your ranch for a while. Of course, I may have added a little to their paycheck, but that's just between you and me!"

"I appreciate that and am grateful for the extra manpower. Rose and I were just laying out some plans for the next little bit and what we should do," Gabriel said as he looked over at Rose and smiled. The last part was b.s., but Malcolm didn't need to know.

"Is there any way I can convince you to change your plans a little?" Malcolm asked.

"What did you have in mind?" Gabriel asked. Now, things were starting to line up.

"How do you feel about traveling abroad?" Malcolm asked.

"Well, I did a fair amount in the military, but it was mainly in the Middle East. Where are you thinking?" asked Gabriel, looking at Rose and winking at her. Gabriel was letting Malcolm do the talking on this.

"I was thinking about seeing if you and Rose would want to come back home with me. I've talked to everyone back home about you, and they all want to meet you. I hope that's okay?" Malcolm said.

"To be honest, I've been kinda lost these past few days. Would it be alright if we continued the conversation from the other day in person? The long-lost family part, not the business part," Gabriel said.

"Sure. I want everything out on the table. We each have a side of the story that the other should hear about. I'd like to know what you're thinking," Malcolm answered.

"How do you feel about ribeye?' Gabriel asked. Having been asked that himself recently, he wanted to make a small joke.

"Best cut on the cow," Malcolm answered, remembering Gabriel's words.

"Words to live by," Gabriel added.

"I'll be over in a couple of hours," Malcolm said.

"See you soon," Gabriel said, then ended the call.

"Well, we'll see how things go after this visit," Gabriel said.

"What are you cooking up?" asked Rose.

"It's about losing one brother only to gain another. I don't know if I should be depressed or happy, and I think my heart is feeling the same," Gabriel said.

Rose stood up from the table and pulled Gabriel up from the table. Staring deep into his eyes, she placed one hand behind his head and the other on the side of his face.

"Listen to me carefully, Gabriel Sterling. As someone who has more or less hidden the past year or so, I have missed being out in the open, not worried about who will see me, not even my ex. You have become my person. My reason for getting up in the morning. So, I guess what I'm saying is, don't miss an opportunity to make your life even better. Even if it means opening an old wound or two," Rose explained.

"Yeah, I need to let things go. I can't live with the guilt of my little brother's death anymore. We all have a path to take. He took his. I took mine. I can do this," Gabriel said.

"Yeah, ya can," Rose said, then leaned in and kissed Gabriel.

"Yes, I can," Gabriel said as he pulled away long enough to catch his breath, then pressed his lips against Rose's for a second kiss. "We both can."

Chapter Twenty-Seven

Gabriel stood watching the main road from his front porch. Time seemed to be crawling while waiting for Malcolm. Rose and he made small talk to break the ice, but mentally, he seemed to be a little unfocused. A big, black truck suddenly appeared at the top of the driveway, which immediately caused Gabriel to come to attention. It was now time to get things squared away. It was time to put his brother's death and that of his parent's behind him.

Malcolm's truck came to a stop with a slight skid in the gravel. The driver's side door opened, and Malcolm jumped out. A cautious smile flashed across his face as he headed towards Gabriel and Rose.

"Howdy! Thanks for inviting me over," Malcolm said.

"Hey, thanks for coming over. I thought it would be easier, at least, for me to explain or, I guess, share my thoughts about what you shared with me the other day. Let's head inside, and we'll talk," Gabriel said, getting straight to the point. Rose stayed close by in case he needed backup.

"Want a beer, water, or tea?" Gabriel asked.

"Beer would be good," Malcolm answered.

Gabriel grabbed three out of the fridge. The third was for Rose. He assumed she would want one as well.

Gabriel removed the bottle caps from all three and gave Malcolm and Rose theirs. All three took a long pull from each bottle.

"Alright, let's get to it. There is something I want to show you. Something that has been on the forefront of my mind ever since we were over at your place," Gabriel said.

He led Malcolm down the hall to where his brother's room was. The door was shut.

Gabriel paused in front of the door before opening it.

The next few moments could change their entire future.

He turned and saw Malcolm was close behind him. Rose was behind Malcolm, bringing up the rear. He glanced over at her and smiled. She gave him a quick smile in return and mouthed a kiss.

"My first question is, when you showed up here and talked to my mom, how long were you here, and did you come inside?" Gabriel asked.

"No, she and I sat on the front porch for some time and talked. I left about an hour or two later and that was the last time I saw her," Malcolm said.

"Did she mention that I had a younger brother? That *we* had a younger brother?" Gabriel asked. He could instantly see the change in Malcolm's demeanor.

"No," answered Malcolm.

Gabriel opened the bedroom door wide so that Malcolm could see inside. So, he could see the folded American flag on the desk and the service medals.

"This is Charlie's room. My parents left it exactly as you see it, even after he died. He followed me off to war because he didn't want to be the only Sterling boy left here. When I retired from the Marines, being here was the only place I wanted to be. It was the only place I could reconnect with even though everyone I loved was gone. I had accepted that a long time ago. I'm sure you know this from your military training, but when we go off to war, we package up what we see the best we can to do our job. It's when we come home that most of us fall apart," Gabriel started to explain.

Gabriel stepped inside the bedroom and sat on the edge of the bed. He folded his hands on his lap and then looked up at Malcolm.

"I haven't packed this part of my life up yet because, until the other day, I wasn't sure I could or even wanted to. Then I met you, and I'll be damned if it wasn't like staring into a mirror," Gabriel said. The emotion behind his words was starting to come through. He could tell partly because he saw tears streaming down Rose's cheeks.

"What are you saying, Gabriel?" Malcolm asked.

"I'm saying that losing this part of my life was hard, almost unbearable, and if I'm going to let you in, all this that you see must mean something to you, too. I know that you grew up without your dad, *our* dad, and what you had with your grandparents was the norm for you, but this was the norm for me, except I lost twenty years of it. I guess what I'm saying is that if you are accepting me in your life, and if that is what you really want, it comes with all of this. I need to know that we are going to become a family. In saying that, I want to be able to pack this room up and make it more than just our dead brother's room. He doesn't need it anymore. My mom is gone. Our dad is gone, and this is my house now. Your house and out there that is your land too," Gabriel finished talking for the moment. He needed a minute to breathe. He swallowed the rest of his beer in a few quick chugs, then set the empty bottle on the bedside table.

"Thank you for showing me this. I was an only child growing up, and it was the norm for me. But to be honest, there was a part of me that felt there was more out there. There were a few things that just didn't line up. So, as I explained the other day, when my grandfather passed, it was here I came to. I needed to figure out things for myself. I had already bought the land and had built my home. For all intents and purposes, I was just like any other rancher out there. I just had some baggage that I needed to be stowed away. When you showed up on my property looking to buy some of my cows, it was like a door had been opened. I never got to know our dad the way you did, but maybe after some time of getting to know each other, I will, in turn, get to know our dad. I'm not just some rich guy who bought some land because he had the money; I was the first to work the land. And then I met Snake. Hell, I even got kicked by a Highland cow. Do you know how bad that hurts? A lot."

Malcolm reached out his hand to Gabriel and helped him up off the bed, still holding tightly to his hand.

"I promise you that I will be the older brother you never had. I will never seek to replace your younger brother or your mom and our dad. I want my own relationship with you and with whomever else you share your life with. All I ask is that you let me in. Let my family in. I promise it will be the second or even the third best part of your life," Malcolm said as he turned to Rose and extended his other hand. "I want the both of you in my life."

Gabriel now had his answer. His heart confirmed it. His gut spoke the truth, and the military had trained him to sniff out liars for the truth. The man standing before him, his long-lost brother, was definitely telling the truth.

He let go of Malcolm's hand, wrapped his arms around him, and squeezed him tightly. For the first time he could remember, this was what it felt like to be home. He now had a family.

Rose joined in on the embrace. She wrapped her arms around both men and squeezed them both.

When they pulled apart, Malcolm pulled out his cell phone, opened a picture, and held his phone out to Gabriel.

"In case things turned out the way they are now, I thought about making a change," Malcolm said.

Gabriel was looking at a picture of an official name change document. He was applying for a name change, or more so, an addition to his last name. Malcolm was adding Sterling to his last name so that he would then go by Grant-Sterling.

"Are you really doing this?" Gabriel asked.

"I was thinking of it, but I wanted to ask you first to see if you would be okay with it. I was never given the option as to what my last name should be, so I'm making the decision to take the name that I should have had the whole time," Malcolm said.

"I think that Dad would be proud and maybe a little upset if you didn't take his last name. I say go for it," Gabriel said, patting his brother on the back. "Welcome to the family, Malcolm!"

"Thank you. I promise to make good on the Sterling last name. It means everything to me," Malcolm said.

"Me too. Now, how about we go eat?" Gabriel said.

"Sounds good to me!" Malcolm answered.

All three left the bedroom, but Gabriel, at the last second, opted to leave the bedroom door open.

It was a symbol to him that he was free of the guilt and accepting of his past.

He was ready to move forward with his life.

Chapter Twenty-Eight

The decision to go to Scotland wasn't all that difficult, but it did cause Gabriel to think about things a little. Was he betraying his mom and dad at all? His dad did keep it a secret from him, after all. His gut was telling him Malcolm was the real deal. Even his heart chimed in and told him to proceed. Rose, too, had been a good counterbalance and was all for the trip. It wasn't that Gabriel was against it, not really. It was more just a new place, new people in his life, and nowhere to go in case something came up between them, and he needed to pull the proverbial escape chute. He wasn't like that, however, so he would deal with it if something should come up.

The official flight plans were made after they had official passports in hand. Gabriel and Rose were on strict orders from Rex to relax and enjoy their time away. No work whatsoever was to be done. Easier said than done.

The flight was direct to Inverness International Airport, where they were met by Malcolm's wife, Elsie, and two daughters, Ava and Aila.

Gabriel didn't have to stand in the shadows too long as Malcolm was swarmed by his wife and beautiful daughters. After the introductions were made, they quickly commenced with the questions.

"Uncle Gabriel, if you have a different mom than our da', why do you look so much alike?" Ava asked.

"Well, little lady," Gabriel started to speak but was entranced by Ava's laughter. "If your dad will allow me, we can share that story maybe tonight after dinner? I promise it will be a good story."

"Uncle Gabriel, are you going to marry Rose? She sure is pretty," Aila asked. Gabriel was not intimidated easily or easily embarrassed, but there was something about the innocence of children and their questions that turned Gabriel into a softy.

Malcolm and Elsie looked at Gabriel with the shock that only parents of children get when their children may have just asked a question or said something no one was prepared for. Gabriel knew how to play this game, though.

"Well, I would have to make sure she likes me first, then I have to buy a ring, and then once I ask her, and she says yes, we have to pick out the place. It's important to have a place to get married in," Gabriel answered.

It was Elsie's turn for approval. She stepped up to Gabriel, looked up into his face, and smiled. Her jade green eyes were speckled with gold flecks staring deep within Gabriel's, almost as if she was looking into his soul.

"I've got just one question for you," she started to say, her Scottish accent coming out. "Malcolm told me about him having to accept your family and all that it came with, and even though you are the last of the Sterling clan, that promise of acceptance comes with equal parts- his for yours and you for ours. Does that sound fair?"

Gabriel had never experienced such questioning, but if he required his brother to accept certain things, the same should also apply to him.

He took a chance, looked down, grabbed her hands, and squeezed them tight. He looked into her eyes and said- "I will love you and your entire family as if they have been mine from the start. I swear it."

Lost in Gabriel's words, she looked like a deer caught in the headlights of an oncoming car. She blinked twice, then looked over at Malcolm and smiled.

"Och. You could take a few lessons from your brother! You Sterling boys sure know how to swoon a woman!" Elsie said. She looked over at Hope and shook her head. "Is he like this all the time?"

"Well, specifically, he took me out one night for a nice dinner but took me shopping ahead of time and let me buy whatever I wanted while he bought his own clothing. Let's just say the desert that night was..." Rose said, not wanting to reveal too much, but she winked at Elsie and smiled.

"Well, it's settled. You're in the family too! Now, let's go before anyone else says something steamy," Elsie said as she wrapped her arms around both Sterling men and headed towards the airport exit.

"Mom, are we having dessert later?" Ava asked.

"No, dear, just your mom and your Auntie Hope. We're just having cake and lots of it!"

"That's not fair! Why can't we have cake?" Aila asked.

"Because this is a special cake, and it's better when it has a little age on it," Elsie said, still smiling. Clearly, she needed some alone time with her husband, but she had to put it into words that only a parent would use to keep things a secret.

They didn't have to walk all that far to get to their vehicle. Once everyone was settled in their seats, Malcolm got them on the road.

Elsie was the first to start the questioning.

"So, is Montana as pretty as Malcolm says it is?"

"For the most part. The Rocky Mountains are the main attraction. There is a lot of open land, which is beautiful all by itself, but when you have the mountains as a backdrop, there isn't another way to describe it other than beautiful," Gabriel said.

"I still can't believe that you two found each other. I know Malcolm started the search, but the fact that you took an interest in Highland cows of your own volition is completely mind-blowing. I definitely think someone or something else was in charge of you two coming together," Elsie said.

"Well, Highland cows aren't as common in Montana, and neither is a man from Scotland. Now, if he had used his accent instead of hiding it, he would have stood out more than the cows I bought from him, "Gabriel said.

263

"Aye, their beautiful animals. Malcolm tells me you have a bull that was friendly from the get-go," Elsie asked. There were certain parts of Elsie's speech where her Scottish accent rolled off her tongue like water down a waterfall. He started to understand why Rose was so entranced when Malcolm let out his accent.

"Yeah, Red, as I call him, he and I bonded before I even made the sale on him. Now, he pretty much walks around the pasture, and every time he sees me or my ranch hand, Rex, Red comes running up like a little kid and wants to be close. Strangest thing I've ever seen," Gabriel said.

"Well, then, you haven't seen anything strange yet. We've got a whole herd that follows my girls around as if they are a part of the herd," Elsie said.

"I'm looking forward to seeing where it all began," Gabriel said.

"In more ways than one, huh brother?" Malcolm said.

The only person left to interview was Rose, who got off easy.

"Can we call you Aunt Rose even though Uncle Gabriel hasn't married you yet?" asked Ava.

Again, the look of shock from the parents said it all. Rose smiled and took it all in. She had always wanted children, but when her ex did what he did, and she hid herself away with her friend, the opportunity to be with a loving man and have children had slowly started fading.

"I'm okay with it if you are, and as far as Uncle Gabriel marrying me, maybe you could talk to him for me and tell him I'm ready whenever he is," Rose said. whispering it into the ears of Ava and Aila, which resulted in the kind of giggle that only little girls could make.

The drive home from the airport wasn't too long of a drive. Of course, it was new scenery for Gabriel and Rose, so they were taking it all in. The Grant homestead was in the countryside just a little way south of Inverness and close to the world-famous Loch Ness.

Gabriel had seen quite a few places in the world, but Scotland was in a league all by itself.

"Beautiful countryside, isn't it?" Malcolm asked Gabriel.

"Yes, I'm starting to wish I would have been born over here," Gabriel asked as he stared out the passenger side window.

"Every time I come back home, I get like that, and especially when I see my wife and daughters, I'm reminded of what is important. Even more so now," Malcolm said, reaching over and squeezing his brother's shoulder.

The drive concluded when Malcolm turned into a long tree-lined driveway that led to an exact replica of Malcolm's place back in Montana.

"I'm either having a case of Deja vu, or your place here looks like the one in Montana," Gabriel said.

"It's an exact replica. I wanted to mimic what was here, but over there also; that way, I always felt like I was home," Malcolm said.

"Well, that makes perfect sense to me," Gabriel said.

"One of the differences is that instead of all the ranch hands living close by, I built their homes farther out. It gave them an opportunity to feel more like they were on their own. I did keep one structure close, though, and that's the family cabin I use for guests," Malcolm added.

"I see that. It's not exactly like the one Millie stayed in, though. It looks a little more elaborate," Gabriel said as he was starting to see some big differences, one of which was a detached three-car garage with all the bays having a vehicle in each one.

"Did I forget to mention I have a thing for foreign cars?" Malcolm asked.

"Here I was thinking it couldn't get any better," Gabriel said as he spotted a familiar American Muscle car - the Boss 429 Mustang.

"That was my granddad's pride and joy. The first and only really expensive toy he ever bought," Malcolm said.

"Still running?" Gabriel asked.

"Maybe," Malcolm said with a sly smile.

"Let's just say he met an auto engineer once that specialized in Mustangs and hot rods, as you Americans call them, and with a little bit of a fee, the engineer maxed out everything he could. It is a thing of beauty," Malcolm said.

Gabriel heard Rose stifle a laugh and turned around and looked at her to see what he was missing.

"Did I miss something?" Gabriel asked.

"I think I spotted Red's twin brother," Rose said as she pointed out the driver's side passenger window.

A bull that looked just like Red was walking along the driver's side, but it was twice as big. Gabriel wasn't sure whether to be concerned or scared.

"Do you let all of your bulls roam free, or is the big fella next to us the exception?" Gabriel asked.

Malcolm checked his side view mirror and smiled.

"That's my best friend. Gideon. He wasn't supposed to get as big as he is, but when he topped the scales at two thousand pounds, I had a vet come out and look at him. Nothing definite was found other than the vet theorizing that there could be a rare gene in the bull that made him that big. The good part is that he is so docile, I trust him around my wife and daughters. I am not that way with any other animal on my ranch, except maybe my pair of wolfhounds I have. They truly guard the place. I've even seen Gideon and the boys roam together. I'll show you them later. It's a site to be seen for sure," Malcolm said.

"Dad, don't forget about my friend," Ava said from somewhere in the back of the SUV.

"Oh, right. I'm sorry, honey," Malcolm said, making sure his daughter knew he was sorry for not pointing out her animal friend. "Ava is my horse lover. She has a Highland pony, but like Gideon, her horse is also on the large side. Also, an animal that I trust. Strange, I seem to bring in animals that are more trustworthy than some humans I've met over the years."

"Hear ya there. I would say that was one of my regrets about being in the service. Unless you served stateside, you didn't have many belongings. I would have wanted a Mastiff, though."

Rose nodded in agreement with the two men. Her big boy, Samson, was her big baby. He was a Chocolate Lab/Mastiff mix and every bit a bull in a China shop when he wanted to, but he had a heart of gold.

"Reminds me of Samson," Rose chimed in.

"You mean the meat thief," Gabriel added, laughing at the end.

"You have a big dog too, Rose?" Malcolm asked.

"Yeah, he's been my protector since things fell apart with my ex. I needed an alarm system at home, but when I found Samson, I realized I had the best home alarm system money could buy," Rose said.

"Except, don't leave your bacon accessible, and it's better to just let him have it if you do," Gabriel said.

"I've experienced that myself one too many times with the boys, which is why I learned to just get them their own supply of meat snacks," Malcolm added, sympathizing with Gabriel.

Malcolm pulled up to the guest cabin and parked near the front door so his new family could easily unload.

A few minutes later, Gabriel and Rose were inside the guest house unpacking, or at least Rose was. Gabriel was sitting on the edge of the bed, staring out the back window of the cabin.

"You okay?" Rose asked.

"Yeah, I'm just soaking it all in. Plus, I was thinking about calling Rex and checking on him," Gabriel said.

"Probably not a bad idea. Even with Millie being there, I would still want to make sure he was okay.

Gabriel agreed and dialed Rex's number but only got his voicemail. Gabriel tried again and then decided to text instead. This was not his favorite way to get a hold of Rex, but he had to consider that he had a little romance in his life now, which tends to do strange things to people who don't usually have that.

Rex, we made it okay and are at Malcolm's place. Call me later or text me back. I just want to make sure everything is okay.

A few minutes later, Rex replied with a text: *Glad you made it. I am fine. Millie has me pretty occupied. ;)*

"Rex just sent back that he was okay, and that Millie was keeping him occupied with a winking emoji at the end. Since when does Rex send emojis, let alone text?" Gabriel asked, astonished that his old friend and father figure was that tech-savvy.

"Love does strange things to people," Rose said, standing in the doorway with a towel wrapped around her and smiling.

"It does indeed, kinda like when a good-looking blonde is standing in the bathroom doorway with nothing but a towel on and smiling at you. It's almost like you're trying to tell me something," Gabriel said, then smiled.

"There's a clawfoot bathtub in here. Do you think I'm about to pass that up, especially with you?" Rose asked, then dropped her towel.

Gabriel launched himself off the bed, kicking his cowboy boots off and his pants in a motion that most kung fu masters would be jealous of. His shirt was next, but it was a button-up, so he just ripped that open and threw it to the side.

"Man, when you wanna take a bath, you really know how to undress," Rose said, wide-eyed like she was at a Chip and Dale strip show.

"Well, there was some incentive standing in front of me, and I didn't want to waste time weighing the pros and cons," Gabriel said jokingly.

"Get in the tub before I change my mind and skip it and just crawl into bed," Rose said in a matter-of-fact tone but with a hint of playfulness.

"Boy, um, there isn't a downside to that except I can't soap you up. Well, I could, but then the bed would get all wet and soapy. Better just stick to the bath," Gabriel said as he slid into the tub filled with hot, bubble-filled water.

Rose's reaction was to scoop a handful of soapy water and splash it at Gabriel, but the sniper saw it coming and quickly went underwater, only to come up right in front of Rose, standing straight up with soap bubbles covering all the right places.

"At ease, soldier, and make room for me. There will be plenty of time for that later," Rose said, giving Gabriel a suggestive wink and a smile.

"Sir, yes sir," Gabriel said, and then gave a mock salute and sat back down in the steamy bath water.

The water was soothing and relaxing to the point where they almost nodded off, but Gabriel's phone went off in the next room, stirring them awake. Disappointed, Gabriel got out, leaving Rose in the bath herself, allowing her to stretch out the entire tub length in the warm water while also soaking in the view of Gabriel's backside.

Gabriel didn't even grab a towel. Dripping wet, standing up to his full six foot two inches, he stood in the doorway reading the text message from Malcolm: *Do you guys feel like going into town for a bite to eat. There is a restaurant I think you'd like. It also has ribeye, so there's that incentive!*

"Who is it, and why are they disturbing my bath time?" Rose asked.

"It's Malcolm, and he wants to know if we want to go into town for a bite to eat at a restaurant that he likes," Gabriel answered.

"Hm, well, I could use some food, and we are in another country, so if you are okay with a rain check on all of this, we'll pick this back up later," Rose suggested.

"Bath included?" Gabriel asked with a smile that suggested he had ulterior motives.

"Whatever your heart desires," Rose answered.

"Oh, well, you left that wide open! We'll be adding chocolate syrup and whipped cream to the bedtime dessert menu," Gabriel informed Rose.

"Well, then dinner better go quickly because I kinda want dessert now," Rose said as she stood up from the bath water.

Gabriel immediately texted Malcolm: *Give us ten to fifteen minutes, and you can take us anywhere you want!*

He set his phone on the bedside table and immediately reached for Rose's hand.

"What did you just send back to Malcolm?" Rose asked.

"That we'd be outside in ten to fifteen minutes," Gabriel said.

"But it's not going to take us more than five minutes to get-" Rose stopped mid-sentence. She suddenly realized why Gabriel gave the time he gave.

Dessert would indeed come before dinner!

Chapter Twenty-Nine

It was late evening by the time Malcolm, Elsie, Gabriel, and Rose were back on the road heading north to Inverness city center. Ava and Aila stayed with Elsie's parents for the night. Malcolm wanted an evening with his brother and girlfriend but promised his daughters a sweet treat if they allowed the grownups to go without them. After some stiff negotiations, parents and children each got what they wanted.

"I hope you two aren't tired of the scenery yet. I'm going to try and take us a little bit east, then north on the A9 highway, and then when we get into town, we'll go back south so you can see the River Ness as it goes through town. It's really pretty at night as the city lights reflect off the river," informed Malcolm.

"There is definitely nothing like this back home. You've seen it. Scotland definitely has the better views," Gabriel said.

"I don't know if I quite agree. Those Rocky Mountains are a sight to behold. We don't have anything that tall and majestic," Malcolm said.

"True. I spent some time in the mountains as a kid, and they are really beautiful. Every sunrise is more beautiful than the last," Gabriel said. "Rex and I used to do some hunting up there, too."

"Hunting, huh? Maybe you and I should give that a try next time I'm over?" Malcolm asked.

"I'd like that. Maybe we should look into getting a cabin. Might be kinda fun to make it a regular thing," Gabriel said, being the first to throw out the idea.

"Only if us girls can go too?" Rose added.

"Sounds like we're buying cur first family cabin!" Malcolm said.

"It looks that way," Gabriel said, looking up at the rearview mirror and seeing Malcolm looking back and smiling.

"So, about where we're going. We're friends with the owner of the restaurant we're going to, and I asked if we could make it at a late dinner. Normally, it's a pretty busy place, so I opted for a less busy time. He owes me a favor or two, anyway. Of course, supplying them with all the Highland beef they can use may have helped grease the palm, if you know what I mean?" Malcolm said, hinting at a transaction that may have taken place that was very beneficial to the restaurant owner.

"Helps to have friends in high places for sure. Do you have a lot of customers throughout the area?" Gabriel asked.

"I'm somewhat selective in who we supply, plus my beef speaks for itself. I have a few international customers that I have a contract with, so that brings in even more money. You'll see once we get up and running back in the States," Malcolm explained.

"I'm looking forward to it. I want to do better than Dad did when the ranch was full of horses. I want to see the ranch succeed and the family name be known for something other than the ranch that went under," Gabriel said with a tinge of disappointment.

"I don't think you ever told me why or even how you decided to get in the Highland cattle business," Malcolm said.

"Honestly, I'm not sure why I went that way. We saw an auction ad for a Highland bull that would be going up on the auction block, so we went, and the rest is history. Although, there was a bit of a tangle with some sore losers," Gabriel explained.

"What happened?" Malcolm asked.

"A couple of guys decided they were going to try and take Red from me. Well, clearly, I have Red back home, so it all worked out in the end," Gabriel said with satisfaction.

"Sore losers! Well, I'm glad you all made it out okay, as well as your bull. I've never understood why people think they can go in and take something that isn't theirs," Malcolm said, angered by the thought of what could have happened to Gabriel, Rose, and Rex.

The remaining ride to the restaurant was spent mostly on small talk and a lot of looking out the window. It was true that Gabriel had seen a lot of things over the years of military service; Scotland, more so Inverness, was not disappointing in any way.

He was staring out the window, lost in the view when Malcolm tapped him on the shoulder.

"Hey, are you going to get out, or are you waiting for curbside service?" Malcolm said, teasing his brother.

"Huh? What?" Gabriel said, slightly confused.

"We're here, and if you would like to join us inside, we'd be happy to have you," Malcolm said, continuing to tease a little more.

"Nope, I'm good, just lost in a little daydream," Gabriel answered.

All four walked into the restaurant and were happily greeted by the owner and a couple of his wait staff.

Malcolm and the owner shook hands and exchanged pleasantries, then when introductions had been made, the party of four was taken back to a corner booth where everyone was seated at a candlelit table.

The owner said he would send out a sampling of appetizers, along with whatever everyone wanted to drink.

Despite his age, Gabriel still ate like he was a growing boy, so for him to see an entire table's worth of food come out of the kitchen, he knew it would be a good night.

The appetizer course was next level. Eating his fill, he was quite sure he had no room for dinner. But as he listened to the dinner options, he not only opted for a ribeye but settled on the roasted chicken with a salad that came with pancetta and polenta. Both of the last two items left Gabriel guessing. Rose ordered the Trofie Pasta Liguria with basil pesto, green beans, and new potatoes.

It didn't take long for the scents and smells coming from the kitchen to take their minds on a culinary journey that also came with an on-switch for their salivary glands. All four sitting at the table resisted the urge to sneak through the kitchen doors and take a peek.

When dinner finally arrived, there were no words to explain the sights and smells of what was in front of each person.

Gabriel sliced the first piece of meat and sat in utter satisfaction as the seasoned meat melted in his mouth. A small amount of meat juice dripped down the side of his mouth. Rose saw it and giggled as she tried to wipe it but was refused as Gabriel held up a hand to stop her.

"I'm not losing a single drop from this meat!"

The other three laughed. Rose had never seen Gabriel in such gastronomy delight. As she took her first bite of pasta, she, too, understood what Gabriel was going through. The pasta noodles and herbs were nothing short of being compared to food that only God himself had made.

The chef was very pleased with the satisfaction of his patrons.

"Well, brother, what do you think?" Malcolm asked.

"I think I'm kidnapping the chef and his staff, and they're coming home with us," Gabriel said.

"Or we could just open our own restaurant," Malcolm said, trying to slip in the idea while Gabriel was still eating.

"You mean, *us* open a restaurant?" Gabriel asked.

"Sure, why not. We would already have the main supply of meat, and as far as the rest of the food is concerned, well, we would have the second restaurant to this one. Did I forget to tell you I'm part owner here?" Malcolm asked.

"You may have forgotten to mention that part," Gabriel said as he wiped his mouth and smiled with satisfaction.

"I guarantee there isn't anything quite like this over there, and like you said- with the backdrop of the Rocky Mountains, I'm pretty sure we would be bringing in a fair amount of income," Malcolm said, trying to further sell the idea to his brother.

"Hm, Rose, that might give those friends of yours a run for their money. You know, the ones that sent those men after me to test me," Gabriel said, clearly not quite over what had happened.

"You know what, you guys should! They were supposed to be my friends, and even though I love them to death, you being tested as to whether you would protect me shouldn't have happened," Rose said.

"I'm starting to think there is more to this story?" Malcolm said.

"So, earlier, when Rose made reference to Elsie about the date I took Rose on, she didn't tell you that two men came after me that night, all just to see if I would protect Rose. I guess Rose's ex left such a bad impression on them that they decided to test me. I call that overprotecting in the worst way," Gabriel explained.

"Did you send 'em packing?" asked Elsie. This shocked Gabriel and Rose.

"Well, they were hurting in the morning, I'm quite sure of it. There are two things I will fight for unconditionally- my family and my home. Everything else, I'll work out the details later," Gabriel said.

"Spoken like a true protector!" Malcolm said as he raised his glass. "To protectors."

"And the family we protect!" Gabriel added.

It was decided that dessert would be packed up and sent home in several containers. Malcolm wanted an opportunity to show his brother and girlfriend a little of Inverness while there was still some light out. Malcolm and Elsie led the way outside as they walked around. They walked along the Loch Ness riverfront. Both Gabriel and Rose were immediately lost in the sights of Mother Nature and Scottish architecture.

The walk led them down the road to St. Andrew's Cathedral, where they stopped. The crisp night air had a chill that Montana didn't quite have yet.

Always the sniper on duty, the watcher of all, Gabriel noticed the number of people still out but was pleased that they seemed scattered about going their own way. Having spent the later part of his service years more or less on his own on various missions or even with a fellow soldier, he very much appreciated smaller crowds; not that he didn't mind the bigger ones, it was just easier to keep his eyes on smaller, quieter settings.

He also noticed a fair number of cars traveling past. One such vehicle, an older model sedan, backfired. The sound was too close and mimicked a gunshot.

Gabriel was the first to react.

Subconsciously, he immediately slipped into military mode, and that backfire sound to him sounded like a round being shot off. His reflexes kicked in as he jumped in front of Rose, Malcolm, and Elsie. It wasn't until his brother called out that they were okay. All was well. It was just a car that had backfired.

Gabriel needed a moment. This had not happened to him in a while.

"Are you okay, baby?" Rose asked.

"I'm okay. I just need a moment. That backfire was too real for me, and sometimes I get triggered. I'm sorry," Gabriel said, breathing irregularly.

"It's okay. You don't have to apologize," Rose said as she held him close.

She was joined by Malcolm and Elsie, who also wrapped their arms around Gabriel.

"All good, brother?" Malcolm asked.

"All good. I'm sorry for the reaction. It's been a while," Gabriel said, trying to apologize for the scene.

"Don't ever apologize for your service! You can take the man out of the soldier, but you can't take the soldier out of the man," Malcolm said, trying to console his brother.

"Words to live by," Gabriel said, agreeing with Malcolm.

"Are you two okay with heading back to the SUV now? Maybe we can pick this up another day and show you around when it's daylight?" Malcolm asked.

"I'm okay with that. Thank you for showing us all of this," Rose said. "I'd love to see more of your city. This country girl could use some time off the ranch."

"Well, depending on what the boys decide for tomorrow, maybe you and I come back into town, and I show you around?" Elsie asked Rose.

Rose looked to Gabriel for confirmation.

"I'm okay with it if you are?" Gabriel asked.

"Looks like I'm all yours!" Rose said to Elsie.

"And it looks like you're all mine!" Malcolm said to Gabriel.

Everyone laughed. There was a hint of excitement with tomorrow's bro date and girl's day out. Neither would equal the other in activities or enjoyment, but both were necessary.

Gabriel needed time with just his brother, and Rose needed time with another female to do female stuff, like talk about guy stuff and other various guy-related things. Plus, Rose really hadn't had a moment to even think without having to share her thoughts with someone else.

On a whole other level of concern, comments about her and Gabriel getting married were weighing on her, and maybe not being with him for part of a day would settle some of those feelings.

She needed a moment to be real with herself. As do most people when faced with life-changing events potentially coming at them.

Chapter Thirty

The following day, as Gabriel watched Rose and Elsie leave, he couldn't help but feel a sense of loneliness already. Too much had happened, too many things had been said between them to not have a connection with her, and with comments being said or bare minimum implied, marriage was inevitable for them. A part of himself was just a little apprehensive about that level of commitment, but then he reminded himself of all he went through as a Marine.

He smiled, knowing that Rose was now the better part of his life. Malcolm, of course, was a new addition and had his own place within Gabriel's heart, but something about being with Rose brought a sense of calmness.

"Well, what do you say we go take a walk around so you can see firsthand what a ranch full of Highland coos looks like?" Malcolm asked.

"I'm ready. To be honest, I'm kinda hoping Gideon pays us a visit. I'd like to see how he compares to my Red in terms of personality," Gabriel said.

"You'll be surprised. The first time that bull walked up to me and nuzzled my hand, I thought my life was over. No two-thousand-pound bull ever comes up to you and says, "Hey, you wanna pet me?" but he did. The second time was when I thought he had gotten out of the pasture gate. Turns out, he had figured out how to lift the latch and let the gate swing open. He and about twenty of his closest friends were walking across the front yard; that's when my wolfhound brothers made friends with him. They were curious about why he was in their territory, and rather than try to intimidate the brothers, he knelt in front of them so they could get a better look at him," Malcolm explained.

"Unbelievable," Gabriel answered.

"You wanna see unbelievable, watch this," Malcolm said, then whistled and called out to Gideon.

There was a return bellow like Gabriel had never heard of. He looked around for the source, but nothing was coming, at least not yet. In the distance, Gabriel could see a fair number of female cows. Suddenly, they all parted as this massive bull walked through the sea of his lady friends.

"Gideon, thig gu dad!" Malcolm called out.

"What did you just say?" Gabriel asked.

"I told him to come to Daddy," Malcolm said.

"And he comes to that?" Gabriel asked, amazed.

Malcolm smiled and turned toward the massive bull now running at them.

"Don't move. Stand next to me and watch what he does," Malcolm instructed.

"Um, he's getting closer," Gabriel said, nervously.

"Hold tight, and you'll be fine," Malcolm said.

Sure enough, Gideon stopped in front of Malcolm, raised his head, and bellowed.

Stephen St. Clair

"How's my big boy, huh? Did you have a good night with all your lady friends?" Malcolm asked as he scratched the surface area of Gideon's enormous head.

It wasn't long before Gideon took an interest in Gabriel. He nudged Malcolm out of the way, took a couple of steps, and stood in front of Gabriel. They were nearly eye to eye.

"Hello there, big fella. I believe I have an acquaintance of yours back home," Gabriel said.

Gideon snorted, then proceeded to lower himself down to the ground.

"Well, this is new. He's never walked up to a stranger and just decided he was going to lay down," Malcolm said.

"Red did this not too long after I got him home. Rose and I were just standing there, and he up and laid down. The next thing I knew, he had his head propped on my lap, and Rose was sitting next to him on the ground, leaning against his belly and rubbing it like he was the family dog. We kept that up for almost thirty minutes, then he got up and went about his business," Gabriel said.

"Sounds like you and I have the tamest bulls in the world," Malcolm said.

Gideon suddenly changed his mind on a potential belly rub, got back up on all four muscular legs, and made a head gesture akin to that of a dog that wants its master to follow. Shocked at this new level of communication, both men followed.

"I think he wants to show you around his place," Malcolm said, amazed.

"Lead on, my friend," Gabriel said as he patted Gideon on the rump.

Men and beast walked around for quite a while. It was as if Gideon was Gabriel's personal tour guide and showing him all the popular sites, mooing at different interest points as if to say, "And over here we have the bale of hay that I eat from, and over here is where I scratch myself."

"He certainly has the tour guide down pat," Gabriel said.

"Yeah, he does. Believe it or not, he's never done this. He's walked with me while I take the lead, but never the other way around," Malcolm admitted.

"It will be interesting to see how Red is once we get back home. Rex wasn't too keen on his taking a liking to Rose and I, and between you and I, I think he was just jealous," Gabriel said.

"It's possible. Rex has all the experience, and you show up and steal his thunder," Malcolm said.

"Good point. We'll see once I get home and how the herd is doing. Although, he's probably gotten his attention pretty well taken up right now since Millie is back in his life," Gabriel said.

"It's funny how ghosts from our past come back into our lives," Malcolm said, referencing their own coincidental pasts.

"So, not to change the subject, but how are you and Rose doing?" Malcolm asked.

"Things are okay. I mean, compared to how they were when we first met each other, we have grown pretty close together. In a strange twist of fate, I've been thinking about the order of things and how they happened- me joining the Marines, only to return home and for her to run to my small town. I'm just amazed how we even got together. Although Rose would say that the Almighty above is responsible because I happened to take on some work at the church she just happened to work at already," Gabriel said, sharing briefly more of his and Rose's story.

"And marriage? If you don't mind me asking. I know my girls were prying, but they are the fact finders, the truth seekers," Malcolm said.

"Well, to be honest, I can see it happening, but I need to work on things a little bit more. You saw what happened last night when that car backfired," Gabriel said.

"Yeah, but that's something that may stick with you for a long time, and the level of psychological evaluation that you would have to have to even remotely come close to making things better," Malcolm said, trying to sympathize with Gabriel. "When I was in the military, I did the minimum and got out. I knew I wanted to at least serve and get that part over. Then, I went to university, and I had an opportunity to see where my true strengths were. Being really good with money helped. I never actually saw any action, so I'm thankful for that, but I saw plenty of other soldiers that were battered and bruised mentally and physically, and it makes me glad that I was stationed where I was."

"I don't blame you. There were plenty of times I wanted to call it quits, but the closer I got to being in for twenty, the more I realized that all I had to do was play it safe, and I would be out. Twenty years in and then retiring gave me a decent amount of pay," Gabriel said.

"Well, I'm glad we both made it out okay. I know your level of service and the amount of time you found yourself in the field comes with baggage, but none of us are going anywhere, so if that means you lean on us for support, then that's what we gotta do!" Malcolm said.

"Thanks for that. I appreciate it. I have my pastor back home who has agreed to help if needed. He was there after Rose and I had our first blow up. The problem is that we *both* went to him for help. A slight conflict of interest, but he got the job done, and Rose and I survived the blowout," Gabriel explained.

"I think you two will do fine. Yes, there may be times when you each need that extra help, but you'll get through it.

Speaking of getting through it. You wanna head back to the house and wait for the girls?" Malcolm asked.

"Yes, that sounds like a good idea. I think what you have here, we ought to be able to mimic back stateside, plus having Rex and even some of your staff from your ranch back at home should make a difference too," Gabriel said.

~(-)~

When Elsie and Rose pulled up, Gabriel and Malcolm had been sitting under the shade of a mighty oak tree, drinking a Scottish ale. Both ladies got out, happy to see their counterparts, kissing them firmly on the lips. It was well worth the wait for the men to receive that kind of welcome.

"Ladies, did you have any fun?" Malcolm asked.

"Oh, yes! It's been long enough since having a girlfriend to shop with that I almost forgot what it was like to actually get more than a grunt when I ask if something looks good on me or not," Elsie replied.

Gabriel's eyes went wide. He had yet to experience such a shopping trip, but by the look on his brother's face, there had been one too many trips where he was not completely forthcoming with the truth.

"I got you a little something," Rose said, whispering in his ear as she went for another kiss.

"Oh, yeah? What is it?" Gabriel asked.

Rose handed him a small bag. He looked up at Rose with a curious look.

"Look inside, but don't do anything else," Rose instructed.

Taking Rose's cue, Elsie did the same thing with Malcolm. Both men looked at each other and shrugged their shoulders, but upon peeking inside the bag, they immediately stood up, grabbed their partner by the hand, and led them to their own place.

"Did you both get the same thing?" Gabriel asked.

"More or less. Mine was a little less, if you know what I mean?" Rose said, hinting at what was in the bag. "You can take it out now. No one is around."

Gabriel pulled out a lingerie garment that had less fabric than normal garments worn on the lower part of a woman's body. His eyes widened with curious satisfaction, and a smile spread across his face.

"I'm not done, though," she said as she handed Gabriel another sack.

"What's in here?" he asked.

"The rest of the outfit that goes with what's in the other sack," Rose said.

Gabriel opened the other sack and saw some red fabric. He pulled it out slowly and saw that it was a long red dress that had a slit up the side.

"For me also?" Gabriel asked.

"Hm, more for you to look at while on me. There is a special musical performance at a performing arts theater near where we were last night, and us girls wanted to treat you guys for taking good care of us," Rose said.

"Well, it seems you ladies will have the advantage over us men. I didn't bring anything that formal," Gabriel said.

There was a knock at the door. Rose went over to answer it.

"Hi, girls! Thank you for this. Tell your mom I appreciate it," Rose said.

Rose turned around with a garment bag.

"Problem solved. Why don't you take a quick shower, and if you're lucky enough, you can watch me put everything on," Rose said, flirting with Gabriel.

In about two seconds, Gabriel was naked and in the shower. He knew when the situation called for action. This was one of those moments.

In less than ten minutes, he was out of the shower, freshly washed, hair combed, and beard trimmed at the neck. He stood in the bathroom doorway smiling.

Rose was shocked.

"Are you sure you took a shower?" she asked.

"Honey, I was in the military for twenty years. Everything we did was set to a timer. You, on the other hand, can go as slow as you like. So, go ahead and get dressed. I'll just be over here watching," Gabriel said, leaning against the bathroom door's door frame.

Rose accepted the challenge. She was going to draw this out. Gabriel wasn't going to get off as easily as he hoped, and he was most certainly going to have to wait to remove the clothing. It was going to be an all-night love affair.

Rose picked up a bottle of body mist. The kind that Gabriel had said drove him crazy. She walked in front of him a few feet and gave the bottle a quick spray, making sure it landed on the right areas of her body.

Next, she slowly slid into the undergarments. With each movement, Rose noticed that Gabriel's jaw opened a little more, and his eyes had a little bit more of a twinkle in them.

The red dress was next. She turned around so he could only see her from the backside. As she slid the dress down over her head and down over her torso, she looked back over her shoulder and asked if Gabriel would mind zipping her up.

Gabriel moved so fast that he nearly lost his towel. Zipping her up slowly and taking in the sights and smells, he was intoxicated by the prospect of undoing everything later that night.

Rose instructed Gabriel to sit in the armchair at the foot of the bed. She lifted one leg, set it gently on his lap, and handed him her red leather high-heeled shoes.

"Help a girl out?" Rose asked, smiling.

Gabriel nodded.

Both heels were on in less than a minute as Gabriel sat in amazement.

"It's almost like you planned this. When did you have time to do this?" Gabriel asked.

"We girls know how to get things done when we need to, and as far as the theater, I kept that in mind, too. I don't want you to worry about certain elements coming up, so the show ought to be really nice," Rose explained.

"Thank you," Gabriel said and leaned his head up for a kiss.

"There is just one problem. I don't have clothes to match what you are wearing," he said.

"That's what your nieces brought down. While we were in town, Elsie and I took the liberty of buying both of you pants, a shirt and tie, and a jacket to match. If you wanna know my opinion, you are going to look so much better than Malcolm," Rose said as she ran her hands up Gabriel's chest.

"You keep doing that, and the only show that will be going on will be me peeling that dress off of you," Gabriel informed Rose.

"Nope, Elsie and I agreed that no matter how hard our man tried to convince us to stay and enjoy things from home, we were going out on the town. You guys have to soak up the view all night long!" Rose said as she slowly turned and walked away. "I'll meet you outside, so you better hurry up!"

Again, Gabriel was on the clock, and he moved like a cheetah chasing its prey. He was dressed in under five minutes and out the door, but as it turned out, he was the last one to the garage. The other three were waiting.

"It looks like you and I have a full evening ahead of us," Malcolm said. "The only question that I have is, which door to open? Rose, you can pick the door to open, and behind it will be the car that you ride in," Malcolm said.

Rose thought for a moment, then chose door number three. The garage door slowly went up, and the light came on. Inside was a long, sleek Bently convertible. The color was red, the same as Rose's dress.

"It appears that you and my car have something in common. You're both beautiful," Malcolm said.

He walked over to the car, got in, started it, and slowly pulled it up in front of the other three. He got out, opened the other doors, and helped his wife in, then Rose. Gabriel climbed in from the other side.

"Now, are we ready?" he asked.

A resounding 'yes' came from the other three. They were off to the show in style.

Chapter Thirty-One

The show they were attending didn't start for another two hours, so Malcolm decided that a drive along the River Ness would be appropriate, plus a drive straight up through town. Gabriel silently wished there would be more drives like these. He enjoyed spending time with his brother and his family.

Regarding children, that was a conversation that hadn't come up yet. He wasn't opposed to them but was a little late to the game. If Rose wanted a baby, he'd be happy to go down that path. For now, he was just going to enjoy what they had.

"How do you like the view?" Rose asked.

"A guy could get used to driving around this town," he answered.

"Not that view, this view," she said and nodded at herself.

The slit in her dress revealed her upper thigh, to which Gabriel tried reaching out and received a playful slap on the hand. Rose smiled.

"That wasn't very nice," Gabriel whispered.

"Remember, you have to soak up the view! It's not always about what you can get at that moment," Rose said with a satisfactory smile.

"That's so not fair!" Gabriel said, now holding both hands in his lap.

"We just wanted to have a good time with the both of you and thought maybe a little eye candy along the way would be kind of fun," Rose said. "Isn't that right, Elsie?"

"That our men must wait until the end of the night? Absolutely!"

Gabriel and Malcolm's eyes met in the rearview mirror, each raising their eyebrows at the other.

"It's going to be a long night, dear brother," Malcolm said.

"Agreed. Maybe we come up with our own strategy?" Gabriel asked in front of the ladies.

"Hm, interesting thought. What did you have in mind?" Malcolm asked.

"Oh, secret spy stuff. You know, top secret," Gabriel replied.

Rose and Elsie looked at each other, neither worried. They knew they had the upper hand. Most women did. The evening was going to be interesting.

The theater came into view. It was a modern marvel for sure, with it being covered in glass, steel, wood, and concrete.

Malcolm parked the car, and he and Gabriel got out and raced to the passenger side. Gabriel opened Rose's door and held out his hand for her to take. Once Rose was out of the vehicle, he and Malcolm escorted their dates to the entrance.

The line wasn't terribly long, but they were standing in the late afternoon sun, making things a little difficult between the sun's reflection and the heat.

Gabriel turned to block the sun from getting in Rose's eyes, and while doing so, he thought of something he could try to get Rose's attention.

He moved his head close to hers to ask her a question. One that didn't need to fall on public ears. "Since you're going to make me wait all night for affection, can I have one small kiss to get me through?" Gabriel asked.

"I suppose, but only on the cheek," Rose said.

He turned to face her, and as he leaned his head in to kiss her on her right cheek, he placed his right hand on her left cheek. He leaned in a little more and drew a breath to catch a hint of her perfume.

He exhaled slowly along her neckline, starting at the bottom of her earlobe. His hot breath sent ripples of excited energy across her skin, which sent a sensation down her entire body, causing her to completely shiver from head to toe.

With his hand still on her cheek, he got nose to nose with Rose to her in the eyes and then deviated from the plan to only kiss her cheek and, ever so softly, barely kissed her on the lips. It was so soft she could barely feel it, but it was enough that her body shivered again.

Still looking her in the eyes and keeping nose to nose, Gabriel whispered, "You're going to be glad we are in a separate building from them. I'm going to do things to you…" and then Gabriel pulled his head back and smiled as he pulled out his cellphone and quickly looked up an image of hot massage oil being dripped slowly on a woman's back. He texted that image to Rose and then returned his cell phone in his pocket.

Rose pulled her cell phone from her purse and looked at the message. She nearly dropped her phone as she saw the image. To any passerby, the picture was acceptable, but what Gabriel had said to her implanted a thought to go along with that image.

She exhaled slowly as she put her cell phone away. Clearly, what Gabriel had said was enough to get a rise out of Rose. It would be a long evening if stuff like that kept happening. The thought occurred to her that maybe an evening with temptations and teasers was not a good idea, but when Elsie looked back at her and saw her skin flush and a bead of sweat run down her neckline, she reached over and grabbed her hand.

"We're going to find a restroom, boys. Hold our place in line, will ya?" Elsie said.

"Certainly. Don't take too long. The opening act starts in thirty minutes," Gabriel said.

"The opening act is nowhere close to starting, Gabriel Sterling!" Elsie said in a thick Scottish accent as she hurried off with Rose to the closest public restroom.

"What just happened?" Malcolm asked.

"I may or may not have scored the first point for the home team," Gabriel said.

"What did you do?" Malcolm asked.

"Well, I read a book once that was talking about nerve endings and sensations, and it said that there was a response in a woman's neckline that, if done properly, could send her into a type of orgasmic shiver," Gabriel said.

"Is that what just happened?" Malcolm asked.

"Well, apparently something worked, but your wife noticed, hence them rushing off to the restroom," Gabriel said.

"I need to borrow that book. So, what's next?" Malcolm asked.

"Play it cool. They know the game is on now, but you need to make a move, too, that lets Elsie know you're in it to win it," Gabriel said.

"I can do that. It's been a while since I've seduced my wife, but I think I still got it," Malcolm said. He suddenly looked up and saw both women hurrying towards them. Rose was in tears.

"Looks like something is wrong. Turn around," Malcolm said, then nodded toward Elsie and Rose.

Gabriel turned and instantly moved towards Rose when he saw the tears running down her face.

"What's wrong?' Gabriel asked.

"He knows," Rose said.

"He who?" Gabriel asked.

"My ex. He and a couple of his friends showed up. He found Emelia and trashed her coffee shop. He said that unless I show back up, more than just a coffee shop will get damaged. We need to go back home, Gabriel. I need to end this now," Rose said.

"It can't be just you, though," Gabriel said.

"He's right, Rose. We're family. We take care of each other. Let's go back home and get packed. The girls can stay with Elsie's parents, and I also have a friend who owns a private plane. He'll get us there," Malcolm said.

"Rose, we're going to take care of things, I promise," Gabriel said.

"He's crazy, though. He'll kill all of you if you get in his way," Rose said.

"I know how to hide, remember? I did it for a living. We'll get him taken care of, so you never have to worry about him again," Gabriel said.

"Come on, let's get going," Malcolm said. I'll call my friend on the way home.

"And I'll call Rex and Pastor Nick and let them know what's going on and that they need to stay out of sight. Rex might be harder to convince, but he'll understand." Gabriel said.

Everyone headed back to the car and got in. As far as what everyone had planned for the night, they would have to revisit it later.

Now, it was time to go monster hunting.

Now, on the plane, a plan would be required for this, and knowing there would need to be at least one stop where they refuel didn't help the stress levels. A call was made to the local police, and all the appropriate info was given. Being told they would handle it didn't settle well with Rose. She knew better.

Gabriel, of course, was thinking of different ways he could hunt the man and his friends down and take care of the problem as if it were a mission back when he was a sniper, but that really wasn't a viable option. At least not yet.

There was another option he hadn't considered-involving the military. After all, they created the monster. They should have to put it down. Maybe a call to a friend still serving could help.

Gabriel got up and said he needed to use the restroom and would be back.

Once in the plane's tiny bathroom, he looked up his friend's contact info and texted: *Jack, it's Gabriel. Do you have a good way to deal with an ex-Army soldier (and friends) who was medically discharged and is now potentially a threat?*

He's my girlfriend's ex and has already threatened to kill her friend.

A few minutes passed, and a text came through: *It depends. If you meet him in a back alley, can you take care of things that way? I'm kidding. In public is the best option. Bait him and have him and his buddies make the first move. If he's smart, he'll draw you out, but with your expertise, this should be easy for you! Good luck.*

At first, he thought his friend Jack was of no help whatsoever, but then he re-read the text and suddenly realized the man was a flipping genius. He left the bathroom and gathered everyone up for the plan reveal.

"I have an idea, but it will take some doing. I have a friend named Jack who has experience dealing with things like this. He suggests meeting your ex out in public. Let's get him and his friends where they must be seen," Gabriel started to explain.

"What if he doesn't want to do things that way?" Rose asked.

"Then I do things my way. I'm not saying I want to do it that way, but the guy and his friends are psychologically unstable, and if I ever find out he didn't go through proper channels when giving them the boot, I'll add them to my list, too," Gabriel said.

"So, how do we start this?" Rose asked.

"Well, if you have his number, shoot him a text. Completely play the scared little lamb that he knew you to be. Let's show him that you're not," Gabriel said.

"I might be able to add numbers to our side," Malcolm said. "Half my ranch hands in Montana are ex-military. I'm pretty sure I could recruit some of them to help. Let me go call Snake and have him gather his people up. Rose, we're going to end your nightmare one way or the other, I promise," Malcolm said.

"I know you all will help make this all go away. I just don't want anyone to get hurt. There is a chance his mental state has gotten even worse. He never went into the V.A. for help, but if you're already missing a nut and a bolt, you might not know to go in," Rose said.

"And if he's not missing any parts and he's this way because of another issue, then drastic measures we'll need to be taken," Gabriel said.

Everyone sat silently for a minute, and then Malcolm got up and called Snake. He was only gone for a few minutes before returning with a thumbs-up.

"Snake said he knows for a fact that at least ten of his guys will help, no questions asked. Now, the bigger question is, where do we trap the guy and his friends?" Malcolm asked.

"I believe there is another auction, one of the year's biggest ones near Butte. We could go there and set things up?" Gabriel said.

"If that's the one I think that is, then you're right. It's huge, and it's also in two days. We should have enough time to get home, get what we need, and head down there," Malcolm said.

"The only thing we are really missing is the actual deed itself. As much as I don't want to do this, I think you'll have to meet him face to face, Rose," Gabriel said, stating what was becoming a more obvious course of action.

Rose went as white as a sheet.

"I'll help," Elsie said. "Rose and I can act like we're walking around looking at the different animals. I'd be an extra set of eyes," Elsie said.

All eyes turned to Malcolm.

"Your call. A family united is a family that will succeed," he said.

"Okay, so, when we get home, we'll make final preparations, then have everyone meet up the day of the auction. We should assume that as soon as we give him the location name, one of his friends will be scoping the place out, so it behooves us to do the same but get there even earlier. Maybe the night before and get as close to the place as possible," Gabriel said.

Everyone agreed. This plan had to succeed, and there were enough people to make it happen. Now, they just needed to wait a bit. With a little luck, things would fall right into place.

There was only one thing left: get a message to the ex. Rose opened her cell phone and found his number. She hesitated before sending a text, but it had to be done. She laid it out there- the where, the when, and the why. Then, to end the text, she made a point-blank statement: *You and I are over with, but if you need to see me face to face for it all to sink in, then let's do this.*

Rose hit send on the screen, probably a little harder than she needed to, but she was desperate for him to get her message and the point.

Chapter Thirty-Two

The day had come. Everyone was up before dawn and heading out. It was decided that those with 18-wheelers would drive down and act as if they were actually there to buy an auctioned animal. Everyone else was there as window shoppers. Rose talked to Emelia and got the description of her ex's friends. Unfortunately, they matched the description of half the men at the auction. Everyone would just have to do the best they could.

Rose would have to keep her head on her shoulders to remain safe. Gabriel decided to try and take up a sniper's vantage point when needed and get where he could see when the meetup would take place. The plan was to get Rose's ex in a tighter area with people still around.

There needed to be a route mapped out and people on standby so that they could take down and restrain the offenders. To help with this, everyone got a walkie with an earpiece, except for Rose and Elsie.

Once the floor was mapped out as far as positioning, people took up their positions and milled around, looking for suspects that fit the description.

Gabriel, Rose, Malcolm, and Elsie met in a secluded area out of sight. Gabriel tried to keep his head covered by wearing a ball cap. Same with Malcolm. Rose and Elsie wore loose-fitting clothes and ball caps.

"There is one more thing I need both of you to keep on you, and I don't care where you put it. Just keep it out of sight," Gabriel said as he handed each woman a metallic, telescoped object.

"These are called ASPs or telescoping batons and are very effective. You just have to get it out in time to use it," Gabriel said and then demonstrated by flicking his wrist. With a sharp metallic snap, the entire length of the rod was visible.

"If you feel threatened and are in an area that you can't escape, this is meant for close combat. Keep it hidden, be ready to use it, and if you do, anywhere on the head or between the legs is your best option," Gabriel instructed. "The other option is if you can't get the weapon extended, you can use it to jam in someone's eyes, temples, ribcage, or anywhere else you see an opening."

Rose and Elsie tucked them in their waistband up front and made sure the asps were secure. Malcolm took Elsie for a minute to have one last talk. Gabriel did the same thing.

"You got this! When you are through with him and his friends, you will never have to worry about him ever again!" Gabriel said. "I will be close by at all times. Malcolm will take the lead, you and Elsie will follow, and I will bring up the rear. Just keep your eyes and ears out. Everyone else is doing the same. This whole thing will be over before you know it," Gabriel said, trying to be reassuring. "Remember, if he is trying to play this smart, he probably won't just come out and talk. He will probably try and take you, so be on alert. Tell Elsie that, too. You both need to be on high alert but not show it."

"I'll make sure to use my sniper senses," Rose said, trying to crack a joke. Gabriel caught the meaning and laughed.

"Be safe, and let's get this done so we can go home and start planning a wedding," Gabriel said.

Rose stared at Gabriel like he had just said something profound, when really what he did was propose to her.

He quickly pulled out of his pants pocket a velvet box. He opened it to reveal nestled inside a gold band with a huge diamond on top and a matching band for the husband.

"I know this is the wrong time, but I need you to know I love you, and we can get through anything together!" Gabriel said.

Malcolm and Elsie watched from a distance, and it was hard not to cheer, so they held their hands in the air. Rose, though, had tears running down her cheeks.

"I've wanted this with you since the first day I met you. Since we wished on a star, and now here we are," Rose said.

"So, does that mean my wish is coming true too?" Gabriel asked.

Rose wrapped her arms around Gabriel's neck and let out a soft squeal as she tried to keep quiet, but it was nearly impossible.

Gabriel slid the ring on her finger and gave her a celebratory kiss, but it was over before it started.

Gabriel's phone and Malcolm's phone started vibrating. Multiple locations checked in and said they saw three men all reporting to look like the one Emelia described.

"Let's go, and please be careful," Gabriel said.

Gabriel nodded to Malcolm and Elsie. One of the things that Gabriel and Malcolm did not discuss with anyone was that they were carrying a small firearm. They were small enough to fit in a hip holster inside the waistband. This was purely a last resort.

The foursome made their way out of their secluded room and started walking down the main thoroughfare of animals and animal pens.

There was no sign of Rose's ex or his friends yet, but Gabriel knew better than to trust that the enemy would simply walk in and take her. He wasn't that crazy. At least he prayed he wasn't.

Gabriel decided to take a chance. He called out to a couple of his watchers, who had seen the three suspects move in just a little towards where they saw them move. This would tighten up the net.

An intersection was coming up, so Malcolm spoke into the mic on the inside of his collar that he was going to post up and act like he was looking at a couple of the cows penned up.

Rose and Elsie needed to walk a little way and then stop and do the same thing.

Gabriel would hang back and act like he was on his cell phone while looking around.

"Everyone, report in. Where are my eyes at?" Gabriel asked.

One by one, reports came in that no one was seeing the three suspects.

"Alright, I need everyone to return to their original spots if they have moved. Let's start over," Gabriel ordered.

He opened his cell phone and pulled up the picture of the three men. While looking at them, something seemed off with one of them. He thought for a minute why the one looked so familiar.

Suddenly, the light came on.

The one in question was a sex slaver. The same one as one of the men he helped put away a while back, but how did he get out of jail? He immediately called the local sheriff's office and quickly explained who he was and why he was calling. The deputy on the phone said he would send all available units to their location.

"Malcolm, we have a problem. One of the men we are looking for is a sex slaver I helped put in jail a while back. Sheriff's deputy said he escaped. This changes things a bit," Gabriel said.

"What do you want to do? If we pull everyone now, we risk losing our foothold," Malcolm replied.

"Give me a minute. It would be nice if we could round these guys up before the deputies show up and blow this whole thing apart," Gabriel said.

"What if we flush them out a different way?" Malcolm said.

"Meaning?" Gabriel asked.

"What if we go to the head of this event and tell them that we are working with an international task force and are looking for three men tied to an international sex slave ring. We could literally turn every single person in the place into our eyes and ears," Malcolm explained.

"I like that, I like that a lot. Do you have your military ID on you?" Gabriel asked.

"Yes, why?" Malcolm asked.

"Have your ID ready if they ask to see it, but in the meantime, grab Rose and Elsie, and let's head for the information booth," Gabriel said. "All spotters move to any and every building entrance or exit you can. We have a new plan, and the sheriff's deputies are on their way. Something new has come up that changes the plan a little."

There was a moment for everyone when the feeling of urgency climbed to high alert, but then, as they moved to a new spot, they calmed down a little.

Gabriel, Malcolm, Elsie, and Rose made their way to the information booth and asked to speak to the head of the auction event. It took a bit of explaining, but when it was brought up that the sheriff's deputies were on their way and were already given orders to turn the place upside down, the head of the event became a little more compliant.

"Do you have an all-building intercom system?" Gabriel asked.

"Yes," the booth person said.

"Good, I need to borrow it," Gabriel said.

The woman working the booth handed Gabriel a microphone and then stepped back.

Gabriel accepted the mic and then stood up on the desk.

He tapped the top of the mic like everyone does when they pick up a mic, and then he stared out into the crowd. He looked down at Malcolm, Elsie, and Rose.

"Keep your eyes open for movement in case the men are close," Gabriel said.

"Excuse me, ladies, and gentlemen, here at the auction. Excuse me, and pardon the interruption. I am Staff Sergeant Gabriel Sterling of the United States Marines, and I need a favor. Among you are three individuals. Three cowardly men are here to try and kidnap my girlfriend, one of the men belonging to an organization that sells women and possibly your children for sex slaves. Now, if you are okay with what I said and don't care what I am saying, feel free to go about your business. However, if you don't want this filth among you, up on every TV screen are pictures of these men," Gabriel paused for a minute to allow his instructions to sink in. He could tell by the looks on most people's faces they were not thrilled by the interruption but even less thrilled that there were dangerous criminals among them.

"Corporal Samuel Stark, come on out. You want to talk to Rose so bad that you are willing to go to her friend's coffee shop and destroy it and then threaten to kill her, then come on out. Let's see what a true coward looks like!" Gabriel scanned the room for any quick movement and didn't see any at first, but then, at the back of the room, he saw the heads of three men with their backs turned towards him, moving toward an exit door.

"Malcolm, I see them. Let's move," Gabriel ordered.

The four hurried out of the booth and to the nearest exit to run alongside the building and cut them off.

"Anyone driving a rig, move it to block all exits out of the parking lot and the property. They won't be leaving except in the back of a squad car. If the deputies show up, let them in, and I'll handle the rest," Gabriel said.

The four made it outside and started scanning the parking lot, then saw movement towards the back along some pens where cattle were being kept, and semis were parked.

"I see them over there by the rigs," Malcolm said.

They started heading towards the wanted men, hoping to box them in.

"Samuel Stark! Come out with your hands up and bring your friends. Especially the one that is wanted for sex trafficking," Gabriel called out loudly.

There was no response.

Gabriel suddenly saw a vantage point he hoped wouldn't come back to bite him or the other three with him.

"Malcolm, see that pen over there with that big black Angus bull in it? Let it out. It should run towards the area the three men are hiding in. While you're at it, let those cows out, too. If anyone questions you, tell them you'll buy them," Gabriel said.

"Great. Always wanted to try Angus for dinner," Malcolm said.

Malcolm ran over and carefully let the big, two-thousand-pound Angus bull out of its pin. The animal was all too happy to go free. It went right towards the area where the three wanted men were. With the bull and the cows loose, the sudden parking lot congestion would cripple any vehicles trying to get out of the lot, mainly the one they were looking for.

Gabriel circled around the far side to sneak up on the men but couldn't see their boots when he looked under the trailers.

"They must be up in a truck now. We gotta find out which one. Whoever is blocking the exit, move out of the way. Standby and watch out for anyone wanting to rocket out of the parking lot," Gabriel said.

Gabriel kept pushing towards the back of the lot. He hadn't seen any movement for a while, which worried him a little. They had either made it out of the lot or hid really well. He had the sudden urge to make sure Malcolm and the ladies were with him.

"Malcolm, are Rose and Elsie with you?" he asked.

"Yes, we stayed back by the door we came out of. The deputies just pulled into the parking lot and headed towards me," Malcolm said.

"Good, send a couple of them towards the back of the lot. I think the trio is hiding out back here somewhere," Gabriel said.

"Will do. Be careful," Malcolm warned.

Gabriel kept moving through the different corridors between eighteen-wheelers. He stopped suddenly. He heard what sounded like voices, but they sounded like they were coming from a trailer.

He pressed his ear against the trailer he had his back to and tried to listen. There was nothing at first, but he had an idea while listening.

He pulled out his cell phone and asked Rose to text Samuel. His cell phone might go off; that would be a dead giveaway.

Within ten seconds, he heard the faint sound of a text alert on a cell phone. It was in the opposite trailer from Gabriel. He was facing the trailer, hiding the man who wanted to hurt Rose and possibly the other two responsible for countless other crimes.

I wish for once that bull was close by, Gabriel thought to himself.

He crept towards the end of the trailer. The doors were slightly ajar. He heard movement in the trailer. The men must have decided to make a break for it.

Gabriel snuck around the trailer and moved over two. He needed a vantage point. Just when he thought he had one, he realized he was being stared down by the black Angus.

"Hey there, big fella. I don't suppose you would help me out, would ya?"

The bull snorted and pawed at the dirt.

"I didn't think so," Gabriel said.

Having that bull there could either help or hurt the situation right now. The next few seconds would make or break everything.

The semi-trailer doors creaked open. Clearly, they did not realize the bull was a few yards away. The first one climbed down out of the trailer and had his back to the bull.

The next one started climbing down and still had not seen the bull.

Gabriel decided to get things going. He stepped out from his hiding place.

"Howdy, boys. You looking for me?" Gabriel asked.

The men saw Gabriel standing there but had still not seen the bull behind them.

There was one more thing the two men didn't see - Malcolm standing behind the bull. Malcolm saw Gabriel and nodded.

"Yaw!" Malcolm yelled, slapping the giant beast on the rump.

The bull immediately shot forward at lightning speed, leaving zero chance for the men to alter their course or jump back into the trailer.

Gabriel knew what was coming. Those men were about to learn what it meant to get hooked.

The bull suddenly dipped his giant horned head down and then lifted upwards. The two men were instantly lifted in the air and went sailing. Their limp bodies slid down the side of an adjacent trailer. They were going to feel that in the morning.

Gabriel stood absolutely still as the bull flew past him. He poked his head around the back of the trailer and saw Malcolm. They gave each other a thumbs up, then moved towards the trailer the two men had climbed out of.

Gabriel made a silent count to three. They threw the trailer doors open and saw that it was empty. Panic instantly set in with both men.

"Let's get back up where Elsie and Rose are. I have a feeling Samuel never got as far as those two, "Gabriel said, motioning to the two lifeless bodies lying on the ground.

As they rounded the last trailer, Gabriel and Malcolm stopped instantly.

Rose was pulling out of the parking lot in the driver's seat of a pickup truck, and Samuel Stark was on the passenger side, holding a gun to her head.

Samuel spotted Gabriel and Malcolm, gave him a friendly gesture, and then ordered Rose to go.

The clock was now ticking.

"Anyone behind the wheel of *any* vehicle, Rose has been taken somehow and is now on the road exiting the parking lot! Get out there and chase them down!" Gabriel ordered. He knew it wasn't his call to order that, and he wasn't law enforcement, but he decided to beg for forgiveness later.

Malcolm ran to Elsie, who was okay, while Gabriel ran to his pickup truck and got in. He was now joining the pursuit.

There comes a time in a man or woman's life when they must decide their next course of action. Gabriel and Rose were at that crossroads now.

While the pickup truck Rose was driving had a decent lead on Gabriel, Gabriel's truck would catch up in the end.

He was driving a 1996 Dodge Ram V10. It had more horsepower than the truck Rose was driving, not to mention the duallies on the back end.

Gabriel would be getting his soon-to-be wife back quickly if God, this badass Dodge, and Fate were all on his side now.

~(-)~

Rose panicked at first and was very much the scared little mouse that Samuel used to remind her that she was, but when they were a little way down the road, she felt something poking her in the lower abdomen.

The asp! I forgot I had it. I'll pull it out and hide it under my leg when he's not looking.

Rose also noticed that he wasn't wearing a seat belt. This was going to come in handy. He may have thought she was a quiet little mouse, but all those stupid guy movies he made her sit and watch were about to become real. She just had to play it out.

She kept one eye on the road and one eye looking at the mirrors. In the distance behind her, she could see a long line of vehicles, no doubt Gabriel and his posse coming to get her.

"So, did you think you could hide for very long?" Samuel said.

"No, I knew you would eventually find me, but I'm not worried," Rose countered.

"Oh, yeah, why is that?" Samuel said with a sneer.

"Look in your side mirror. See that big black Dodge truck coming. Do you know what its name is?"

"No, what? And who names their truck?" Samuel asked.

"Real men do, that's who. And that truck's name is Fury, as in Hell hath no Fury!" Rose said, accelerating. While her ex was distracted, she quickly pulled out the ASP and put it under her left leg.

Rose looked down and saw that the speedometer was nearing 110 m.p.h., which was way too fast for her liking. She needed to speed her plan up a little. She needed to prove she was no longer the mouse he thought she was.

"Did I also mention that the man driving that big black truck is my husband and a former Marine sniper? I wouldn't be surprised if he has his rifle mounted on the dash looking down the scope right now." Rose knew that sounded absurd, but she needed a moment where he was thrown out of focus for a minute.

"That makes no sense at all. Are you stupid?" Samuel asked.

"What? Marine snipers were taught to use their weapon with both hands, unlike Army flunkies like you, who only were taught to use it with one hand," Rose said, making an obscene gesture with her right hand.

Samuel was about to pop. A vein in the middle of his forehead was pulsating, and Rose could see it from where she was sitting. It was getting closer to when she needed to end this once and for all.

"Ha, nice try! Maybe I only needed one hand to use my weapon because then I could use the other to choke out scared little girls like you. Sounds fun. Maybe we should try it!" Samuel said.

Samuel moved like he was going to scoot over closer and try to choke Rose, but instead, he smacked her upside the head with the butt of the handgun he was holding.

Rose saw stars but managed to keep the ruck on the road.

"How's your head? You need some aspirin, little mouse?" Samuel said, a stupid smile plastered across his face.

"Fine! How's yours?" Rose bit back.

"Huh?" was all Samuel could say before Rose slammed on the brakes. Rose kept in her mind that Samuel wasn't wearing his seat belt and would use that to her advantage. Now was that time.

Samuel instantly went into the windshield headfirst, cracking it. Blood was running down his face. Simultaneously, the truck's tail end fishtailed violently, but Rose was determined to keep it on the road. She got the truck back under control just in time to see Samuel's bloodied face staring at her.

"I'm going to kill you the first chance I get!" he screamed, rage building with every second that passed.

"Not before I do!" Rose unleashed. With her right hand reaching across her lap, she grabbed the asp and jabbed it into Samuel's throat hard.

He began to sputter blood. Coughing and choking up mouthfuls of thick blood. Panicked and angry, he pointed the gun at the side of Rose's head, the barrel of the .45mm pressed against her temple.

She wasn't done, though, and she was willing to risk it all.

I love you, Gabriel! she said silently, then hit the brakes hard one last time. At the same instant gravity took effect, she raised her right arm up and hit his arm so the gun, for a fraction of a second, would be aiming behind her head and not at it.

The gun went off, blowing out the rearview piece of glass.

Samuel hit the windshield again, cracking it even more and causing more damage to his face.

Rose's head bounced off the center of the steering wheel, where the horn was. She was okay, but she was seeing stars again. She fought with all she had to remain conscious.

She closed her eyes and prayed this nightmare was over once and for all this time.

Chapter Thirty-Three

Gabriel, now in his truck, remembered why he named it Fury. After all these years, it indeed had some fight left in it. He slammed the pedal to the floor, causing the V10 Dodge Magnum to rocket down the road. He could just barely see the truck Rose was in, but he was going to be there very soon, and he was going to take care of business.

His cell phone went off. It was Malcolm.

"Is Elsie okay?" he asked.

"Yes, she's fine. Are you?" Malcolm asked. It was a stupid question. He knew his brother was not mentally okay.

"I am, but he won't be when I catch up to them," Gabriel said.

"Brother, you got this!" Malcolm said.

"Aren't you supposed to tell me to let the law enforcement take over so they can do their job?" Gabriel asked, shocked by what his brother said.

"Hell no! I'm from Scotland. I take care of shite myself! Now, get that truck down the road and take care of that piss ant!" Malcolm said, letting his Scottish brogue out in his voice.

"Sir, yes, Sir!" Gabriel replied.

The pedal was down to the floor, but somehow Fury kept increasing speed. It knew the target was ahead and wouldn't rest until it was off the road.

Seconds later, Gabriel saw the truck Rose was fishtailing, causing the man with the gun pointed at Rose's head to hit the windshield hard, but not before the glass behind Rose's head exploded.

There looked to be an exchange of words between Rose and Samuel, and then the truck fishtailed again, but worse this time.

"Rose!" Gabriel yelled.

The second fishtail allowed Gabriel to catch up. He bumped the rear of the truck in front of him, which was dangerous, but he needed to get Rose's and Samuel's attention.

The truck in front of him fishtailed again, then slowed. Gabriel watched as it slowed a little more, and then the driver's door flew open, and Rose jumped out, followed by Samuel's gun going off, possibly emptying the clip where Rose's head should have been. Gabriel watched in slow motion as he saw Rose land in the ditch. She was going to be torn up, but she would survive. Samuel? Probably not.

Rose slammed on the brakes again but then threw the transmission into neutral. While doing so, she undid her seatbelt and jumped out the side door. The ditch was coming up at her fast. She hit the ground hard and blacked out. She was safe now.

Gabriel saw that Rose was free and clear and slammed his truck, aptly named Fury, into the back of the truck in front of him. He continued to push it down the road for quite a distance, leaving some serious rubber on the road as well as pieces from the front of Gabriel's truck. The nightmare was just seconds from being over.

Gabriel managed to push the other truck hard into the ditch on the incoming traffic's side of the road; that's when he saw Samuel's body fly out the now completely shattered windshield.

He hit the brakes of his own truck to keep it on the road. He didn't need his vehicle in the ditch as well. He quickly exited his truck, and just as he was about to circle around the front of his truck to potentially finish the job, he heard Rose's voice calling to him. He changed course and ran back to her.

Rose had blood running down the side of her face, and her shirt was torn in more places than had fabric, but at least she was alive. Gabriel carefully scooped her up in his arms and held her tight.

She had survived being kidnapped, just as Gabriel said it might happen, but for Rose, it needed to happen. She needed him to physically assault her so she could become the lioness and not the mouse. The mouse that she had once been was no longer alive. The new Rose stood, bloodied and beaten but victorious.

As she took one last breath before Gabriel set her back down on the ground feet first, she heard a bloodied gurgle say something that sounded like her name. Samuel stood in the middle of the highway about thirty yards in front of her and Gabriel.

"Rose!" Samuel said, then spat a mouthful of blood. "I'm not done with you yet!" spitting more blood, he took another step, then raised his gun and pointed it at Rose.

Marine sniper Staff Sergeant Gabriel Sterling saw it coming and, in one fluid movement, set Rose down behind him, reached behind his back, pulled his Smith and Wesson CSX, and without thinking or even remorse, emptied the clip into the man who tried to kill Rose. His Rose.

The echo of shots fired rang out for miles as the man who had almost killed Rose fell to the ground, now with 13 rounds fired into him with deadly accuracy.

The thing about snipers, at least the well-trained ones like Gabriel, was that they had muscle memory, and while Gabriel was reacting to the threat in front of him, his body knew where to place the gun, and his trigger finger knew when to pull the trigger. The result was a dead criminal lying on the ground.

His story was over, but now Rose and Gabriel's was about to start, officially, this time -now that a new page was turned.

Chapter Thirty-Four

The morning sunlight flowed through the stained-glass windows in the chapel hall at Mt. Hope Church. Its warm rays reflected off Gabriel Sterling's silver buttons on his Prince Charlie suit jacket that matched with his Clan Sterling kilt. The thought of wearing a kilt had never crossed Gabriel's mind, but what little time he had spent in Scotland recently was enough to imprint on him just how important family and the clan structure really were, even more so, the new additions to his family.

"How are you feeling this morning, brother?" asked Malcolm.

"Surprisingly, I'm doing pretty good. Maybe a tinge nervous, but you know, okay," Gabriel answered.

"Good, and may I say how good it is to see you wearing the clan colors. Dad would be proud," Malcolm said as he admired his brother.

"You don't look so bad yourself," Gabriel said as he turned to look at his brother.

"Good things are coming, coming for the both of us. You need to know, too, how proud I am to call you my brother. I'll admit, when I first met you, I was quite sure you would walk away the moment I shared the story we shared with you, but you took it in and embraced it. My only regret was not getting to know our dad," Malcolm admitted.

"Me too. I should have gotten out years ago. Then maybe Mom and Dad would still be around," Gabriel said as he looked out one of the chapel's side windows.

"I think that all played out long before you and I were even born. Let's make our future and that of our children's future count, okay? We have so many things coming up that it excites me to know that I get to share those things with you, my brother, my only family," Malcolm said.

Malcolm was correct in saying that, even though he had distant relatives on his grandparents' side. His true family was right in front of him. The only family he truly needed.

One of the side doors on the stage opened, and Pastor Nick appeared, wearing a smile that only a loving pastor could give. He was proud of how things turned out for Gabriel and Rose, and in the next few minutes, he would be joining them together as husband and wife. He was a proud shepherd of his ever-growing flock.

"Gabriel, I believe you have a bride that is about ready, are you?" Nick asked.

Gabriel and Malcolm looked at each other and nodded, but there was one last thing he needed to do. He needed some last-minute fatherly advice from the one man who had stepped up to the plate when his own father had not. He needed Rex.

"I need a second with Rex, if that's okay," Gabriel said.

"Of course. I'll go get him," Nick said, leaving the stage.

"I'll meet you at the back of the chapel," Malcolm said, then patting his brother on the back.

A few seconds later, Rex came out of the same door Nick had just exited through.

"I heard you were looking for me?" Rex asked.

"Yeah, I just wanted a minute with you. I wanted to tell you how proud I am to have gotten to know you and for you stepping up to be someone you didn't have to be," Gabriel said.

Rex looked straight into Gabriel's eyes. He was standing before the only person he considered his family, his son. Gabriel was correct. Rex didn't have to play the role that he did with Gabriel, but when he saw Gabriel's own father become more involved with the everyday life of the ranch versus his own son's life, he became attached to the child just as a father should.

"Nothing has made me prouder than to watch you grow into the man that you have become. I know your mom and dad would feel the same way if they were here," Rex said.

"But you are the one standing here, and that is all that matters. Thank you, by the way, for wearing the kilt. I know you were completely against it, but it means a lot to Malcolm and I," Gabriel said.

"Well, anything for my boy. I'll just be happy when I can put on some britches again. This whole thing about not wearing anything underneath ain't right, although Millie was kind of fond of me when I was gettin' dressed earlier," Rex said with a smile.

"I agree. I don't know if I'll ever get used to wearing this, but it's all about the family," Gabriel said.

"You're damn right!" Now go get yourself hitched so we can get to celebrate'n!" Rex said as he left the stage.

Gabriel was now alone on the stage with his thoughts. Things were finally coming together.

He was no longer haunted by his past, not when he had everything he ever needed in his present. It was his future that he was concerned about. Everything he had worked for, everything he had done, had led him to this moment. He was about to make the biggest commitment he had ever made, but it was with the woman he was about to share his life with, so really, there was no hard choice there.

Although he knew there would always be those uphill battles, those arguments, those moments that kept him up at night, he knew he was on the right path, and it started at Mt. Hope church the day he walked in and met Rose Callahan.

The time had finally come. Gabriel stood looking out over the packed chapel as he awaited the music to start playing, which meant his soon-to-be wife would be coming up the aisle to meet him.

He had taken on missions that were more stressful than this, yet he found himself with more butterflies in his stomach than he had ever experienced. At the same time, however, in the rest of the chapel, there was a feeling of peace in the air as everyone remained respectfully quiet and talked amongst themselves, no doubt about what the bride would look like as she passed through the double oak doors.

Gabriel's attention was suddenly brought front and center as the piano played the bridal entrance song.

The doors suddenly creaked open, and there stood Rose.

She wore a long white dress with a beautifully laced neckline. A gold necklace and earrings to match. The dress was at a length that it did trail behind her, but not enough that it needed someone to bring up the rear.

What drew the attention of onlookers was the addition of the Sterling clan colors to the dress itself. No one in attendance had seen Scottish formal attire and watched in awe as Rose slowly walked down the aisle.

She was met at the bottom stage stairs by Rex, whom she had chosen to give her away; that too had become another defining moment for Rex.

When asked by Pastor Nick who was to give Rose away, Rex accepted the duty and handed her off to the eagerly awaiting Gabriel Sterling.

"You look so handsome," Rose whispered.

"You look amazing," Gabriel replied.

The couple, hand in hand, presented themselves to Nick, who in turn would be presenting them to the congregation as well as God above.

"Ladies and Gentlemen, brothers and sisters of the church of Mt. Hope, we are gathered together today to join these two together. Now, the story of Gabriel Sterling and Hope Callahan started long before they were even born. It started in the stars above when God looked upon each of their souls and gathered them together as a Father would his children, kissed each of them, and then sent them down to Earth," Pastor Nick said as he opened the ceremony. There were already tears flowing among those in attendance.

"I would like to open this ceremony with prayer, but I would like to ask that each person in the rows place their hand on the person in front of them so that each and every person becomes a chain," Nick said, then gave everyone a second or two to do as he asked. He bowed his head in reverence but did something he had never done. Led to do so at that moment, he raised his right hand towards the heavens as if reaching out to God himself.

Gabriel reached for Rose's hand and held it tight.

"Father of all, I come to you now to present to you this man and woman, your children. They humbly ask for your blessing and love and to join in holy matrimony here today. Bless them, Father, with a long and fruitful life. We, the congregation, ask you to protect them and keep them safe from all that seek to do them harm. May they walk in the footprints you left behind so they may be on the path to righteousness. May they always feel your love and grace. In your Son's name, amen."

Pastor Nick gave everyone a moment to reset, then continued with the ceremony. He had prepared long and hard for this ceremony as Rose and Gabriel became two of his closest friends. He had known their struggles and triumphs, and now he would know of the victories as he joined them together in marriage.

"Rose, when I met you, I had only been stateside for just a short time, and as you know, I just finished up the hardest, darkest time in my life. When you accepted me and gave me shelter in your own life, my old life started to fall away. I no longer needed to hold onto that part of my life any longer. You became my life. As I stand here today, I promise to give you my life, my love, my heart, and my respect. I love you, Rose Callahan," Gabriel said.

Rose was now crying but holding herself together by a thin strand.   She had reached that moment in her life that she never thought she would.

"Gabriel, when I saw you that first time you had come to do some work for Pastor Nick, I could feel your presence before I had even walked into the chapel here. When I looked you in the eyes and saw your smile, I knew you had a good heart, but I also knew you were running from a past that you were trying so desperately to leave behind. I, too, was running from something, but when we met that day, we collided together, and the story of our lives suddenly became one. It is my hope and prayer that you will spend all your days walking with me in this life and the next, living, loving, and laughing as we face the challenges of everyday life together. I love you, Gabriel Sterling. Thank you for choosing me."

It was now Gabriel's turn to slowly unravel. No one in that room had seen Gabriel cry, but tears ran down both cheeks and onto his suit coat. It was time to let it all go so that his union with Rose would be free and clear of any residue from his former life, from either of their lives.

"In closing, I would like to offer one piece of advice to this couple. Gabriel and Rose, we are granted but a short life here on Earth. It is my prayer that the two of you spend your lives together making memories, sharing laughter, dancing in the rain, and everything you can possibly get out of this life so that you can live it to the fullest! May God grant you his blessings as you go forth in this life together as husband and wife. To all those in attendance, the church of Mt. Hope, I present to you Mr. and Mrs. Sterling!" Pastor Nick said as he presented Gabriel and Rose to the congregation and the world.

Everyone rose to their feet and cheered loud enough that people in the street could hear. Gabriel and Rose headed down the aisle toward the front of the church, where a stretched limousine was waiting for them and taking them to where the reception was being held- the park where they shared their first meal together.

The reception, of course, was to be the second highlight of the day. Gabriel and Rose both dressed down for this. Post reception was going to be spent on a plane back over to Scotland, where they had a cabin by River Ness waiting for them.

The afternoon was spent eating, drinking, and thanking everyone in attendance for coming.

There was one part of the reception that time slowed down for - the husband-and-wife dance.

Everyone watching the bride and groom looked on with wonderment as they held each other tight, stared into each other's eyes, and smiled while they spun around in circles, dancing to their favorite song. A song that, for them, said it all.

Gabriel and Rose were now free to live their lives without fear of who might be next in line to try to do them harm or to give mission orders.

Their only mission in life, now, was to live for each other. To love each other and to make memories to last a lifetime.

Despite having been spent running from someone or something, their lives could now be spent running towards each other.

They were now nearly complete in every way.

Nearly...

Epilogue

The plane landed with only minutes to spare. A stressed-out and angered Gabriel Sterling ran alongside his brother Malcolm Grant-Sterling to the fueled and waiting SUV sitting on the airport tarmac. It was going to be a close call.

"I got this, brother. I'll drive, you get in. You'll need to be the one talking to Rose, not me," Malcolm said. Gabriel did not disagree.

Rose was on her way to the hospital. She was in active labor with twins- the boy they had named after Gabriel's brother, Charlie, and his sister's name was Hannah Grace, after Rose's mom.

"Rose, we're in the car headed your way," Gabriel said.

"Okay, honey. Please hurry! I can't do this without you," Rose said as the pain from the contractions intensified.

"We're just a few minutes out. We should arrive at the same time as you. When we pull up, I'll jump out as soon as we get there, and then I can wheel you to the labor and delivery," Gabriel said.

"I'm scared," Rose said, her voice shaking.

"I know you are. I am, too, but you can do this. We can do this," Gabriel said, trying to reassure Rose that she was going to make it.

Both vehicles pulled up to the hospital at the same time. Gabriel was the first one out of his vehicle and over the ambulance's rear doors as the medics lowered the gurney to the ground with Rose, trying her hardest to keep her babies inside her until they reached the hospital.

The trip up the elevator felt like an eternity, but once they reached the labor and delivery floor, it was go time.

Gabriel was taken one way so he could put on a sterile gown and sterile footwear. Rose was taken another way so she could be prepped accordingly.

Gabriel stood waiting in the operating room for them to finish.

Everyone raced around the room to get things going, and then, finally, Rose was wheeled in. She had been given an epidural and just in time, too.

The doctor responsible for the delivery of the twins sat at the foot of the bed, waiting like the catcher of a baseball team.

From the beginning, Rose and Gabriel were told that delivering twins was no ordinary feat. It would take all that she had and more.

That moment had now arrived.

Baby Charlie had taken the lead to come out first. Push after push, coaxing after coxing, Rose delivered her first healthy baby. The doctor held it up, and immediately, baby Charlie cried out at the top of his lungs, announcing to the world he had arrived.

"Charlie's here, baby! Charlie is here. One more time. You can do this. Let's get Hannah cut and into the world," Gabriel said, trying to encourage Rose.

When it was time, Rose started to push again. Within just a minute or two, baby Hannah's head was crowning, and she was on her way to meet the world alongside her brother.

Alarms started going off, though; Rose and her baby's vitals were going down, and her blood pressure was rising. The baby was in distress.

"Rose, you gotta push. Your baby needs help. She's gotta make it out, or she'll be in trouble," the doctor said.

Gabriel looked at Rose. Both had panic in their eyes.

"Gabriel, I'm scared," Rose cried out.

"I know, baby, but you gotta do this. Please, give it one more push, and Hannah Grace will be here. Come on, you can do this," Gabriel said.

Rose repositioned one hand on the railing and the other in Gabreil's hand. She was going to give it all she had and more.

The next contraction came, and Rose pushed down with all her might as she cried out. Within seconds, Hannah Grace came out fighting for her life. She was free of her mother's womb, but Rose was not out of the woods.

Hannah's umbilical cord was wrapped around her throat, and in exiting her mother, internal damage was done, causing Rose to bleed extensively. As soon as baby number two was handed off, the doctor began to quickly seek out the source of the bleeding and stop it while making sure the afterbirth was removed.

Gabriel's gaze stayed locked with hers as the baby was born, and the minute the doctor said there was bleeding, Gabriel immediately held onto his wife's hand even tighter.

"Rose Sterling, don't you go anywhere. I need you here. Those babies need you here. Stay with me!" Gabriel cried out.

In the distant background, the cries of both babies could be heard, inconsolable until they could be with their mother.

"Doc, we gotta do something!" Gabriel said.

"I'm trying. I just can't seem to find the source of the bleeding."

"Put the babies on Rose, let them feel her. It will work, I promise," Gabriel said.

The doctor nodded to the nurses, and both babies were immediately brought over and placed on Rose's chest with Gabriel's assistance, who helped distribute the weight with his arms.

"Rose, Charlie and Hannah are here. They need their mommy," Gabriel said.

Both babies immediately stopped crying, and with a hand from each baby, they reached for their mother and managed to touch her face.

"I got it!" the doctor cried out. "The bleeding is under control. Make sure both bags are open wide. Let's get her topped back up, so she can get to taking care of those babies!" the doctor said.

Panic disappeared when life returned to Rose. Gabriel shook his head in relief as his wife looked at him with tears running down her face. She was out of the woods now officially.

"Look at our children, honey. We made those!" Gabriel said, overcome with emotion.

"Our little babies!" Rose said. She kissed each of her children's heads, and then the nurses took them for a final check.

"I'm so proud of you. You carried those babies for nine months and made it!" Gabriel said, wrapping his arms around his wife the best he could while she was being cleaned up.

"We did it. We made it together, and I wouldn't have made it if you hadn't been here," Rose said.

"Our little family is complete now," Gabriel said. He smiled, knowing that he now had everything he had ever wanted.

I wish you were here, Mom, Dad, and Charlie. You would have loved your new family, Gabriel thought to himself, but he knew in some way that his family above was the reason why he had been blessed with the family he now had.

Gabriel Sterling's life was now complete.

Where once he ran from a life he didn't want to live, he now ran toward the life he couldn't be without.

He would do anything and everything possible to protect what was his - at any cost.

About the Author

Stephen St. Clair works as IT superhero during the day and author by night.

He now has 8 titles under his Scottish sporran and many more in the works.

Stephen St. Clair currently lives in the middle U.S. with his wife of 24 years, who is also an author. Together they have five kids and share a plethora of dogs and cats that always seem to find mischief around the house.

He is the Host of The Crafted Quill Podcast and co-content creator for their YouTube Channel - *Have Fate Will Travel.*

You can follow him on:

Twitter as @craftedquill

Website: stephenstclairauthor.com

Email: craftedquill@stephenstclairauthor.com

Made in the USA
Monee, IL
22 October 2023